THE DAY THE SUN VANISHED

THE DAY THE SUN VANISHED

DEXTER LOKO

For my father, Max
who unintentionally introduced me to a world of magic when I was
only ten.

And my mother, Josephine
who drove several kilometres around the city, with purpose, to find
me all the books I so desperately wanted.

Together, you've done an amazing job.

TABLE OF CONTENTS

THE DAY THE SUN VANISHED

Kofi had turned seventeen the day before yesterday but had never seen daylight. No one knew exactly what had happened to the sun. Everyone had their own theory and no two stories seemed to agree. Some said the sun had simply exhausted all of its energy. Others swore it was the agents of the netherworld at play. Others believed it was the final days of the world and their village was the last remaining stronghold … And so, and so, the speculations went. But if there was one thing on which everyone agreed now, it was that the darkness had come to stay. That was certain.

Those who had lived during the days of the sun were naturally the elders. They spoke with pride about the glorious bright days and made those like Kofi, who were born in the darkness, feel somewhat … smaller.

Kofi was a smallish young man and, in his childhood, his peers had teased him a lot. But everyone agreed he was wise, far wiser than other young men his age. *You're an old man trapped in a young man's body.* Those were the exact words of his mother, who was only twelve when the sun vanished.

'We were setting fish traps by the river when it happened.'

This was a story Kofi had heard one too many times, but his mother recounted it anyway, and he would fall absolutely quiet as he listened, a small smile on his smooth face and heavy hope in his childish heart.

'That day, the sun was exceptionally bright and hot. The sky was so blue, and the waters of the Volta River sparkled like diamonds.' His mother's voice echoed softly in the hut that was lit only by a few burning logs in the corner. 'It was almost as if it was preparing to say goodbye.'

'One last burn,' Kofi piped up, excitement in his voice.

'One last burn,' his older brother mimicked in a teasing voice as he entered the hut.

'Shut up, Kankan!' Kofi shot at him.

'The sun is gone and is never coming back.' Kankan dropped the stack of firewood he was holding near the fireplace and was looking crossly at their mother. 'He should be out working, Mama, not listening to bedtime stories this early in the morning.'

The light flickered over Kankan's face, and Kofi smirked and imagined him as the devil.

'The stories give him hope,' Mama said, managing a small smile. 'As they should you.'

'The stories make him lazy.' Kankan's brows furrowed. He stared point-blank at Kofi, and Kofi could have sworn he saw horns on either side of his head.

He stifled a laugh as his brother's mouth twitched in irritation.

'If we don't gather enough wood in the next few days, we'll all freeze to death anyway,' Kankan said to both of them before storming angrily out of the hut.

Kofi looked at his mother and burst into a laugh.

His mother chuckled and added, 'Don't laugh at your brother. You know he means well.'

'So what happened, Mama?'

'The sun continued to burn,' she said. 'Then it got so hot, too hot! I remember wishing I could take off my skin.' She sighed deeply before finishing her usual story. 'My friends and I dipped underwater to cool off, and when we emerged seconds later, the sun had vanished.'

'Without any warning?'

'Just like that,' Mama told him. Kofi listened, wide-eyed. 'Those who witnessed the last few seconds said it just grew smaller and smaller until it left us with only darkness.'

'And it took the moon too, along with everyone's happiness?' Kofi asked.

'Not everyone.' His mother grinned. 'As you can see.'

Kofi laughed again, even more heartily than before.

'Your happiness should never depend on anything but yourself. I am glad you have always remembered that.'

'Do you think it will ever come back?'

This was a question Kofi had never asked his mother before. Everyone said the sun had left them forever and put monsters in its place, but he wanted to hear it from her lips.

He regretted his question immediately. First, because he suspected what her answer might be, and second for putting her in perhaps a rather difficult situation; she may have to lie to him.

'Go and help your brother.' She smiled weakly as she tugged playfully at some of his dreadlocks. 'I would help too, but I don't feel quite well today.'

He got up, put on his thick cloak and picked up his staff, which was nearly as tall as him. He lit its darkened tip and ventured out into the frosty darkness.

His mother's pleading voice followed him from the hut. 'Kofi, don't wander towards the edge, I beg of you.'

Her frail voice saddened him terribly. The lack of sunlight made his mother quite sick, just like most of the older people in the village. His father had passed away six years ago when his bones became too frail for him to even stand. Kofi fought back tears as cold swept his insides. The chill had nothing to do with the weather but was caused by the vivid pictures swimming in his head, painfully teasing him that his mother could meet the same fate.

As he walked steadily down the icy, muddy path with shrivelled moringa trees on either side, he greeted several people, who just like him were beginning their days by going to farm or fish whatever was possible before the Sabremouths emerged.

Sabremouths were vicious, six-legged creatures that killed humans for no reason. The Sabremouths were herbivores, but that didn't stop them from mauling any villager they sighted and bathing in their blood.

The Sabremouths had arrived the same night the sun vanished. In the early days, they lurked only around the hills at the edge of the village, but in recent years, a number of them had ventured further into the village in the evenings, so that by morning, people were found lying in their own blood, dead on the streets and torn into shreds.

Some people said it was because of the dwindling river and greens around the edge. Others said the Sabremouths had just become more bloodthirsty. No one seemed to have the answer – nor did they for many other questions. Rainfalls were scarce but appreciated by the villagers, especially the heavy ones because it meant the vegetables could thrive and the Sabremouths never came to the village whenever there was a thunderstorm. Heavy storms apparently were the only things the Sabremouths feared.

However, Kofi was certain he was more afraid of losing his mother to the darkness than confronting an entire pack of Sabremouths. He watched a man drag a dead deer past him. *Lucky chap*, Kofi thought, as he returned the man's greetings. The man and his family would eat well for the next month, at least. A good number of the village's livestock had died out over a decade ago, either from the darkness or by the paws of the wicked Sabremouths. The handful of them that roamed around now could not reproduce as quickly as they were being hunted.

He looked up at the dark sky. The morning was almost done. The villagers used the stars up above to tell the time, and everyone knew that gathering wood was best in the mornings and fish were more plentiful in the river in the afternoons. Good vegetables peaked in the evenings, but the best ones were only available at night. Harvesting those was a perilous task very few were willing to undertake, but Mama would never get better if she kept eating the worst of the yields.

Kofi wiped a tear as someone thumped him painfully on the back.

'Kofi, you're late!' came the voice of a girl. The fire from her staff revealed her tired but pretty face. 'Did you just wake up? Everyone would have gathered the best wood by now.'

'Sorry, I was catching up with my mother.'

'Let me guess – listening to stories about the sun again?' She raised one of her brows at him.

Kofi shrugged and bit his lip. Nadia was his best friend and one of the many villagers who believed the sun was never coming back.

'If you want to waste your time, that's fine, but next time I won't wait for you.'

Kofi cracked an old familiar joke to douse the tension and, as always, Nadia softened at it. It worked every time.

'Sorry,' she whispered. 'I didn't mean to be grumpy. It's just that I don't only need the wood to keep the hut warm. I'll need to cook something proper today too. I've been on a plant-based diet, against my will, for the past fortnight. Even finding chunky snails these days is proving to be a Herculean task.'

'Why didn't you ask?' Kofi asked pointedly. 'I would have brought you some.'

Nadia simply blinked. Kofi made a mental note now to remember her needs because he knew she still wouldn't ask later. Nadia was stubborn and a little too proud for her own good. This annoyed Kofi because he enjoyed doing things for Nadia.

She hurried him up the path and towards the forest, where the villagers gathered wood for cooking and keeping warm. Her breath shot into the air with every word she spoke.

'I swear this winter is ten times colder than the last,' Nadia said, limping slightly as her pace increased and not minding her tattered blue cloak that was gathering dirt at her feet.

'You say that every winter,' Kofi said hastily as they climbed.

Nadia snorted and then tripped over something so that she fell with a heavy thud.

'Stars! I can't afford to have two bad legs,' she spat as she picked herself up quicker than Kofi could help.

They steadied their staffs and peered down to see what the culprit had been. It was the frozen body of a man. The top part of his green cloak was severely ripped and red from his own blood. His head had been crushed beyond recognition, and he bore several deep claw marks on both arms, and large chunks of flesh were missing from his stomach, allowing his insides to spill out of his corpse.

'Sabremouths,' he and Nadia chorused quietly.

'These attacks are becoming more frequent,' Kofi said, looking away instantly and fighting back the urge to vomit.

'And more vicious,' Nadia added.

She continued to stare at the corpse as if expecting it to reveal more answers.

Nadia was brave. She always had been, for as long as Kofi had known her. She had lost both parents in the last five years to illnesses from the darkness. Growing up, her laughter had always warmed Kofi's heart and brightened his days, but he barely remembered what it sounded like now.

Her mother had died first. On odd days, she would still smile, perhaps because her father still lived, but when he got sick, she ventured towards the hills to get better vegetables to aid his recovery. There, she almost lost her life when a Sabremouth nearly ripped her left leg clean in two. Her father had died the same day upon her return from the hill and, just like the sun, Nadia's laughter and smiles were lost forever.

Now sixteen, she lived all alone in her parents' hut, fighting for her survival in the darkness like everybody else in the village.

'How is your mother?' Nadia asked as they returned downhill after gathering their wood.

'She's getting worse,' was all Kofi could say.

Nadia said nothing for what seemed like an eternity, and just as the silence was becoming haunting, she spoke. 'What if there was a way to help her? To help everyone.'

Nonplussed, Kofi stopped in his tracks and turned to face her. 'What do you mean?'

Nadia hesitated, eyes darting to all corners except towards Kofi.

'Nadia …'

Kofi's gaze was fixated on her face. Nadia's eyes met his, and she spoke solemnly. 'Before my father died, he told me about a plant.' She broke her gaze again and looked down at her feet as she continued. 'Sun plants. They only grow in the valley over the edge. They're supposed to have the power to bring back the sun to our village.'

'But your parents didn't believe the sun could come back,' Kofi said, still refusing to shift his gaze from her.

'I lied,' Nadia whispered. 'I didn't believe, but they did.'

'Nadia …' Kofi started. 'When you got mauled by the Sabremouth on the hill, were you going to …?'

'Yes.' And now she had tears rolling down her cheeks. She looked even more tired than ever as she adjusted the stack of wood that was slipping from her one-handed grip. 'I didn't want to tell you because I knew how hopeful you already were about the sun. The last thing I wanted was to put your life at risk by asking you to follow me over the edge.'

'So, you just went alone and nearly got yourself killed?' Kofi asked in disbelief.

'I had to try to save my father, at least, even if there was only an infinitesimal chance, and I couldn't ask you to do that with me.'

'It could have saved the entire village. All of us!' Kofi's voice was rising.

'What if it isn't real?'

'What if it is?'

'This is why I didn't say anything.' Nadia sobbed. 'You'd only try and get yourself killed.'

Kofi laughed drily. 'But it's okay for *you* to try and get yourself killed?' he thundered at her so loudly that the two passing women clutching their own stacks of wood and fiery staffs slowed to glance at them.

'Kofi, I—'

'Myth or not, you should have told me,' Kofi said, his voice lowered back to normal. 'And in case you haven't noticed, Nadia, we're all dying anyway. If the darkness doesn't kill us, the Sabremouths will.'

Leaving her sobbing on the spot, Kofi walked angrily back home. He refused to talk to his mother or Kankan for the rest of the day. Nadia had been selfish in withholding that information. They were supposed to be best friends. He continued to brood in silence and remembered that Nadia was barely thirteen when she made that decision, and she, too, had suffered a terrible loss. Then, remembering she had no one else now, his heart softened. She also needed something decent to eat. He picked two large snails and one frozen salmon from the chiller in the corner of the hut and stuffed it inside the deep pocket of his cloak.

Then he lit his staff and made to leave the hut.

Kankan's voice boomed from behind him. 'Where are you going? It's nearly midnight.'

'I – I'm off to find some good vegetables.'

'I already got us enough this evening,' Kankan informed him and pointed towards the mound of mushrooms and radishes in the basket right next to the chiller. 'We're done for the week.'

'But the best ones are only just blooming, you know.'

Kofi raised his hood over his head and prepared to leave but their voices appeared to have woken their mother.

'It's not safe out there, Kofi. Please, listen to your brother.' She coughed amidst her words.

'I promise I won't be long.' Kofi faced his brother, voice low and almost pleading. 'I need to see Nadia – it's urgent.'

Kankan frowned at first, then he dipped his hand into his cloak and retrieved a small, corked bottle with contents that resembled lightning and swirling grey smoke. He sighed and handed it to Kofi. 'My last bottle of Hayaki. If you sense *anything* dangerous, use it.'

'But … this is very expensive,' Kofi said hesitantly.

'And you said this is important.'

Kofi nodded slowly.

'Then make sure you return home safely,' Kankan said and reduced his voice to a whisper. 'I cannot take care of Mama alone.'

Kofi smiled as he took the tiny glass bottle from his brother and wandered into the night. The paths were just as icy as they had been that morning.

The only difference now was that no one was out on the streets. His heart raced as he passed the boulder that meant he was approaching Nadia's hut. He heard small growls but convinced himself that it was just his mind playing tricks on him. He had questions that could not wait until morning.

He knocked on Nadia's wooden door with his free hand. After a few more attempts and fearing his flame could attract the wrong attention, he pushed the door open.

His fire brightened the cold hut. There was Nadia, shivering and drenched in sweat on her bamboo bed. The light revealed her pale skin, and she seemed too sick to show any surprise.

'Nadia, you're sick?'

Nadia nodded ever so slightly.

'But you looked well this morning.' Perplexed, Kofi placed his hand on her burning forehead.

'It gets worse every night. Plus, how else would I gather wood if I didn't get up in the morning?' Nadia said with chapped lips and between slow-paced breaths.

'Damn it, Nadia! I would have done it for you,' said Kofi. 'Were you even going to tell me?'

'Eventually,' said Nadia. 'But I planned to get better first.'

'What is it?'

'Mama Agbo said it's the long-night sickness.' She looked at him and, for the first time, he saw fear in her hazel eyes. 'And I may not have very long.'

'Nonsense!' Kofi spat. 'I will go and bring the sun if I have to.'

Nadia held his hand, and her eyes brimmed with tears. 'You were always so brave, Kofi. It's why I've always liked you.'

'I will make you say that again tomorrow,' said Kofi, squeezing her hand as he smiled.

And then Nadia grinned for the first time in years. Even now, she looked beautiful, and Kofi's heart warmed as if the sun had truly returned. His own eyes welling up with tears, he sprang up quickly from her side. He emptied his pocket into the small basket beside the dead fireplace. With a serious look, he faced her again.

'By morning, I will return with the sun,' Kofi declared.

Nadia still had tears rolling down her cheeks as she smiled with a nod. Turning his back on her, Kofi left the hut and broke into a run, the tiny glass bottle bumping into his chest from inside his cloak pocket.

Kankan was seated by the small fire when Kofi reached home like a father waiting upon the return of his wayward son so he could chastise him.

'You didn't have to wait for me,' Kofi told him, keeping his tone as low as possible.

'I wasn't. I just couldn't sleep,' Kankan said, staring at the logs that burnt with a gentle crack.

Kofi knew he was lying. Kankan was only eighteen months older than him but had been forced to become a man after their father passed away and mother took ill. And even though Kofi didn't always agree with Kankan's methods, he understood them. Kankan was also overprotective, and while this could be utterly annoying, Kofi was grateful for it.

'She's getting worse,' said Kofi.

'I know.'

'And it's not just her—'

'I know,' Kankan said again, and this time he looked at him knowingly.

'I can't just watch,' Kofi said, his voice breaking. 'I have to try.'

Kofi told his brother his plans while their mother snored lightly at the other end of the hut. 'I know it's stupid, but—'

'It's stupid, to be honest,' Kankan said. 'But it's worth a try.'

Kofi stared at Kankan in disbelief.

'You're crazy if you thought I'd let you do this alone.'

'But Mama—'

'We'll be back before she wakes,' Kankan said seriously. 'So we better leave now.'

And so the brothers walked in the darkness, neither of them saying a word to the other. The only sound that could be heard were the crickets in the bushes and the occasional gentle thud of their lit staffs upon the earth. Kankan appeared to be buried in his own thoughts; Kofi certainly was. They had trekked at least three miles when Kankan suddenly stopped. Kofi stopped beside him.

'Stars – I forgot my knife.'

'But you carry it everywhere.' Kofi turned to face him, fear rising in his voice.

Fire and steel would barely be enough to stop the Sabremouths as it was.

Kankan continued to curse. 'Stars, stars! I changed my cloak earlier because it got wet, and I forgot to take the blade out.'

'Take mine!' Kofi said without thinking.

'Don't be stupid, you can't fight those monsters with only fire.'

'Neither can you – but you're a better fighter.'

'Which is why you need it more than I do,' Kankan said with a smile. 'Also, there's no turning back now.'

And before Kofi could argue another word, Kankan strode up the hill that rose before them. They continued again in silence, but this time, the atmosphere was eerie. There were no chirps from crickets or hooting from owls. Instead, they were greeted by a rather dirty smell. The villagers called this 'mutua' – the smell of death. It was as if hundreds of decaying corpses hid behind the trees on either side of them.

'We're getting close to the edge,' Kankan told him in a whisper. 'I can see the trees ending.'

Kofi swallowed and pulled out the knife from his cloak. It was an old knife with a battered leather handle, but its blade had remained sharp from all its hard work on the fields.

'Kankan, is this normal?' Kofi asked, anxiety getting the best of him. 'We're in Sabremouth territory – why is everything so quiet?'

'You ask like I've been here before,' said Kankan. 'And keep your voice down, man! I know we're legendary, but if we can avoid getting noticed by Sabremouths, I'd rather that.'

As silence fell between the brothers again, something rustled behind the trees.

'Did you hear that?' Kofi jumped.

'Shhh!'

'Kankan! Something is behind there.'

'Don't stop! Keep walking. Look up there, that's the edge.'

'Kankan—'

Kofi didn't finish because this time Kankan stopped too. Tiny red lights dotted the area either side of them, and soft growls rose around them.

'Sabremouths!'

'Run!'

Kankan led the way, swivelling his staff as he ran forward towards the edge. Kofi took to his heels behind him, clutching his knife even tighter.

The growls grew louder and, within seconds, dozens of Sabremouths were chasing them towards the edge, bringing mutua with them. Kofi looked back breathlessly. The six-legged beasts were nearing them, their strong limbs moving rapidly but barely touching the earth. They appeared to be gliding with ease. Even in the darkness, he made out several jagged, twisted teeth in their open, drooling, rotting mouths. These things were worse than anyone had ever described them, Kofi thought as he passed his brother, who continued to twist his staff as they ran.

Kofi thought of his mother as the Sabremouths closed in on them. There was no way they could outrun these beasts. They were going to die here and their poor mother would be all alone until she died from the heartbreak of losing her foolhardy children to the forces of the darkness.

Kofi's throat dried as his thoughts drifted to Nadia. She, too, wouldn't last long because the long-night already had her. Slowly, the entire village would be filled with nothing but decaying corpses.

'Do you still have the Hayaki I gave you earlier?' Kankan asked amid fast-paced breaths.

'Yes,' Kofi answered quickly, checking to feel if the tiny bottle was still there.

'Take it out and open it,' Kankan said, reaching to take the blade in Kofi's right hand. 'Quickly!'

Kofi dug his fingers into his pocket and pulled out the bottle. He put it straight to his teeth. As the cork came off, a surging burst of electricity emerged from it and shot into the sky. Mist gathered over his head and quickly formed a swirling, thick grey cloud that shot down cracking streaks of lightning.

'What are you doing?' Kofi's eyes opened wide as Kankan stopped in his tracks. 'Get in, you idiot!'

Kankan smiled but his eyes carried sadness. And for the first time since they were children, Kofi saw real fear in his brother's eyes.

'The bottle contains protection for only one.'

'I-I don't understand.' Kofi's mouth was dry. 'Just stand with me, it'll be okay.'

Kofi started to move towards his brother, but Kankan yelled sharply. 'No! It can only take one.' Kankan's voice was breaking. 'And it won't last for very long. Find whatever is over the edge and save Mama, save Nadia … save everyone.'

'No, no. Kankan – I can't. Please, I can't.' Kofi shook his head and sobbed as the cloud above him opened with rain. The water quenched the fire on his staff and drowned the tears that were rolling freely down his face.

'Go, Kofi! Get out of here now! If we both die, then this will all have been in vain.'

Kankan fell to his knees as the Sabremouths surrounded him. He swished his staff and blade wildly so that he cut and burnt some of them. Many of them screeched in pain, but many more snapped their teeth with dangerous longing, their eyes glowing even redder with the wildness of bloodlust.

'Take care of Mama,' Kankan said.

At the same moment, Kofi closed his eyes and turned his face away. His heart was heavy, but his legs were even heavier as he struggled to run forward. Rain and streaks of lightning continued to pour down on him as he ran to the edge, followed by the loud thunder that Kofi was grateful for. He couldn't bear to hear what remained of Kankan writhing in agony.

He reached the end of the trees and lost his footing when his sandal got stuck under his wet cloak. He shut his eyes again and felt himself tumble down the other side of the hill. For several minutes, he feared to open them. The rain had stopped falling, and he waited for death to come. But now, something was warming his face, like a friendly burning fire from above. Slowly, he opened his eyes, and above him was a vast bright sky with a small yellow patch. It was too painful to stare at directly, so he sat up instead. Here, there was no smell of death. Only the sweet smell of fresh grass and the sound of healthy trees rustling gently in the wind. Eyes welling up with tears, he picked up his staff and walked towards the endless sea of sun plants.

ANANSI

Nearly forty-eight hours had passed since their boat hit the rocks and capsized off the Gulf of Guinea. The waters were calmer now, and only small patches of grey clouds remained in the sky. It was difficult to imagine that, not too long ago, all three fishermen were battling for their lives with the incredible force of nature.

The fishermen had all made this trip many times over their fishing years, but none of the men had ever experienced a storm of that magnitude.

'God has kept us alive for a reason,' the youngest of the fishermen said now. His name was Zed.

'There is no God,' the second fisherman huffed instantly. He was heavily bearded and had long matted locks. This was Tega.

'Don't say that!' Zed stared at him as though he had just committed the greatest crime. 'Look around, we are all God's creation.'

'Look around,' Tega repeated in mocking imitation, throwing his skinny arm into the air. 'If there was *a god*, all of this shit wouldn't be happening, would it?'

'That's rubbish,' Zed continued. 'Life is a test. God tests us every day, and I believe this is one of those tests.'

'What do you think?' Tega asked the third fisherman.

Both men turned to the huge, dark-skinned man lying on the edge of the wooden plank. The man had said nothing so far and said nothing now. He didn't even acknowledge that he had just been spoken to. Instead, he continued to stare, arms behind his head, into the sky. He was called Tvka. The three men didn't know each other per se. They were fishing contractors, and every day they would go to the marina in search of work. And for a daily fee, they would join a fishing boat that went deep into the parts of the sea where fish were aplenty.

So, every day, each fisherman met a different fisherman from the ones he had met the day before. Occasionally, you would meet the same men, maybe even know their names or become friendly. But not to the point of distraction. Out on the seas, everyone was for themselves and themselves alone. The more fish in your net, the more money, so Tvka had never cared to know faces, names or be friendly.

Every morning before sunrise, he would be at the marina, moving from pier to pier, looking for the best fishing boats to join so he could do what he did best – fish.

Experienced fishermen knew what to look out for when selecting their conveying boats. After all, that was part of the trade. The fishing boats were all skippered by androids, so looking out for the helmsman would not help a fisherman's decision. But one could tell from the hull of the boat. The markings and lines on it could tell you all you needed to know – like how many times the boat had ventured out to sea and how well it had fared in the storms it faced. That was all a good fisherman needed, as long as he had good hands too, of course.

At the start of their journey, their android had displayed the passenger's headshots on the wonky screen as it called out the names of all the fishermen on board and announced all safety protocols and emergency procedures. Over a dozen men had been onboard; now only three remained.

'We could've easily been one of our fallen compatriots, but God kept us alive,' Zed said to the man on his other side.

Not for long though, Tvka thought. They had not been able to salvage any food or water from the sinking boat. No other fishing boats had ventured anywhere close to them in the last two days, and it was only a matter of hours before the high tides or another storm came to finish the job. He raised his wrist to his face. *Quarter past five.* The face of the old brown leather watch was now severely cracked, and bits of water had slipped through the glass, but otherwise, it had survived the ordeal.

This watch, this beautiful precious watch that he'd received as a gift several years ago. He'd never really fancied timepieces, especially ones he had to keep strapped to his skin, but this one, he loved this one. He valued it beyond everything else he owned and would cherish it forever … or for whatever time he had left.

'Are you saying this god of yours kept you alive because you're better than the others?' Tega asked with a raised eyebrow. The sarcasm was clear as day in his voice.

'No, but he kept us alive because we have a purpose.'

'And the other eleven men didn't?' Tega asked again; this time one could sense the growing irritation inside him.

'Perhaps their purpose on earth had already been fulfilled.' Zed sounded convinced by his own words. 'Ours is just starting. Either that or we've been given a second chance.'

Tega sighed and he, too, turned to face the sky. 'Well, if there is a god, I'd love to see him get us out of this one. I'll need proof to believe. Sorry.'

'Do you believe in love?' Zed asked Tega.

'What is the correlation?' Tega said, eyes still glued to the sky.

'Do you believe?'

'Yes,' Tega said calmly.

'Why then, you can't see it, can you?'

'Oh yes I can.' Tega faced Zed once again. 'I see it in my woman's eyes. I feel it when she touches me or when I call her name and she answers. I can't say the same about your gods.'

'*The* God,' Zed corrected him quickly. 'Again, I tell you to look around, my friend.'

Tega sighed wearily. 'Evolution and science built this. We built this.'

'Only because God gave us the wisdom in the first place,' Zed said, undeterred.

'Whatever. I guess if that makes you sleep better at night, then fine.' Tega adjusted his weight on the floating plank as he spoke. 'As for me, I'd rather spend my final hours thinking about my woman's kisses than a mythical sky-daddy.'

'You are married?' Zed asked.

'I am to be in three weeks,' Tega said with a small smile. His smile faltered, and his tone betrayed some notes of bitterness. 'I waited too long to ask her. I kept frolicking around with other women even though I knew she was the one. I was a fool.'

'Ah, look, my father had a saying, better late than never.'

Tega scoffed. 'Your father didn't come up with that though. You know that, right?'

Tvka snickered and the two men turned to him in surprise. However, he still refused to meet their gaze.

'But I'll tell you what,' Tega said in a renewed tone of seriousness. 'Maybe I'll invite you to the wedding if your god manages to keep us alive.'

As the sun slipped under the horizon and night came, the tides grew just as they had expected. The thick, wide plank that held the men from death bobbed up and down with the growing restless waves. Their faces lost colour as each man battled hunger and thirst in silence. There was also no escaping the chill that surrounded them.

'What do you reckon will get us first?' Tega asked amid icy breaths after many hours of silence.

'Huh?' Zed muttered.

He clearly hadn't been paying attention. He seemed to be shivering the most.

'I said what do you think will kill us first? Hypothermia, thirst or sharks?'

Zed remained quiet for a bit, then he began to sob. Tvka appeared or at least pretended not to notice, but he, too, was shivering slightly.

Tega spoke out again. 'I'd say hypothermia.' He frowned as though he were deep in thought. 'Thirst would be a close second in my opinion and definitely way less painful than being shark food.'

Zed sobbed even louder now and, while Tega remained poker-faced, Tvka finally turned to him and spoke in a deep, calm voice.

'There're only tiger sharks in these parts, and they won't attack humans. Also, you can last another day without water.'

Both men turned to look at him, relief apparent on their faces.

'So, hypothermia it is,' said Tega.

'Why has no boat come by since?' Zed asked. He was no longer sobbing, but one could hear the defeat taking over his voice.

'We're way out of any fishing zones,' Tega said as a matter of fact. 'No one comes this far out.'

'But I thought the androids send out SOS signals to the marina in times of danger.'

'Ha! Not when the boat is that old,' Tega said slowly. 'I'll bet everything I own that the alarm system for that boat wasn't even working. It was one of the oldest boats in the marina.'

'I always thought I knew I had to look out for the good boats.' Zed sounded even more broken. 'Clearly I was wrong.'

'Man, none of us saw this coming. *Andromeda* was a damn good boat, even though she was old. I've used her many, many times,' Tega continued in all seriousness. 'That storm wasn't normal. No new boat would've pulled through that, even if she had the latest android system.'

'What if we swam? We're all excellent swimmers, right?' Zed asked, turning to both men as he spoke.

'We won't make it very far. We haven't eaten in two days.' Tega bit his lip as he finished. His teeth were chattering.

Zed pressed on. 'We'll only have to swim until another boat finds us.'

'We'd die within hours. The water is too cold,' Tega said drily. 'Also, how many people fish in the middle of the night, man?'

Both men fell silent once more, gazing up at the stars in the endless sky. If the circumstances had been different, it would have passed for a beautiful night. So far, there had been no sign of another storm. That was a good thing; it could buy them at least another day of survival. Perhaps until a travelling boat passed and rescued them or they died from one of the impending dangers. Whichever came first.

The wooden plank bobbed gently as small waves splashed its sides. Eventually it would become weak from all the water it had soaked up and they would drown anyway. It was a miracle it had held their weight thus far. The night grew colder, and while all three men were now shivering, Zed appeared to be suffering the most. He would sob occasionally but didn't stop shivering, so much so that the other two feared his unsettling vibrations would sink them faster.

Tvka removed his coat and wrapped it around the young man.

'Th-thank you,' Zed managed.

Tvka barely let out a grunt in reply as he warmed himself uselessly with his large veiny hands.

'My wife is expecting our first child. I needed to make more money before our baby arrived. That's the reason I started coming out to sea seven days a week,' Zed told no one in particular. 'I can't believe I won't be there for them.'

'I thought you swore God was going to keep us alive because he has a purpose for us all?' Tega said.

It was hard to tell if he was being honestly hopeful or downright condescending.

'If God existed, he wouldn't have let this happen,' Zed said, his voice teary. He was still shaking as he had been earlier. 'If God exists, he shouldn't make me beg for a chance to at least say goodbye to my wife.'

Tega said nothing and, after a while, he, too, removed his coat and lumped it upon Zed, who was now quiet. Silence fell upon them once more as clouds gathered above and sent all the stars into hiding.

'What about you, big man?' Tega asked after Zed had fallen asleep. 'Any woman in your life?'

Tvka's face gave away no emotion. It was impossible to know what he was thinking. Arms still wrapped around himself, he took short loud breaths but remained silent.

'I'm sure a fine-looking man like yourself must have a woman anticipating his return, eh?' Tega asked with a knowing smile. 'Ah, I see, several women, then?'

But Tvka continued to warm himself in silence, eyes transfixed at the ever-growing dark clouds.

'Or maybe you're all alone because all you did was fish,' Tega pushed. 'That's alright. I know some fishermen that are married only to the trade.'

Still, Tvka said nothing. Instead, he turned to his side, so that all Tega could see was his broad back.

'Fine then,' Tega said calmly. 'Let us just die in silence. Sound way to go.'

They were awoken a few hours later by thick painful drops of lashing rain and, not long after, heavy gusts of wind that threatened to blow them off the plank. Drenched and confused, all three men sat upright on their floating saviour, each thinking of his own end. A streak of lightning ripped through the sky, revealing nothing but vast seas for miles on end. The loud thunder that followed took the shape of the wind and spoke with authority. Its voice was calm, even though the waters were not.

'I can deliver a message for each of you,' the wind said. The voice was neither male nor female. 'What shall it be?'

Zed, who had been weeping since he awoke, spoke out first. 'Tell my wife I want her to know how much I love her.'

The wind made a rushing sound of acknowledgement, and Tega went next. 'Tell my lady I am sorry,' he said, staring wildly at nothing. 'I am sorry for wasting so much time pursuing money and not spending my days with her.'

The wind made another rushing sound, but nothing further came. The two men stared blankly at Tvka who, again, had no readable expression on his face.

'Surely, you must have someone waiting to hear from you?' Zed asked the silent man.

But Tvka said nothing.

'He has no one,' Tega informed the waiting wind. 'He was married to the sea.'

'So be it,' came the powerful voice of the wind.

'Wait!' Tvka called as they felt the wind turn with a sigh. 'I have a message for someone.'

The other two fishermen turned to him with looks of sheer curiosity as the wind waited.

'His name is Anansi,' said Tvka, looking quite defeated. There was unmistakable panic in his voice. 'Tell him I'm still at sea, but I'll be seeing him soon because God will bring me back to him.'

FIRESTARTER

No one knew her name or her age, but everyone knew she was a witch. After all, she always wore the same black robes, as dark as midnight, and her face was barely visible through her hood. She came to the town's market once a week, unfailingly. And each time, she was greeted by loud curses and snide remarks from the townspeople. Children laughed and threw small rocks at her, and the older people spat at her feet and questioned why she was allowed to dwell among them.

Technically though, she didn't dwell among them. No one knew where she was from originally or even where she lived now, but several people said she lived deep in the forest, alongside the wild animals that were just like her. Some swore she didn't even live in the realm of men, that she only came to the market for food because her realm was a barren wasteland filled with the bones of the men, women and children she had devoured.

'I saw her disappear one time,' one boy told his gullible friends as soon as she walked into the market square today.

'Really?' one of his friends asked, open-mouthed.

'Yes, of course,' the storyteller said convincingly. 'She chased me, but I was way too fast for her.'

His friends gasped and stared at him with keen interest, so he continued. 'I saw her face!'

'No!' This time it was a girl with a squeaky voice that spoke. 'Is she as ugly as they say?'

'Even worse,' the encircled boy said with dramatic effect. 'She's a monster. She had sharp teeth like a vampire, and her eyes burned red with fire like the devil.'

Several more of them gasped, and the girl with the squeaky voice screamed and ran away from the circle, crying hysterically as she made her way to her parents' stall.

The witch continued through the stone path, making her way from stall to stall. Each time, she was cursed at and turned away.

'Get out of here, you witch!'

'Don't bring your bad luck here.'

An older woman sucked her teeth as the witch approached her stall; the witch wasn't worth her words. So she gave her the silent treatment.

Undeterred, the witch continued steadily down the path, clutching her empty woven basket. She felt the eyes behind her head as she stopped at a particular stall. The young man in charge swallowed and stared back at her, but said nothing. He had kind eyes, but he, too, knew that everyone was watching them.

The witch spoke in a very young, very human voice. 'How much for a kilo of rice, please?'

The man seemed surprised but still didn't utter a word. Instead, he peered at her keenly and even twisted his head a bit, perhaps to catch a glimpse of a human face under her dark hood, but he could only see her pointed chin.

The soft voice came again. 'If I could also have a jar of olive oil too, and a small sack of salt.'

The man looked around, then shook his head slowly. 'Sorry,' he whispered.

'I beg of you – I haven't eaten in days.' And now one could hear her voice crack. 'I will pay more than the usual price, please.'

'I can't,' the shopkeeper said abruptly; he stared around wildly. 'I'm sorry.'

With that, the witch walked away, basket as empty as it had been upon her arrival.

'You better not return!' someone spat as she headed for the trees.

Another person threw a small rock that missed her head by inches as she disappeared into the forest.

* * *

As the sun began to set and the marketers closed their shops, the young man filled his satchel. He was extremely careful to make sure no one was watching him when he made his way into the forest.

She had to live somewhat close, he thought as the trees swallowed him. He considered turning back after every five minutes, but he didn't. This was stupid, he told himself again. Yet he continued to search for any trace of her. He heard a sound behind the trees, but it was only a small fox. So he walked in silence in the twilight until he heard footsteps behind him. Bandits had ambushed him.

He knew even before he turned back to have a look. He wanted to make a run for it but knew it would be futile and foolish; he was surrounded in no time.

There were three of them, all wielding sharp daggers. They were clad in black with masks that concealed much of their faces.

'I have no gold,' the young man said uneasily, quickly throwing his arms above his head. 'Only an old watch given to me by my father.'

One of them inched closer to him; he had the demeanour of the leader. 'Gold is nice, but that's not what we'll be needing of you today.'

'What then?' the man asked, sounding quite alarmed.

The masked man stuck out his tongue in a tease and pointed his dagger towards the man's chest.

'I don't understand,' the young man said. His heart was racing now.

One of the other bandits smacked him hard across the face with knuckle-ringed fingers so that he tasted his own blood.

'You seem young and healthy. Your sweet heart should be worth a lot on the black market. We'll take that, if you don't mind,' the second bandit said with a sneer.

'And I happen to like those boots you have on,' said the third who had smacked him earlier. 'That's some nice quality leather, mister.' He finished with a sinister laugh.

'I'll take that nice satchel he's carrying,' the first of them said. 'But you guys can share items later. Remove his heart and whatever else we need. We have quite the journey ahead.'

The man tried to run, but he tripped and the men laughed. Two of the bandits approached him, sharp daggers pointed as he lay on the ground shaking in terror. He blamed no one but himself; this was what you got when you followed a strange girl into the forest.

'Wait! Let Osi do it,' said the first bandit again, with the authority of a leader. 'Last time you cut too deep at the arteries and lost us decent gold.'

The second bandit retracted his knife reluctantly, allowing the third to inch his sharp blade towards the man's chest. The young man sobbed, and as he closed his eyes, he heard his thick garment rip apart.

'Hurry! It'll be nightfall soon,' the leader said with a tone of urgency.

'Fully-grown men who are scared of the dark? Interesting,' said a female voice from behind the trees.

The bandits turned wildly around, and the frightened young man opened his eyes. He could make out a hooded figure a few metres away. The figure drew closer in the semi-darkness but her large hood made it impossible to see her face.

'The tales of your inhumanity precede you, but I have one question,' the hooded woman said. 'Why the hell would you attempt to rip out a man's heart without the mercy of slitting his throat first?'

'Who the fuck are you?' the leader of the bandits asked, brandishing a long dagger in her direction.

'I see you're rude to boot,' the woman said as she came even closer to the scene.

This woman is fearless, the young man thought, still lying on the ground. Or perhaps she was just foolish, thinking she could take on three armed men. Then it dawned on him. His brows furrowed, and his small eyes widened in a matter of seconds. It was the witch from earlier. The young woman he had come looking for. He saw a bit of her pointed chin now as she drew a shiny knife with a hooked end from inside her robes.

The leader laughed alongside his men. Then he spoke out, irritated. 'We're running late already so we might as well make our wasted time worth it.' He switched into a confident pose, grimacing as he held his dagger in front of him. 'Boys, we have two hearts now. A crying man-child and his saviour bitch.'

The other two laughed again as they, too, switched to fight mode. The three men surrounded her.

'To think that I even considered mercy,' the witch said calmly. 'Thanks for making this easy.' And with that, she attacked.

Leaping gracefully and spinning on the spot, she slit their throats in one clean sweep. Her twisting motion made her hood fall. She stood there with her back turned to the man who now had blood splattered across his face. The bandits wheezed and clutched their necks uselessly as blood gushed out. Seconds later they lay on the earth, unmoving.

'This part of the forest isn't safe for travellers,' she said, still with her back to him. 'You shouldn't be here.'

'I'm not a traveller,' the man said, picking up his satchel and rising to his feet. 'I came here to look for you.'

The witch remained silent, but she used her free hand to draw her hood back to her head.

'Why?'

'I … brought you some food.'

'You're the trader from the market in town.'

'Yes, my name is Etim. I'm really sorry about earlier,' he said, and he meant it. 'You see, I couldn't sell to you because … because—'

'I'm a witch?'

'The people are scared of you and—'

'I don't blame them,' she said slowly. 'I'm a monster, and you shouldn't be here.'

'A monster who just saved my life?' Etim asked, inching towards her.

The witch took a few steps forwards and asked, 'Tell me, why are you really here, Etim?'

''Cos I know you are not the monster they make you out to be and you just proved it.'

'Do not speak of this to anyone.' Her tone was not commanding; instead, it sounded like a plea. 'I appreciate your kindness, but please never return here.' And with that, she walked briskly, deeper into the forest.

'Hey! What about the food?' Etim asked as he hurried after her, but she continued to hasten.

He started a small jog to keep up. 'I promise I'll sell to you the next time you're in the market,' he yelled after her.

She continued to walk down the path, and he increased his speed. Etim chased after her until he tripped over a thick, overgrown root. He cursed out loud as the bottle of olive oil came rolling out of his satchel along with the small bag of rice and a handful of spices.

'Alright, alright,' Etim yelled at her, feeling somewhat defeated. 'You won't take the food, but at least tell me your name.'

The witch stopped in her tracks and seemed to consider for a while.

'Please,' Etim muttered, and he was unsure if she had heard him or not.

'Zenaida,' she said softly, and with that, Etim saw her robes disappear completely behind the trees.

* * *

Five weeks had passed, and Zenaida hadn't shown up to the market or anywhere near the town. At first this didn't trouble Etim, but by the beginning of the eighth week there was still no sign of her, and it was clear she was intentionally staying away. Perhaps she assumed he would have told the townspeople she wasn't just a witch but a murderer too, Etim thought as he stood in the ferocious midday sun.

He would never do that; he was still grateful to her for saving his life. Did she slaughter three men in the process? Yes, but it was either the bandits or his and her hearts on the black market. He continued to ponder silently as he pushed the canopy of his stall further out to block some of the sun.

He had thought about her a lot after that day. And every day, he couldn't help but fix his eyes on the edge of the forest, hoping to see a hooded figure carrying a woven basket. But at the end of each day, he was left disappointed.

Today he remembered how fierce she had been and how she had ended the bandits within seconds to protect him, and it gladdened his heart. It made sense since she was a witch. *If she was a witch.* Regardless, she was tougher than several men he knew, himself included.

'Why are you smiling like a sheep, Etim?' said the owner of the stall beside his. 'You've barely made any sales today, so what has you so cheerful?'

'Tell me, Tobi, is there ever a day that goes by when I am not cheerful?'

Etim beamed and Tobi eyed him with a frown. Etim thought Tobi always had the most readable facial expressions.

'It's a new girl, isn't it?'

Etim said nothing but continued to grin as he waved away the flies trying to perch on his fresh cabbages.

Tobi smiled too. 'That witch stopped coming into the town and now everyone has found new luck with love. Everyone except me, anyway. Even my younger sister now has a boyfriend.'

Etim laughed nervously, avoiding the gaze of his friend.

Tobi was the closest thing Etim had to a best friend. The two couldn't remember when or how they became friends, only that they played tree and river a lot as little children and had always lived in the same quarter. They had grown up together, set up their stalls at the market on the same day, and basically told each other everything.

'Well then, who is she?'

Etim swallowed drily and was grateful when a woman with her young daughter, who was dragging a stubborn goat by the horns, stopped by Tobi's stall to ask for the price of carrots.

Etim waited until they were done haggling and, when the customers left, he picked up his satchel and turned to Tobi. 'I forgot to pack a lunch today. Can you watch the stall while I rush home?'

Tobi had barely nodded when Etim rushed off. He went through the streets in the direction of his house, and when he was certain no one could see him, he detoured into the forest.

He walked until he was near the scene of the attack, intentionally avoiding the exact spot in case the corpses of the men still lay there. And after what seemed like an aimless search, he stopped because he could sense someone was behind him, watching him.

'You must teach me how to be so stealthy,' Etim said, turning on the spot to face the hooded figure.

'Why are you here?' Zenaida asked, her tone cold but voice calm.

'You stopped coming to the market. Why?' Etim inched closer to her as he spoke.

She continued to face him but took several steps back. Even with the light leaking through the trees, it was impossible to see anything other than her chin.

'I told you not to come back. It's not safe—'

'Should I be afraid of you or forest bandits?'

'What would it take for you to stop coming here?'

'Have lunch with me and perhaps I'll never come back.'

'Perhaps I could just kill you.'

'You're not a killer,' Etim said.

Zenaida snorted. 'You know nothing about me,' she said. She turned her back to him and started to walk away. 'Also, did you see how easy it was for me to kill those men? I can do it again.'

'You don't frighten me, Zenaida,' said Etim, walking slowly behind her.

Zenaida stopped and spoke. Her voice was gentle again. 'You're not safe here. Please leave.' And then she turned and continued her brisk walk.

'You have two options,' Etim said dauntlessly behind her. 'You could kill me, or you could share my bowl of shrimp rice with me.'

Zenaida stopped once more before letting out a loud sigh. 'I find your persistence quite annoying, Etim.'

Etim smiled because even this warmed his heart.

* * *

Etim forgot to pack a lunch daily, much to the annoyance of Tobi, who now found himself tending to two stalls for several hours every afternoon.

'So, are you going to be gone every lunch hour now?' Tobi asked him one afternoon upon his return.

'My mother prefers to make fresh lunches these days,' Etim responded quickly.

'Yes, that explains exactly why you're gone for longer with each passing day.' Tobi bit on an apple as he eyed his friend sceptically.

'Exactly, you know how mothers are.'

'Since when did your mother start making you lunch, by the way?' Tobi asked on another afternoon as Etim picked up his satchel in preparation to rush off. 'You've always cooked your own meals.'

'Oh, you know. She saw how I struggled to wake up early in the mornings, and since she's mostly home in the winter doing her pottery anyway, it works for us both. Who'd say no to that?' Etim said, chuckling nervously.

'Very kind of her,' Tobi said, forcing a small smile too.

'Yeah, very.' Etim gave him a quick wave and hurried through the streets before doing his usual detour.

Zenaida liked Etim's shrimp rice, but she particularly enjoyed his cassava porridge. So he made it a duty to make more of those. He loved seeing her gobble down the food as she laughed at his jokes. It was the first time a girl had told Etim he was a good cook and called him *hilarious*.

'Come in, I want to show you something,' Zenaida said one afternoon after a delicious meal.

She lived in a shabby shack deep in the forest. Etim had never been inside because they always had lunch on the bench right in front. She had never invited him in, and he had never asked. Etim suspected the inside of the shack was sacred to her craft, so he had let things be.

'Are you sure?' Etim asked as Zenaida led the way up the steps that comprised three flat boulders.

'*Oh, please.* I know you are dying to,' she said, and they both laughed.

Zenaida opened the flimsy wooden door to reveal a fairly large, dingy but tidy room. Etim first noticed the mismatched chairs. The curtains had been cut incorrectly too and were so old and dull it was difficult to make out their colour.

He counted six different knives hanging on the wall, all of them shiny and ready. He saw the worn-out bow and a few arrows arranged neatly in a pile by the corner next to an empty fireplace. It was almost as if Zenaida had sensed his discomfort because she spoke immediately.

'I only use them if I have to. I have to protect myself,' she whispered, quickly ushering him to the farther end of the room where several abstract paintings were jumbled up on the wooden floor with small jars of paints. Two uncompleted canvases hung lazily on the wall.

'You did all these? They're beautiful, Zenaida,' Etim said, running his finger over the splashed canvas of a blue and yellow oil painting.

'This is how I make a living,' Zenaida said, with a little pride in her voice. 'I move from town to town, selling them. I am lucky if I make a few coppers, but I get by.'

'Why?' Etim asked perplexed. 'Why do you live like this? Don't you have any … family?'

'My story is complicated.' And now her tone was etched with sadness. 'But I am not a witch.'

Etim believed her and instantly felt sorry for her. And for the first time, he felt an urge, a real urge to protect her.

'Zenaida.'

'I can't be saved, Etim. I told you before, I'm better left alone.' She turned to face him but kept her head facing the floor.

Etim leaned closer, and slowly, he started to push down her hood. Zenaida gripped his hand with tremendous speed. 'Get out!' she barked at him.

'I-I don't understand,' Etim began. 'You wanted me to come—'

But her booming voice cut him short. 'I don't want to ever see you again,' she yelled in such anger that Etim had to take several steps back.

'If I d-did something to upset you …' he started again. 'I'm sorry, I just—'

'I said, *get out!*'

And with that, Etim hurried out of the shack, nearly tripping over the boulders of the steps. Jaw clenched in anger and tears stinging his eyes, he ran non-stop until he got to the town.

* * *

'Etim … Etim!'

It was Tobi calling out his name because a customer had been standing in front of his stall for a while and he had just stood there, staring blankly.

'Oh,' was all Etim uttered as Tobi continued to stare at him perplexed. 'Sorry,' he added to the old woman, who smiled and nodded curtly.

After she left, Tobi rushed over and stood with arms akimbo. 'Man, what's going on? You've been acting like a zombie for the past week.'

'I'm alright, just feeling a bit unwell.'

'You don't look unwell.' Tobi hadn't taken his gaze off him. 'You look heartbroken. This have anything to do with that new girl you've refused to tell me anything about?'

'There's no girl.' Etim didn't look up at Tobi. 'I don't know what you're talking about.'

'Yeah right, so you were just having secret lunches with yourself the last couple of weeks, then?'

Now Etim stopped spraying the vegetables in the stack with the watering can and turned to his friend. 'You knew where I was.' He faked seriousness. 'I was home having lunch with my—'

'Mate, your mother stopped by last week,' Tobi said without breaking eye contact. 'She came to deliver some ceramic bowls to a vendor and was surprised you weren't here.'

'It must have been one of those days I—' Etim started, but a visibly irritated Tobi cut him short.

'I thought we told each other everything.' And he looked away. 'I'm not mad, I'm just disappointed you think I'm that stupid or that you can't trust me.'

'Tobi, it's not that, of course I trust you. It's just—' Etim was cut short again by the sudden rising voices in the market.

'The witch is back!' someone yelled.

'What is she doing here?' another whispered not too far from him. 'I assumed the town chief told her to never return.'

Etim looked to the edge of the forest and there was Zenaida, walking straight with purpose, empty woven basket on her arm and the hem of her robes dragging the dust on the stony ground. She stopped in front of Etim's stall, and the raised voices were reduced to scattered murmurs. He could feel Tobi's eyes on the side of his head. Everyone was watching now, wondering.

'I'd like two tubers of cassava, a bag of salt, and a jar of olive oil, please.'

Etim said nothing at first. His jaw was clenched, and his head felt tense. He was still furious about how she had treated him the last time they met, but he could not ignore the sweet feeling in the pit of his stomach. Even with everyone still watching and the whispers steadily rising around him, Etim was truly glad she was here.

'You promised,' Zenaida muttered.

'Five coppers.'

Etim gathered what she had requested and heaped it into her basket as she dropped five reddish-brown coins on the wooden ledge.

'Would that be all?' he asked.

'I know it's not for sale, but I'd like your forgiveness too.'

Etim blinked foolishly, bit his lip and nodded slightly. 'I forgive you.'

And with that, Zenaida turned away and went back to the forest, leaving rising murmurs once more in her wake.

Tobi slowly tilted his head to stare at his friend and, at that moment, it was impossible to tell exactly what he was thinking.

* * *

'I told you my story was a complex one.'

Etim was seated opposite Zenaida on a rusty swing attached to a great acacia tree outside the shack. She sighed heavily as if she was getting ready to retell something that caused her great pain. But Etim was curious, so he sat there patiently, waiting for her to continue.

'My parents had wanted a child for the longest time,' she started. 'Too long. They tried everything but nothing worked. They prayed and offered sacrifices to a hundred gods, and still, no child came forth.'

She shifted uncomfortably in her seat, a lowly stump from an old tree that had been cut ages ago.

Etim watched her closely, saying nothing. He had waited so long for this; he dared not interrupt.

'Just when all hope seemed lost,' Zenaida continued, 'an old woman appeared to my mother in her dream. She claimed to be a priestess of Abike, the goddess of fire and vengeance. Upon waking up, my mother went to find her shrine. There, the priestess told my mother she would conceive a beautiful girl, but Abike demanded something in return.'

Now, Zenaida looked to the earth, and Etim could tell she was frowning, because he saw her chin tighten.

'Abike wanted my mother's service.'

'What service?' Etim had to ask.

'The priestess was dying, and Abike wanted a virtuous woman to take her place,' Zenaida said. 'Apparently, she found that in my mother. Now, you see, my mother had gone to the priestess without my father's knowledge. She didn't even tell him about the dream. They'd got their hopes dashed too many times in the past. I suspect she wanted to be certain before roping him in this time around.'

She raised her head and paused for a bit before speaking again. 'My mother became pregnant exactly one moon cycle after her visit to the priestess. My father was overjoyed, and he threw an enormous feast at the news. My mother, however, was a mixed bag of emotions. She was happy to finally be granted her heart's desire, but sad for what was still to come.'

Etim continued to watch Zenaida in silence; her body language exposed her discomfort for the story she was telling.

'Zenaida,' he mumbled. 'If it's too painful—'

'No. It's important you know this.'

So, once again, he fell silent as he waited for her to carry on.

'Shortly before my birth, my mother told my father the circumstances of my conception. And it was only then that she explained to him the depths of her contract with the goddess of fire and vengeance. She had agreed to serve Abike as her priestess after giving birth to me and that entailed leaving everything from her past life behind.'

It was as though Zenaida had read Etim's mind because she spoke immediately after. 'Yes, including me, her newborn child and her beloved husband of many years. My father insisted they run away where the goddess wouldn't find them, but my mother knew that was impossible. She wept and pleaded for my father's understanding, but he wasn't losing his wife to the goddess's service. My mother eventually succumbed, and in the middle of the night, they ran away. I was born in a makeshift shed in the swamplands. We were at peace until one year later, when the priestess died. Mother began having renewed dreams where Abike commanded her to return to the shrine. This time, she told Father, who made us pack and run again, even farther this time. We moved here to this shack, which they built. My parents became ostrich farmers; they reared eight of them here in our backyard, and we were finally at peace again. It even seemed like Abike had forgotten us until the morning of my eighth birthday. I went out to the back of the shack to greet my parents where they'd been gathering freshly laid ostrich eggs, but when they turned to face me, I struck them with blindness.'

Zenaida's voice croaked now as she wiped tears from her eyes. Etim just sat there, unsure of what to do. The last time he had touched her, she had nearly bitten his head off. So, he sat there and empathised.

'I ran to get help and met a group of men hunting, but upon looking at me, all four men went blind.' Zenaida was sobbing. 'I couldn't believe what was happening. I was so confused I sat underneath a tree and cried for hours until a family travelling through the forest saw me. The man among them asked me what the problem was, but I couldn't say because I didn't know. They were so kind to me and refused to leave my side until they were certain I was alright. The man's wife asked me to look up at them and wipe my tears. Upon gazing at me, they, too, went blind. I still remember their screams of agony as I ran away from them. The cries of their two young daughters still haunt me when I sleep.'

Zenaida was sobbing and shaking uncontrollably, so Etim went to her and held her close.

'I'm cursed. I told you, I'm a monster!'

'It's no fault of yours,' Etim said. 'And you're not a monster.'

'I've ruined people's lives, and I've killed several men,' she cried.

'You had to protect yourself; it's not your fault.'

'It's all because of me.' She cried some more into his arms. 'I'm not worth it, Etim.'

Etim remained with her for what must have been hours. Later, without uncovering her face, he found her lips and kissed her tenderly.

'You don't scare me,' Etim reminded her and she giggled. 'I'm not going anywhere.'

The sun had begun its descent when Zenaida held his hand and led him to the back of the shack.

It was a large, fenced space with overgrown shrubs, even on the bamboo sticks surrounding it. Etim could make out several deep claw marks on the bamboo panels at the end of the field.

'The ostriches did that after I blinded them,' said Zenaida. She was pointing in the same direction Etim was looking.

'Zenaida. Whatever happened to your parents?'

She continued to stare towards the centre of the field.

'I don't know if it was your townspeople who had long accused my parents of practising voodoo or Abike who wanted vengeance, but when I returned home that day, I found them here.' She pointed a few metres away from where they were standing. 'The ostriches had blood on their claws,' she said, with no emotion now. 'Their chests were cut open and their hearts had been ripped out of their bodies.'

* * *

Spring came, bringing light showers and fresh air along with it. Wildflowers blossomed in their hundreds, and bees buzzed noisily as they suckled on the scented petals with gentle taps.

Zenaida would smile to herself as she watched Etim from the doorway of the shack. He particularly enjoyed watching the plumage of golden pheasants as they passed by on their migration route.

'My *husband*,' Zenaida would tease, 'lunch is ready.'

Etim would rub his palms together and come running towards her with a wide grin on his face. They had gotten married in a secret ceremony seven weeks ago.

Etim became ostracised from the township after he married 'the witch of the forest' without his family's blessing. No one knew where the young couple's shack was located, but Etim's parents were certain the witch had their beloved son under some powerful dark spell. His father had tried speaking sense into him, and his mother had rolled on the floor weeping about how she had lost her son forever.

'Mama, I'm not lost, I'm just in love.'

'Where is this witch?' she cried. 'Let me beg her to give me back my son!'

'I'm still here, Mama.' Etim stared at both his parents with tears in his eyes. 'I'm not dead.'

'If you take this road, you're as good as dead to us,' his father said with a sort of finality.

'You misunderstand her,' Etim pleaded as he fought back the tears. 'If you just got to know her, you'll see she's not what you think—'

Etim stopped because there was a savage look in his father's eyes. His father turned his back to him and helped his wailing wife up from the floor. Etim knew this was it. He had made his decision, and they had made theirs.

The only person who knew the whereabouts of their shack rarely visited. Tobi had remained somewhat friendly with him and brought them food supplies once a week, typically after sunset. Etim always invited him inside, and each time, Tobi politely declined. In the beginning, they spoke at length about town news and mutual friends, but as time went on, Etim was lucky to get more than a few words out of his old friend.

'I need to return to the town,' Tobi would say hurriedly. 'No one must suspect I come here, and you know the forest isn't safe after dark.'

'The risk you take is greatly appreciated,' Etim said this time. 'Zenaida and I are in your debt.'

Tobi smiled weakly and gave a sharp nod towards the shack at Zenaida, who always kept her distance too. Then he turned abruptly and disappeared into the darkness.

'You don't like him.' Etim scowled. 'Why?'

'*He doesn't like me.*'

Etim sighed. 'He fears you, and you don't make it any easier for him.'

'And I don't trust him, so let's keep it that way.'

'He risks his life coming here all the time!' Etim found his temper rising.

'And we always offer to pay him for his services,' Zenaida said matter-of-factly.

'Which he never accepts.'

'Yes, because he is such a great friend.' Zenaida made her way into the shack. 'All I'm saying is he might have other motives.'

'Such as?'

'Ugh! I don't know. Maybe he's spying on us. Feeding information to your parents, to people in your town?'

She fiddled with the stove, with her back to him. He inched towards her and squeezed her shoulder firmly.

'He's the only one who's stood by me,' Etim said softly. 'By us.'

Zenaida said nothing; instead, she tugged herself forward slightly as if to get away from his grip. This shack had been her safe space, long before Etim, and long before Tobi.

'Do you want milk in your tea?' she asked.

* * *

Etim spent the bulk of his time on the farm behind the shack. He grew lots of vegetables in small patches, but he was most proud of the tomatoes. How the morning dew kissed them with tiny drops of water when he came to check on them in the morning. Zenaida spent most of hers painting. She mostly worked inside, but sometimes she came out so they could both enjoy the sun. The other town was several miles away, so Zenaida avoided it too, unless she had to sell a few paintings. Some days she managed to make quite a few coppers, and on other days, like today, she returned tired and rather downcast. That evening, as she took a bath, Etim walked in unannounced.

'What are you doing?' Zenaida yelled, turning her gaze to the bathroom wall so fast that Etim burst out laughing. 'Are you mad?'

She chuckled nervously with her eyes still on the wooden walls. But Etim continued to come closer until he reached the tub. He saw the goosebumps form on her skin as he ran his fingers through her curly red hair to the back of her neck and down her spine. Zenaida shifted uneasily in the warm water.

He dropped to his knees, and his voice became low. 'It's been eight months.'

'Etim … don't,' she said in feeble protest.

Zenaida stretched her hand down towards the floor in a useless attempt to grab her hooded bathrobe.

'You're my wife.' His breath was just behind her ear now.

'Etim—'

Etim held Zenaida's head and turned her face to his, but her eyes were closed tightly shut. His chest was pressed against hers, and her heart was racing as fast as his. He felt the blood rush downwards. He was alive.

'I am ready, Zenaida.'

* * *

'When did this happen?' Tobi asked when he finally came around.

He had not shown up in nearly eight moons. Etim had been worried sick because now he could not have gone to the town in search of Tobi even if he wanted to. He smiled as he pushed his guiding stick around him, trying to feel Tobi with it.

'I feared the worst when we didn't hear from you.' Etim smiled. He could smell the mint leaves on Tobi's breath.

'I was being watched closely by the town guards. I couldn't risk it.'

'Does anyone know?'

'I can't say for certain, but I suspect so.' Tobi sounded serious. 'I'm only here to tell you personally that I can't make these trips going forward.'

Etim nodded. 'I understand.'

'There's also been rumours.'

'What rumours?'

'I hear your parents plan to take you off the witch's spell—'

'She's not a witch!' Etim raised his voice a little higher than he had planned. 'She's not a witch, Tobi. You know this. She's my wife.' Etim reduced his voice to a whisper. 'And she's with child. My child!'

What followed was a prolonged silence between the two men until Tobi spoke again. 'Then I must warn you as a friend.' Tobi sounded grim now. 'Take your wife and leave. I've heard they've got the permission of the chief's guards. They will use force if they have to.'

'We'll be alright, brother,' Etim said, staring blankly at where he knew Tobi stood.

'Did she do this to you?'

'What do you mean?'

'You're fucking blind, Etim!'

'On the contrary. I've never been able to see more clearly.'

* * *

Zenaida got really angsty when Etim told her the details of his conversation with Tobi. He could tell by the sound of her heavy steps as she paced back and forth in the room.

'We have to go,' she finally said. 'It's not safe here anymore.'

'Since when is the fearless Zenaida, *killer of men*, scared?'

'This isn't a joke, Etim!'

'What's not safe is us running away in your condition.' Etim rose from the chair to meet her. 'We have a baby on the way, and this is our home.'

'You don't understand, Etim. I have a very bad feeling about this. We must leave!'

'Since when did you take the words of Tobi seriously? You never even trusted him.'

'Precisely.'

He held her head still, up near his, and kissed her lips. He felt them quiver a little upon his. 'I'd die before I let anyone take you from me.' Etim rubbed her heavy, protruding belly. 'You both.'

'I've been h-having dreams, Etim.'

And now she sounded truly scared. Zenaida was never scared.

'Abike is coming for me.'

'What? How can you be certain? Why didn't you tell me?'

Something was rising and twisting inside his stomach, and he did not like it.

'I thought if I pretended the dreams weren't happening, they'd … go away. It started sporadically after I conceived, but now I see her every time I close my eyes, and her instructions are clear.'

Etim swallowed anxiously.

'I must leave my old life behind and become her priestess.' Zenaida was crying now. 'Now do you see why we must run?'

'We're going nowhere,' Etim said adamantly. 'If we keep running, it'll never end. My family, the town, Abike. It'll never end.'

'Oh, Etim.' She cried into his shoulder. 'This is all because of me, and now our poor innocent child—'

'—will be protected because we will fight whatever comes, together,' Etim assured her with another kiss.

As Etim held Zenaida close and felt her skin upon his, he remembered the first evening they had made love. It was the day her beauty had struck him blind. It had only been less than a second of gazing into her eyes, but the memory remained fresh and would last him an eternity. Her full face had been radiant like the sun, and he could only describe her beauty as aggressively breathtaking. Her untameable flaming red hair had seemed to match her eyes, because his eyes had burned with fire right after. Now, he barely remembered the anguish, only the immense pleasure that had followed.

* * *

They named their son Koa, and he was the most beautiful boy in true testament to his parents. For several nights after his birth, all Zenaida did was cry, for there was no greater pain for a mother who could hold but not look upon her child. Painfully, they had decided it would be best to blindfold him with a piece of cloth. Koa cried a lot in the beginning, but eventually became a happy child even with his temporary blindless.

'It's for the best,' Etim had assured Zenaida. 'When he's older, he can decide for himself. Tell me how beautiful he is again.'

And with that, Zenaida would giggle as she described their child to Etim, bringing Koa close enough so his father could feel his features. No one knew where they lived, and the only one who knew did not care to visit. Abike had also stopped appearing in Zenaida's dreams. They lived, they loved, and they farmed. All was well.

On the night before Koa turned eight, Zenaida had announced that she would set off to the big town in the valley between the highlands first thing in the morning. The large painting she had been working on for months was finally complete and ready for a new home.

She woke before Etim and Koa. In high spirits, she wore her finest and brightest robes; the blue one she had worn on the day she and Etim tied the knot. She clasped the robes around the collar with a small silver brooch and went merrily on her way with the cloth flowing behind her like some expensive silver curtain.

She sold her most prized painting yet and bought a very fat pig. She would make a nice pot of pork pepper soup for Koa's celebratory dinner, and the remaining meat would last them weeks. Feeling rather pleased with herself, she rushed home just after noon.

The shack door was ajar when she arrived, so she tied the pig to the front baluster and went in. There was no one in the shack, so she went to the backyard. Koa loved helping Etim on the farm. He was obsessed with tomatoes, just like his father.

'Lemongrass!' Zenaida yelled as she neared the back. That was the safe word they had all agreed to use whenever she returned home, to give Koa the chance to tie his blindfold.

She chuckled as she reached the fence, opening her mouth again, ready to give them both a light scolding for leaving the door open so they were all at the mercy of mosquitoes later at night.

Right there, in the middle of the farm, with freshly cut tomatoes lying around, were her husband and her son. Crimson liquid covered their fronts. It was difficult at first to tell if it was from the squashed tomatoes or their ripped-out hearts. She pushed her hood back and ran to them, falling to her knees with grief and wailing so loudly that the committee of vultures perched on the acacia tree nearby dispersed in terror.

Even in death, Etim looked happy. He had the faintest smile on his face, and he was clutching Koa's arm tight to his side. They both had the same short, jet-black hair. Since he had been in the safe care of his father, Koa had indeed removed his blindfold. It was the first time Zenaida was seeing his eyes. They were big, brown and beautiful, and they stared back at her blankly as tears continued to pour out of her eyes.

The vultures had returned and were flying low in a ring above her head now. Flies, too, had gathered on the fresh, open wounds. As she got up and turned her back, one bold scavenger landed on Etim and pecked inside his gaping chest.

Zenaida made her way into the shack. The tears had stopped flowing, but her throat remained dry and her chest heavy.

Trading her periwinkle blue robes for her old onyx black, she took a pair of rounded Damascus knives from the wall. Their blades glistened momentarily when she met the sun. Without thinking, she cut the rope from the baluster that held the grunting pig. The animal, suddenly sensing its freedom, pelted towards the forest with the rope still trailing behind it.

She took purposeful strides now. Eyes transfixed ahead of her, she clutched the ivory hilts of her knives so tight her hands went from hurt to numb to oneness. She would find the time to bury her dead later; this could not wait.

Today was midweek and by extension, market day, so the entire town would be gathered, buying, selling and gossiping, laughing at the problems of others and ignoring their own. She supposed this made people feel better about themselves. She was certain it would be packed, and the bustling noise proved her right as she approached the target area.

She reached in and tapped the power reserve inside her. The currents jolted inside her body like naked electrical wires. Zenaida opened herself to them. There was something she'd told no one. Something she'd refused to admit, even to herself. Abike's curse had given her something else. Unnatural speed and superhuman strength. Once or twice, she'd harnessed fragments of them, but nothing more. Others might have seen the goddess's touch as two sides to a coin; a blessing and a curse. For Zenaida, though, the only blessing she'd ever known had just been yanked away from her, and for that, everyone had to suffer. Suffer as she was suffering now. *Humankind and gods alike, they will pay!* So in that moment, she embraced the curse and its by-products, and accepted the monster that she truly was.

As soon as she emerged from the forest, it was Tobi who first caught a glimpse of her. Zenaida smirked malevolently when she saw his eyes widen in fear as she dropped her hood. Tobi's screams of agony alerted the market square as Zenaida launched forwards. Several people clutched their eyes in anguish as they fell to the ground or tried to flee, but she was too quick for any of them, and her blades, sharp and unforgiving, delivered strong and precise fatal cuts.

She slashed the blades swiftly through the warm air with newly reawakened vengeance, spilling the blood and guts of men, women and children. Everyone around her yelled and writhed in pain as their eyes burned upon her gaze. There was barely any time to escape before the witch's blade met and sliced their flesh. Their cries of misery were her heart's melody. When she was certain she had gotten all the people, she tore through the livestock for good measure. Then she set fire to every structure that stood. Even the trees and bushes around were not spared.

If anyone miraculously survived this inferno, the town would be uninhabitable.

Still vengeful but momentarily satisfied, Zenaida drew her hood up once more and retreated.

A smouldering carnage remained in her wake, and it reeked of flesh, blood and burnt wood. Behind her, thick smoke turned the day into night. Her sheepskin boots printed red patches on the shiny stone path while her blades dripped with the same substance. There were no more screams now, just her own long, slow breaths in the quiet as she disappeared into the shadow of the trees without looking back.

Now, to Abike's shrine.

Last Train to Rukuba

The driverless locomotive finally pulled to a grinding halt. A well-dressed young man sat patiently on an old bench by the platform. The Plateau Express train left here daily, every six hours unfailingly until six forty-five in the evening. The man had planned to be on time for the twelve forty-five afternoon train, but today the delivery boy, who was always on time with his medicine, arrived an hour late, so he'd had to wait. He never went anywhere without his medicine and his best pair of shoes.

He was slightly annoyed that he had missed the train because this shattered his strict schedule, but still, he had been patient. There was no other choice, after all. He had arrived at the station just as the train he should've been on pulled away, so he'd actually seen the back of it leave. He had set down his ageing brown leather suitcase beside him and endured a boring six hours of reading nine newspapers from the free newsstand. There had been nothing of interest in any of them.

Picking up his suitcase now, the man looked at his ticket before walking steadily onto the train where he found his private compartment.

Meanwhile, outside the grand station, a young lady was sprinting towards the front entrance. She attempted to be ladylike as she crossed the street, almost graceful even, but this was near impossible and, quite frankly, she didn't care how she was perceived at this very moment. If she missed this train, she was screwed, literally. She frowned as she entered the terminal and looked at the massive digital boards for the departure schedule, but there was only one line of text. 'RUKUBA – Final Call' flashed dangerously at the top.

She slammed her paper ticket on the glass scanner. It beeped and flashed a quick red before turning to green, granting her access to the platform. She smoothed her skirt unconsciously with her free hand as she boarded. Looking one more time at her ticket to confirm her coach number, she opened the door; already seated was a good-looking man who was impeccably dressed. The man looked quite surprised to see her. She gave him a small smile before putting her suitcase in the overhead storage compartment and then took a seat opposite him. She stared out the large panoramic windows but sensed the man's gaze fixed upon her. She ignored it at first, but then it was beginning to make her uncomfortable, so she looked him square in the face and tried the politest tone she could muster.

'Everything all right, sir?'

The man looked slightly insulted, perhaps angry even, but when he spoke, he sounded just as polite as she had been to him. 'You're in my coach,' he said simply with his legs still crossed.

The woman's eyes darted automatically to his shiny, well-polished black shoes. 'Excuse me?'

'This is a private coach.'

This time, the man was fully aware of the arrogance in his tone, but he had paid for a private coach for one reason – to have privacy.

And so he wanted nothing more than to be alone.

'It says here – 4C,' she said, peering again at her ticket. 'Hold on, aren't the first five coaches typically first class?'

The man shrugged unknowingly but he suspected she was right.

'Oh, I'm sorry. There must have been some sort of mix-up with my ticket.' She brandished the small piece of white paper at him quickly before getting up to leave. 'I definitely didn't pay for first class.'

She chuckled nervously as she withdrew her suitcase hurriedly from the overhead compartment. She gave the man another small smile without meeting his gaze as she spoke once more. 'Sorry again for the inconvenience.'

This time he returned her smile ever so slightly and nodded curtly as the door shut behind her.

The man lit a cigar as the steam train sped along on its tracks. The sun was slowly going below the mountains, so he looked at his watch. It was time to take his medicine. The pill had barely gone down his throat when the coach door slid open again.

'Oh, for fuck's sake!' the man said with a heavy sigh. 'This is a private—'

It was the same young woman from earlier. She looked terribly flustered, and the man only noticed now that she was pretty. But the last thing on his mind at the moment was a woman, so he couldn't have cared less if she had just walked out of a magazine's cover page.

'I'm awfully sorry. I've checked everywhere, it seems the train is full.'

The man stared at her without saying a word. This was a terrible inconvenience, but the rail company sold her the same coach in error, he thought. Reluctantly, he tipped his bowler hat at her before making a sweeping gesture with his hand towards the seat opposite him.

She threw him a broad smile and rushed to sit down, bringing distinct notes of her devilwood perfume along. 'Thank you so much! This has never happened. I should have looked and checked, but I got my ticket online at the last minute.'

The man nodded but said nothing. He barely even looked at her; instead, he focused on one of the newspapers he had already skimmed through earlier.

'I am used to being in third with eleven other people in a coach, so I don't mind sharing with only one person for a change.'

The man tilted his head and looked up at her, then realised she was trying to use humour to break the ice, so he chuckled drily. He really wanted to travel in silence, so he hoped she would cease the small talk and enjoy the view instead, or read a newspaper. He was happy to lend her one or two for the sake of his peace.

The woman looked out of the window now, to his delight.

'It's so beautiful.' Her eyes widened with her words. 'These windows are massive.'

She tapped her fingers lightly on the glass and coughed a few times, but the man didn't apologise for blowing his smoke into the air in front of her. The woman was sizing him up and down with her eyes, and he could sense it.

'Do you always travel in first?' she asked.

The man nodded as he took a long drag of his cigar.

'And do you always get private?' she asked again.

'Always.'

He blew more smoke, and she coughed once again, but less now.

'Fancy,' she said, with a look that reeked of faux admiration. 'A man who likes to travel in style.'

'Peace and comfort,' he corrected her quickly.

Her lips curled a bit immediately after he had spoken.

'I prefer to travel in peace and comfort, not necessarily style,' he continued as he blew more smoke into the air, and this time the woman didn't cough.

'Well, I think style is always necessary,' she said with a serious face. 'Regardless of whether you travel in first or third.'

The man couldn't help it; he chuckled in agreement, and the woman noticed his dimples. He had them on both cheeks, and they were symmetrical, just like his jawline. It was obvious the man was in his early thirties, despite his rather boyish looks.

An hour later, amid a few smaller talks and some pockets of silence, the two found themselves deep in conversation. They seemed very different people, and there were things they didn't agree on, many things. But each time it came to this, one of them was respectful enough to drop or change the subject.

'I assure you I keep my political views as mine and mine only,' the man said in a final sort of way.

'With such strong views like that, you'd better,' the woman said, shaking her head from side to side so that her bouncy hair was loose on both sides of her long face, 'or it'll get you in a lot of trouble.'

'Won't be the first time, trust me.'

'Oddly enough, that's the first thing you've said this evening I believe wholeheartedly.'

He burst out laughing for the first time. It was loud and rich and revealed his perfectly white teeth. The woman pretended not to notice and instead turned her attention upwards to his eyes, which apparently did him even more favours. So, she looked out of the window again and formed a particular interest in the snow-capped mountains standing gloriously in the twilight.

'This view never gets old,' said the woman. Her voice was slightly higher than a whisper.

'I find it rather distracting and annoying,' said the man, sounding unimpressed.

'Distracting?' The woman turned back sharply to stare at him as though he were insane. 'And annoying, you say?'

He bent his head and glared at her with pursed lips. It was obvious he was trying very hard to stifle a laugh.

'I'm convinced you boarded this train today solely to disagree with me.'

The man looked upward and laughed again. 'Alright, I confess, I like that view too. I've just seen it maybe a thousand times.'

'So have I, but from a tiny window down in third.' She eyed him teasingly. 'Now let me enjoy the moment, alright!'

Palm under her chin, she struck a dreamy pose and gazed out as the train rode closer to the lakes with the mountains now behind them.

'This is one of nature's finest arts, and I'd frame it right in my bedroom if I could.' She smiled without removing her gaze.

The man stared at her now, with purpose. Her soft heart-shaped face was a little too dreamy even from the side view. There was something about her skin too, almost as if it generated its very own glow. He watched as her supple fingers caressed the space between her lower lip and chin, it had to be butter soft.

She could sense his intentional gaze on her. The cabin grew a bit hot, or maybe that was just her. She could have turned to look at him to force him to break his gaze, but she indulged him by continuing to stare out of the window, even though the mountains and lakes were well out of sight at this point and the darkened golden fields of hay were of no particular interest to her.

After another bout of silence, the man asked her, 'So what takes you to Rukuba?'

'I have a job interview at the federal secretariat.'

She lied. The man didn't know this though, how could he? In reality, she was running away. Escaping an abusive marriage to a man she had lived with since she walked down the aisle at nineteen. Her husband had come to know all her family and friends in the five years they had been married, and there was no hiding from him back in Rokam city. She had tried twice in the past, unsuccessfully of course. But that was a story for another day. Today, all that was important was that she was running far away, and Rukuba was the only place her husband wouldn't find her.

She wasn't going to tell this to a handsome stranger, was she?

'What about you?' she asked the man calmly.

'I'm just going to close a business deal.'

He had also lied. But there was no way for her to suspect this either because they both looked their part. He smiled as he relit his dead cigar. He was, in fact, dying and going to spend his final days in the only place that held some sort of meaning for him.

'So, you take the train often, then?' he asked.

'Same time every week, but in third.'

'And I don't suppose it's an interview taking you every time.'

She giggled and rolled her eyes. 'Could be different interviews. Maybe I've been very unlucky.'

'A faraway interview every week.' He grimaced. '*Tsk tsk.* I'd hate to be you.'

'Oh, don't mind me, most of my family lives in Rukuba. So it's mostly visits. I take it you visit quite a lot too?'

'Same business schedule every week—'

'But in first, and private,' she finished for him. 'It's no wonder we've never met.'

They both smiled and said nothing else as they looked into each other's eyes once more, and in that instant, both wished silently that they could have been more truthful to the other.

The woman had in fact always travelled in first class with her wealthy husband, being the type of man he was, proud and all. He had always insisted they only travelled in a private coach, as if rubbing shoulders with other well-to-do people in the same coach was far beneath him. It was his money, so she had never complained. There was also the fact that she was sure to get a telling off if she did, or a slap across the face, depending on his mood that day and her luck at the time.

She had seen these panoramic views on all those trips. The views were always welcome, but they also left her with a bitter taste knowing what awaited her after the train reached Rukuba. She knew her husband would never search for her here; as a matter of fact, it would be the last place on earth he would think she could be. After all, he loved that city to bits, and she hated it with every fibre of her being, and he knew that. At least that was what he thought, and what everyone else who actually knew her also thought.

Today was the first time she had felt truly happy seeing those snowy mountains behind the lakes. She was free, and the anticipated smell of the Rukuba sea air sent a wave of excitement that filled up her stomach with new-found bliss.

As far as the truth went, the man had only ever ridden in third. He could barely afford a third-class ticket, never mind a private coach in first. Between his daily ten-hour shift in the coltan mines that paid next to nothing, where he was typically surrounded by scores of men covered in soot and bunking in a room with another dozen men somewhere in the slums of Rokam, he had barely had any alone time in nearly twenty years.

Two days prior, he had bought a one-way ticket for this train with his two months' wages, the most luxurious thing he would ever do. He had also emptied his savings in the bank to pay for the last prescription of his medicine, a second-hand suit, and a nice-looking suitcase. The shoes, he had always had, but wore only once a year on special occasions like Christmas, in order to retain their shine. He had never smoked a day in his life, but he picked up an expensive cigar this morning as well. He had always admired the cigar-smoking men in their sharp suits going about their business, just as he was today.

He was going to spend the few days he had left in the most beautiful place he remembered, the seaside town of Rukuba. The last memory he had of his mother was over two decades ago, on this very train – in third class. It was the only time he had ever been on a train too, and all he remembered of it was his mother pointing towards the white mountains in the distance through the small coach window.

He longed for his bare feet to be buried under the sand again. The one time he had been truly happy.

A flurry of movement and sound coincided with the train arriving at the station. The woman got up first, retrieving her suitcase and preparing to leave.

'Hey,' the man called abruptly as she reached for the door. 'I forgot your name.'

She stared at him for a moment. 'That's because you never asked.'

'Well,' said the man, blinking rather stupidly. 'Are you going to tell me, or do I have to suffer?' He blew fresh puffs of smoke.

'I'll tell you the next time we meet. I promise.' She opened the door.

'Aren't you going to ask for mine?' His hat was slightly askew now, and his tone carried a mix of mild amusement and slight hurt.

The woman stood at the door, eyeing him carefully as he continued to grin at her, his face even more boyish and handsome than it had been at the beginning of their three-hour journey. 'We take the same train every week, don't we?'

The man nodded slowly, refusing to break eye contact as he spoke. 'Indeed we do.'

'So you can also tell me your name then.'

And with that, she tucked some loose hair behind her ear and gave him one more smile before leaving their compartment. A smile the man couldn't return.

Alone once more, he stared at the small plastic bottle that contained the last blue pill of his prescription medicine. It had his full name printed on the white sticker in front.

'My name is Jon,' he affirmed quietly to himself. 'Jon Bunando.'

THE DRAGON LORD

Class, titles and family names meant everything in the empire. They were even worth more than gold. People had very little use for gold in these parts anyway, so that was to be expected. Sure, the people of the empire loved material things, just like any typical society. The newest garments, boots and riding gear. There were also fancy dinners at the palace if you were noble enough to get an invitation, and drinking in the public houses because that was most accessible to all. So, on the contrary, the people of the empire had a lot of use for gold – it just wasn't nearly as important as those other things.

But honour, that was a different thing altogether. It was without a doubt the singular most important thing across the empire, worth more than all the gold in the empire's treasury and worth more than class, titles and even the most ancient family names. It was the one thing everyone in the empire agreed upon, whether rich or poor. That and serving the emperor with unwavering loyalty.

And while it was an honour to be called to join the imperial (land) horse guards, there was no greater honour than being a sky guard, a member of one of the dragon families. The dragon families comprised of a few ancient families scattered across the empire with trained dragon lords. A dragon family could have as many as a dozen lords in one household – a true thing of pride – or as few as one. If an older lord from a dragon family died with no younger lords amongst his heirs, his entire family was better off dead because of the shame. In such rare instances, it was not uncommon to see families change their surnames to enter obscurity or even self-exile from the empire to save face. The least honourable option as that was.

Melie was the only child of his parents, so it was not strange that, as he walked through the large striking gates of the academy, it was with a very heavy heart. He saw the empire's formidable coat of arms, a horse and a dragon leaning on two crossed swords, cast solid on the thirty-foot rusting metal frames.

Unlike every other boy here, he had not been looking forward to turning fifteen because it meant the looming cloud over his head was about to come pouring down. The academy was all he had heard about since he could walk and understand any words. This was his family's legacy and his destiny, except it was a path he had absolutely no say in.

Bayelsa Academy was the only official institution where prospective dragon lords from select dragon families came to acquire their ranks before joining the noblest guards. Boys began their training at about fifteen and, within the next two years, every boy was expected to find, tame and bond with a dragon. They also had to learn how to fly them and wield various weapons simultaneously without falling to their deaths. If unsuccessful, a boy could neither graduate nor join the imperial sky guards as a dragon lord. Not forgetting the dragon in the room – failure would also bring total dishonour to the boy's family name.

'Has this ever happened before?' a nervous Melie asked his father, as their personal carriage waited out front, the morning before he was to begin at the academy.

'Never,' his father replied sharply and cast him a brooding look. 'Not in my day, anyway, and I hope to heavens, not in yours.'

That had been the end of that conversation.

Now as Melie stood waiting silently in a sea of a hundred boys in the large courtyard, he pondered over his father's words. What if he found a dragon that wouldn't bow to him? His busy mind flooded with images of him taming a weak dragon and falling off its back to his death on the first flight. Disgraceful. Or even worse, what if he failed to find his own dragon? A winter chill ran down his spine even under the scorching sun.

'Melie Fugah—' boomed the bald man up front.

Melie only raised his hand after the third call because he hadn't been paying attention. The man glared at him so that his ugly, heavily scarred face made him appear almost dragon-like. Coincidentally, he was standing next to the black stone statue of Chidi the Great. The statue was a replica of the gigantic one back at the capital's central square. Chidi sat on the half-spiked back of his legendary dragon, Keziah. And the look on his face was the same one he carried in all sculpted depictions of him. The look of unmistakable bravado.

When the man opened his mouth to speak, Melie made out several broken, yellowing teeth. 'You'll need a much sharper attention span here or else you'll be first to fall off the dragon's back,' the man said before looking at the parchment he was holding again.

The courtyard broke into laughter, mostly from the boys on the right. They, too, wore the same full-length uniform of earth tones. Most of the boys at that end were taller than the boys on the left where Melie stood. He noticed nearly all of them had cords around their necks with what looked like colourful whistles made from large scales hanging like pendants. He recognised this instantly and knew he was going to hate every second on this island.

'Jago Azizi!'

A boy raised his hand in front of him.

'Are you the son of Modibo?' someone asked Melie.

Aware of the eyes peering at him, Melie nodded uncomfortably without looking at who had asked. Some of the boys murmured, and he could have sworn he saw one of the older boys point him out to his mates.

'Silence!' scary dragon-faced man thundered, and order was restored instantly. He went on to finish calling the names on his list before introducing himself as the commandant of the academy. He wore no other jewellery except for the coin-shaped silver badge pinned to the breast pocket of his brown shirt. He was called Simo, but Melie suspected that name wouldn't stick. Simo raised the large scale roped to his neck and blew a low but shrill whistle.

At first, nothing happened, but shortly after, in the silence, a soft and steady rush of beating wings in the wind could be heard. It seemed to be coming from behind the group of trees a few hundred metres away. The rapid sounds grew louder until a large emerald-coloured dragon came into clear sight. The dragon's smooth scales shimmered sporadically under the sun like broken precious stones as it landed neatly behind its lord. The commandant climbed on via its large wing before flying away to *ooh*s and *aah*s from the new boys on the left.

Bayelsa Academy was a sprawling institution with massive stone buildings grouped around six quadrangles and smaller brick structures scattered irregularly on the campus. A former maximum prison, half of its original premises were in ruins now, an aftermath of the last imperial war. The emperor at the time had declared war after the vicious Black Axe insurgents somehow learned to tame and fly wild dragons. They seized control of several ministries and killed the emperor's favourite daughter, Princess Shilily. What had started as a *nonsensical skirmish* eventually turned into a full-blown bloodbath. A seven-year war that led to the creation of the empire's first sky guards – the emperor's dragon lords.

The parts that remained stood quite well, though. The lawns were pristine, and the halls were grand. All six courtyard floors were scrubbed once a week and hot water flowed into the baths in the mornings. And every evening, there was a feast, because the emperor spared no expense towards the training and wellbeing of his prospective sky guards.

Each year, around fifty beta boys made the island their new home and training ground while roughly the same number of alpha boys left the island as freshly ranked dragon lords for the great empire. Ten overlords taught the boys in the mornings in classrooms, and the same lords trained them on the grounds at noon. Evenings were left as free time, and night lamps were to be turned off across all twenty halls three hours sharp after dinner.

Thirty-five staff, all male, served as cooks, stewards and ground staff. There was also Lord Sparko, a stout man whose tanned arms were always covered in fresh burns and shiny old scars. Sparko, as all the boys called him, was the keeper of Bayelsa's tamed dragons; he fed them and nursed the sick ones back to health, too. He had a chronic speech impediment from a throat injury he'd sustained while taming his giant dragon, Red Shrimp. Many whispered that Sparko's disability was the only thing keeping him away from being the commandant of the academy. For even though he had a longer tenure than all the other overlords, he couldn't teach in the classroom or give orders on the battlefield. And yet, that never seemed to stop him from always smiling. Sparko got on well with everyone and even played the occasional evening game of speedball with some boys.

Every boy was advised to carry a bead of vellom on their person at all times. The commandant had said something about always being prepared, or something along those lines. Melie's mind had wandered at that exact moment. Vellom was sought after, especially amongst dragon houses. Its life cycle, however, was strange. The seeds were pulled from the thorny fruits of the dwarf trees found in the northern marshes, but only grew into usefulness in the southern hinterlands of the empire, where the climate was just right for the bipolar plants. And even at that, it was still rather tricky to grow, and it wasn't uncommon for a farmer to only harvest less than a hundred stalks out of over a thousand planted.

The seeds were useless elsewhere but worth a lot to the experienced farmers down south, who planted the seeds and tended to the stalks until they were ten feet tall and mature enough to cough out the soft, gel-like silver beads. Melie had seen his father ingest one small bead at a time whenever he was due to take to the skies. The properties of vellom were not completely unknown to him. He'd heard it made riders more alert, more tolerant to pain, and less prone to losing any stamina, even after prolonged periods. A week into Bayelsa, Melie had received his own small sachet of twelve vellom beads with mixed feelings. The possibility of actually finding and taming his own dragon in a terrain so vast seemed truly exciting, but the equal possibility of failure had also filled him with dread that immediately swallowed him like a black hole.

Bayelsa, although large in itself, only occupied a quarter of Dragon Island. The island was surrounded by several smaller islands dotted around, long rumoured to be nesting and hunting grounds for all sorts of dragons. And although there were several untamed dragons scattered across the empire, especially in the uninhabited outskirts of the cities, Bayelsa's environs were widely known to contain most of the dragon population. There were no official census records, but it was rumoured to be over a thousand strong. The mountains and volcanoes apparently housed most of the beasts up north, followed by the thick rainforests of the east, where a good number of them lurked. The western points of the island were mostly elevated plains that opened up to jagged cliffs whose foundations danced with the sea. There were also fertile lands here that grew the academy's vegetables and housed its livestock. And the south was predominantly beaches, some of them quite pristine and a popular spot for the young lords.

'On a lovely evening, you can see dragons flying near the beach at sunset,' one of the training lords told them one morning during Draconology class. 'It's not all misery and gloom here,' he told them. 'Although I agree, it is mostly misery and gloom on most days.'

The class laughed, and now Melie felt a small sense of relief knowing he wasn't the only miserable person here.

'As most of you already know, considering your backgrounds,' the overlord continued, 'being a dragon lord is more than just finding a dragon and bonding with it or naming it after your pets back home.'

More laughter erupted.

'Oh, trust me,' the overlord said, shaking his head and smiling. 'I've heard some weird dragon names in my time here.

'And no judgement here, gentlemen, at least not from me. My dragon, for instance, was called Sweet-tooth,' he told the listening class with a proud chuckle. 'A name that had nothing to do with her, that's for sure,' he finished with a quirky mumble.

The overlord's attention was now turned away from the class, past the tall, unshuttered window, and onto the sunny grounds. His beige poncho billowed gently, matching the rhythm of the soft afternoon breeze. He continued to pace back and forth for a while, whispering to the air before him and clearly lost in a world of his own creation. After what must have been half the lesson time, he seemed to regain himself because he rolled down the large paper board so it revealed the next slide, depicting several dragons that varied in colour and size.

'Dragons outlive their masters in nine out of ten cases, and I bet you didn't know dragons could die from heartbreak too. Oh yes, they can,' he finished, closing his eyes as if anticipating their shocked murmurings.

He was right, because the class began to talk in excited tones until he hushed them with one silent wave of his scarred hand. 'Can anyone tell me why a dragon can be tamed by a new lord after its former lord's death, but a lord can never tame another dragon if their dragon dies?'

No one answered. He stared around at the lot of them as they all shook their heads.

'Even as learned dragons lords, some things we will never fully understand.' He gazed outside the window onto the grounds again as if deep in personal thought. Only this time, the look plastered upon his face was rather grim. 'One of the many mysteries of our world,' he said in what was almost a whisper, before catching himself. 'Right, well, open to page four. The first three pages you should know, unless you've been living under a rock.'

Melie flicked the first couple of pages of his copy of *Dragon Fundamentals: A lord's guide*.

'Dragons possess different volumes and ranges of flames or ice depending on various factors such as breed, nesting environment, diet and even moods. In tamed dragons, who now share a bond with their lords, these moods can often include those of their riders.'

The overlord went on for ninety more minutes, explaining several things in detail and sharing loads of information. A lot of it Melie already knew from conversations shared between his father and his fellow dragon lord visitors, or from all the books he had been forced to read as a child, but some of it he had never heard. So he paid attention anyway – inking things down onto his moleskin. They finished the entire chapter just before the end of the class, and when the overlord told them they were dismissed, a boy with admiral-blue hair asked a question that Melie found surprising and interesting at the same time.

'Sir, what about ice dragons?'

'What about them?' the overlord asked in what seemed to Melie like feigned ignorance. 'I'm pretty sure all sorts of dragons are mentioned in your textbook, fire and ice alike.'

Some of the boys chuckled, but the boy seemed unperturbed by his classmates' mocking laugher.

'I understand they're extremely rare, but can we find them here on the island?' the boy asked plainly. The look of sheer determination on his face was almost comical.

Now it was the overlord's turn to roar with laughter, much to the embarrassment of the boy.

'Well, let me put it this way. You have a much higher chance of being reincarnated as the emperor himself than you have taming a beast that breathes out sheets of ice.'

And with that, he walked out of the class laughing, and the beta boys could still hear him, even when he reached the end of the corridor.

* * *

Melie kept mostly to himself. A month had passed since he arrived at Bayelsa and he had settled into the routine just like the other boys, but he dreaded each new day he woke up here and, as the days went along, the tiny knot of fear in his stomach had morphed into a full-fledged beast. Any day now, he, along with his cohorts, would be expected to venture out of campus grounds to do what primarily brought them here. He excelled in all theoretical tests but struggled terribly in practice on the field, not because he was smaller than most of the boys in his year, but because he was quite *soft*.

His father had said it. All the boys here said it. He knew it himself too.

'I actually refuse to believe his father is Modibo. As in *the* Modibo!' one boy said when Melie fell off his wooden dragon back while spearing a fast-moving watermelon on a pole.

'I heard his father only sent him here because he had no other sons,' another said on the day he fell face first after missing a simulated fireball in the chest by a whisker.

The boys jeered as the hot water balloons burst with a splash, drenching the front of Melie's dragon completely. The overlord in training that afternoon frowned at him before gesturing him to get back onto his dragon at once.

Melie had got used to these taunts from boys in his own year and the year above. It was clear he was lagging behind, but he was determined not to show any further weakness, not just because of the possibility of more ridiculing here, but because of the reprisals he would receive from his father should he fail.

Today wasn't going particularly well for Melie either. The morning class had been an extra-long and boring one – dragon diet, nutrition and digestive system. He had also skipped breakfast because he hated oatmeal. The sun didn't help matters either; it was an exceptionally hot day, one of those days that made one lose the will to live, so Melie was already struggling and was near breaking point, but nothing could have prepared him for the afternoon training. They had to run several laps, go over a slippery ten-foot wall with nothing but a flimsy rope and a nail in order to reach their dragons and dodge massive blasts that kept coming in rapid succession from the enemy.

Melie's shoulder sagged under the weight of his water-soaked wooden shield. One of the overlords passed in front of him, his lined face wrinkling even more when he frowned.

'In real battle,' started the overzealous overlord, who everyone called Blackbird, after his dragon of the same name. 'Your shield would carry the emperor's crest and would be twice as heavy. You must carry it upright with pride at all times and not just for defence.'

Another overlord, Kumagar, added promptly, 'Not to mention, it's one of the few things that could protect you when you're up in the skies. That and a functioning brain, anyway.'

'Exactly!' Blackbird chipped in. 'Vellom won't protect you. Its effects barely last thirty minutes. You'll be foolish to keep swallowing beads up in the sky instead of focusing on possible threats.'

'But, sir,' one boy started, 'I heard vellom can—'

Blackbird raised a hand to silence him. 'You heard wrong, lad. Your mind may tell you that you're *superhuman* for another hour or even two, but that's only the remnants of the drug lingering in your brain. A placebo effect, if you ask me. A true dragon lord doesn't need such things.'

Kumagar raised one eyebrow and frowned now but said nothing to his fellow overlord. Blackbird had called vellom a drug, clearly showing his disapproval towards it. It was true that some more traditional dragon lords saw the use of vellom as cheating. A sort of steroid that altered the mind and body, wrecking it in the long run. Melie had once heard his father argue for vellom against another visiting lord who swore vellom was a slow poison.

'Your concerns are valid but completely unfounded,' Modibo had said in his loud rich voice. 'There are studies you can avail of, Lord Jiltan. Countless research has been carried out extensively over the years, and the fact remains that vellom has no potential long-term risks. Possible side effects, maybe – yes, of course, as with many things, but if you take one too many beads in a short period of time, then the onus of a head-shattering migraine is your own cross to bear.'

Melie never like Lord Jiltan, with his extremist views and that ostentatious golden walking cane he always carried, even though his legs worked fine. Dragon riding was dangerous. Everyone knew that. *What was so bad about getting an extra boost?* Moreover, vellom didn't exactly give lords any special skill; it simply heightened their abilities and perhaps lowered the odds of them slipping off their dragons and plummeting thousands of feet to their deaths. Melie decided he didn't like Blackbird either. Melie also decided that even if vellom was the slow-killing poison that the hardliners professed it to be, he'd still consume it if it gave him even just a little more *edge* in the skies.

The overlords split the class into two groups, attackers and defenders, for winning points' sake, and the losers were to do the farm duty for the next fortnight. Amid all the yelling, trying to follow orders from cohorts and overlords blaring incoherent instructions, a flustered Melie got hit by two streams of hot blasts square in the face, making him close his eyes in panic. He fell off his dragon and twisted his ankle.

'Down twenty points for team two,' one of the presiding overlords shouted immediately from the side of the field.

Several boys hissed in frustration and cursed loudly as Melie's eyes watered from the searing pain that shot right through his ankle. He tried to stand up but was met by looks ranging from the deepest irritation to sheer disgust.

'I knew we were doomed the moment they put him on our team,' the blue-haired boy from his class said to another.

'Freaking princess needs to go home and learn to ride a horse instead,' another boy on the team spat.

But Melie couldn't make out who said this as he collapsed in pain and broke into a fit of tears. He would have run if his ankle had let him, so he wished the ground could open up instead and swallow him whole.

'Half of you would piss yourselves if you ever came remotely close to an actual battle,' said an unfamiliar voice near him. 'Piss off and leave him alone.'

The voice asked him directly now, 'Are you alright?'

He felt someone's breath close to his face. Whoever this was, the person had taken the trouble to squat near the ground.

Still, Melie refused to look up. He just lay in a foetal position, holding his ankle and sobbing into the dry grass. He felt a firm hand on his shoulder.

'Get him off the field!' someone yelled irritably.

This voice Melie recognised. It was the impatient overlord they all called Sniper. His voice was loud even from a distance.

The rugged hand pulled him up and spoke in the same calm voice from earlier. 'Let's get you to the infirmary.'

Melie tried to stand now, wiping his eyes with his free hand as the boy pulled him up.

It was one of the boys from his year. Melie recognised him from their shared lessons and the opposing team of their simulated battles, but they had never spoken until this day. His arms were muscly, and Melie thought he was quite handsome too. He had the gentlest-looking eyes and a thin shiny scar that ran from under his left ear to the middle of his thick jaw.

'My name is Zayad,' he said, stooping a little to allow Melie to wrap his arm around his shoulder.

He was much taller than Melie and looked slightly older too, even though Melie knew they had to be around the same age. He was patient as Melie limped beside him, wincing in pain with every step. The clamour of battle continued behind them as both boys left the field.

'Heavens!' Zayad chuckled. 'I needed the break too, so thanks for taking the fall.'

Melie eyed him, unsure if he was being sarcastic or not. Zayad smiled so Melie tried to smile back, but all that came out was more wincing.

'Melie … I'm Melie,' he said finally after they had left the field.

'Son of the legendary Modibo,' Zayad said cheerfully. 'Everyone knows who you are.'

'Oh, I'm sure they do,' Melie said and let out another grunt of pain.

* * *

Six months into their time in the academy and Melie could say he had finally made a friend. Zayad was the first real friend he'd ever had, if you didn't count all the ones he had back home whom he had only been forced to interact with because of their shared dragon family ancestry, and many of whom he had absolutely nothing in common with and would rather have played with grass than endure the mechanical conversations whenever their families visited.

So, in the true sense of the word, this was the first friend he had ever made. He was grateful for Zayad, who now made his days at the academy somewhat manageable. Zayad, it seemed, felt the same way; he was always first to seek out Melie, keeping a seat for him during meals in the dining hall and waiting on him after classes like some sort of protector.

They were assigned to different dormitories, so they usually met in the *junior rotunda* and sat by the plump armchairs in the corner near the fireplace. The beta common area was a large circular room with floor-to-ceiling windows that allowed in bursts of sunlight and moonlight. A towering bookcase with a slidable ladder by its side lay idle and gathering dust since most of the boys used the library in the east tower that held the same books and more.

The tall indoor plants in the corners and the small, trimmed bushes that ran the length of the room gave it a rather homely feeling, unlike the many other halls of the academy that often felt cold and lacking despite their large windows, bright lamps and lit fireplaces.

Here, Melie and Zayad always scrambled to complete their essays, usually a day before it was due. Sometimes, they played *guess the constellation* as they gazed at the sky through the clear ceiling. But most times, they simply laughed and talked a lot of nonsense, like how Dragonface came to be so heavily scarred. Their conclusion had been that his dragon, Storm-bringer, had burned him when it sneezed accidentally upon him.

Zayad grew up in a small town six hundred miles from the capital. There his family were the only dragon lords. Before coming to Bayelsa, he had never left his town, but he was not naïve or unexposed. Melie thought he seemed to know something about everything. Zayad was athletic and popular on the battleground, and thus liked by the entire class. He also seemed to be popular with the alpha boys – he could often be seen having chats with several of them along the corridors. So what benefit he had from this friendship, Melie failed to understand.

'Don't you ever worry?' Melie asked one evening as they sat by the beach just before twilight.

'Of course I do, everyone worries about different things,' Zayad said with a smirk.

Melie slapped his shoulder and looked at him knowingly. 'You know what I mean.'

Zayad stared at him but said nothing, then he pointed a finger at the blue crab that was scuttling sideways into the sea. Melie smiled as the water swallowed the crustacean, then he closed his eyes. He could hear the gentle crashing of waves and the laughter of a few boys in the distance who were attempting to surf.

'Everyone thinks I ... am weird.' Melie opened his eyes again and looked down at his feet buried in the sand. 'And you are popular – even the overlords like you.'

'You are weird, Melie, and I am popular.'

'Heavens,' Melie said in amused frustration. 'You're like a five year old, aren't you?'

'Hey! Question anything, but never doubt my intellect.' Zayad frowned, feigning injured pride. Then he broke into a roaring laughter and lay fully on the sand so that his back and calves were flat now.

Melie simply shook his head, smiling a little.

'I stand by what I said.' Zayad looked at him, and he, too, was serious. 'We all worry about different things. Also, I'm not that shallow.'

Melie turned from the sea and looked at him. He, too, lay flat on his back so that they were both gazing at a beautiful patchwork of light purple and deep orange that was the sky.

'I wasn't always popular,' Zayad said quietly.

'Please, don't start a pity party. I find that hard to believe,' Melie said with a tired sigh. 'You mean to tell me you didn't stand out as the young stud in your little town?'

Zayad sighed even louder. 'Melie, I have six older brothers.' There was a certain pain in his voice as he spoke while his fingers gently ran over his scar. 'My brothers all came here to the academy. My third oldest brother tamed his dragon in three weeks! He beat the record set by my father over thirty years before him. And my other brothers all tamed their dragons within six months of being at Bayelsa.'

Zayad was still lying hand under head and facing the sky. Melie remained silent, but he suspected where this was headed.

'My brothers always made fun of me, and my father never stopped them. He said it was innocent sibling rivalry, but I suspect he thought that would've made me as tough as them too. My mother never interfered because she'd always been afraid of my father. Probably scared of my brothers too these days with the bloody size of them. When I was nine, I tried to ride White-shoes, my eldest brother's dragon. That didn't go so well.'

'That's how you got that scar,' Melie said, eyeing the side of Zayad's face.

'Yup. He barely scratched me with the tip of his tail, but that was more than enough to cut deep. Apparently, I was *very stupid* and *very lucky*. Could've been my eye.'

'Being a pirate would have suited you,' Melie added brightly. 'We can't all be lords.'

Zayad showed him a middle finger, and Melie let out a loud guffaw.

'Unfortunately, that still wasn't enough to prove I was tough. It's extremely difficult to stand out when you have six stellar men before you, seven if you count my father.'

And for the first time, Melie saw him.

'This is our ninth month, and no one in beta has tamed a dragon.'

'We will, you will—' Melie started.

'Yes, but even if I did, I'm already way behind the rest of my family,' Zayad said. 'This won't be an extraordinary achievement. Much more is expected of me.'

'Try being an only child of the most decorated sky guard in the empire.' Melie bit his lip. 'The continuous honour of my family's loyalty to the empire lies with me, and I can't even stay a full hour on a stupid wooden dragon.'

Zayad's eyes widened theatrically, and both boys burst out laughing as the waves came within inches of their feet.

Zayad started again. 'I guess when I saw you being picked on, it reminded me of myself, you know … being the constant plaything for my brothers.'

'Never mind, you're tall and strong,' Melie said, imitating a crying face.

'Oh, have you seen my brothers? They are all built like dragons themselves,' Zayad told him. 'I look like a little puppy next to them.'

Melie laughed. 'I'm certain you'll make a great lord soon.'

'And you too – the most ferocious rider once you take to the skies on the ugliest, scariest fire-breathing beast.' Zayad smiled as he nudged him on the arm with his elbow.

His smile faded at the panicked look that swept Melie's face.

'You have flown on dragon back before, haven't you?'

Melie swallowed and remained silent. A fine spray from the high waves landed on their faces like nature's sudden gentle sneeze.

Zayad raised his back from the sand so he could get an honest look at his friend. 'You must have ridden on your father's dragon, surely!'

Melie looked at him, still saying nothing. Upon seeing the perplexed look on Zayad's face, he was forced to shake his head. Zayad grinned at first, then gasped in horror at the magnitude of the revelation.

'My father believes no one should ride on a dragon they didn't tame,' Melie told him squarely. 'That automatically cancelled out any leisure rides for his wife or son. And honestly, Luxor is very scary, so I was never really dying to get on her back.'

Zayad eyed him with what seemed like a look of understanding and newfound pity. Zayad rested a firm hand on Melie's shoulder and squeezed tightly as the cool, salty air filled their nostrils. Melie wished both the air and Zayad would never stop.

* * *

The rampant croaking of bullfrogs around campus was the harbinger of the monsoon season, and their tenth month at the academy was marked by the season's heaviest rains. It was also the month Zayad tamed his dragon, making him the first to do so among the beta cohort. Melie would always remember that weekend morning vividly. Over a dozen soaking wet boys, including some alphas, had barged into the rotunda, where Melie sat writing an essay on how best to treat one of the six most common dragon ailments. The sudden racket had caused him to jump in fright and knock his ink bottle over with his long arms, sending half of the purple liquid all over his paper.

Melie had groaned in frustration and cursed through gritted teeth as the boys stopped in the centre of the high-ceilinged room; the soles of their heavy boots pounding the old terrazzo floor and carrying a drenched Zayad and chanting the empire's war song until their voices reached a crescendo. Zayad beamed with pride as he punched the air and brandished a dazzling electric-blue dragon whistle in his right hand. They passed him from shoulder to shoulder until some overlords came in to congratulate him personally and thump him on the back.

It was as if the heavens, too, had wanted to honour him because lightning had flashed brightly through the glass dome of a ceiling, announcing the thunder that followed shortly after with a great rumble. Dollops of rain pattered against the high stained-glass windows as several more beta boys trooped out of the dormitories to see what all the fuss was about. When Zayad's eyes finally met Melie's, they exchanged wide grins, and at that moment, Melie had forgotten all about his ruined essay and had been truly happy for him.

The celebration continued well into the new week, with the commandant giving Zayad a handshake in front of everyone in the courtyard. Their schedules had long changed since the sixth month began. So, after morning classes now, all boys who were yet to tame dragons were allowed to skip afternoon battle simulations so they could venture out alone or in small groups for more successful searches.

'I can't believe the one morning I wasn't with you, you go and find yourself a nice little dragon,' Melie told Zayad in disbelief as they walked towards the nesting lair one wet morning.

'What? I'm not the one who decided to have an extra lie-in that morning.'

'You know I was wrecked from training the day before.'

Zayad was taking him to meet his dragon – Big-bull. Several of the beta boys and some of the alphas had bombarded Zayad with requests to see his dragon at the keep. But apart from Dragonface, Sparko, and a few of the overlords, Zayad had not obliged. 'I told them I had to show my best mate first.'

'Nice try – I'm almost tempted to forgive you,' Melie said with a snort.

'Oh, I've suffered enough. The bastard nearly melted my face before he finally bowed to me.'

Melie laughed. 'Well, that would have been sweet karma for being such a sly.'

They reached an opening the size of a hundred halls, and Melie froze in his tracks at the colourful sea of dragons. There were scores of them here, from the downright ugly to the magnificent. Some were only slightly larger than horses, but most were as big as medium-sized boats. And a few of them could even compete with the large office buildings in the capital. Most of them were deep in slumber now, although their collective soft growling snores quaked the earth ever so slightly.

Zayad blew his whistle, and instantly one of the larger dragons stirred gently and took several steps towards its lord with its wings mid-air as though ready to take flight any second.

'Come on.' Zayad beckoned after noticing Melie was hesitant in taking another step. 'Tamed dragons won't attack except on their lord's command,' he informed Melie.

'I know that,' Melie snapped.

'Well, come on then!' Zayad signalled. 'He won't bite.'

Zayad stroked under Big-bull's stomach so that it let out a soft snarl, and then he smiled at Melie, who was behind him. Melie, a bit more comfortable now, took calculated steps until he was standing beside Zayad. He stretched out a hand towards Big-bull, and Zayad nodded eagerly. Big-bull's fine blue scales felt like glossy leather, and Melie gave a small cry of excitement as the creature snarled even louder, letting out small puffs of smoke in the process. Zayad tapped its side, and Big-bull lowered its wing flat for his lord to ascend.

Zayad fished inside the pocket of his khaki trousers and popped something into his mouth. He offered Melie a tiny silver bead with the same hand. Melie blinked, realising what it was, took it and swallowed it without thinking. The effect was instantaneous. A small fire burned within him. It started in the pit of his stomach, then it spread to his lungs so that he inhaled and exhaled it. The warmth shot up to his brain too, and now his fingers, toes and every strand of hair were consumed by the power of vellom. He could see the insects flying around him. They seemed … magnified. He could hear the sounds of the forests that surrounded them, the inner sounds, and every fibre of his clothing rubbed against his flesh. He pulled at his khaki shirt and allowed it to rest upon his ribs again, eyes and mouth widening with new interest at the sensory relationship between the tan material and his skin.

'Don't just stand there,' Zayad called and chuckled as he adjusted himself along the dragon's spine, 'climb on.'

Melie frowned. 'Wait! Don't we need crash helmets?'

Zayad rolled his eyes. 'Oh, come on, man. We're not riding into battle, plus we have the great power of vellom! Get on!' he called again; he looked comfortable atop Big-bull's back. He grabbed one of the dragon's spikes with both hands.

Confident in vellom and trusting in Zayad, Melie climbed on and, just as he wrapped his arms around Zayad's waist, Big-bull jerked as his lord yelled a command. A couple of wing flaps later, they could see the terracotta rooftops of the academy below them as they flew towards the open sea. Pockets of Bisons that were reared especially for the tamed dragons' sustenance roamed and grazed on the fields.

'Heavens!'

'It's amazing, isn't it?' Zayad called back at him.

'It's unreal!'

First time on dragon back and Melie didn't hate it as much as he had imagined he would. As they flew over the waters, the reverberation of beating wings met the rushing wind. And when Melie rested his head on Zayad's back, the echoes of Zayad's roaring laughter were all he could hear. All that mattered.

* * *

Zayad's success seemed to have opened the door of luck for the rest of the beta year; several more boys tamed their dragons in the weeks that followed. Each morning the number of boys out on the search dwindled and, at the end of the year, only Melie and the blue-haired boy from his class, Maten, remained without dragons. Worse than the increased taunting, which Zayad tried to stop as much as he could, was the fact that his father was to preside over the ranking ceremony this year.

'Your father, the general, will be here tomorrow to represent the emperor for the ranking ceremony,' Dragonface told Melie as he rushed out of the hall after breakfast. Sparko stood nearby, with his arms behind his back. Short and stocky but agile and sharp. The man had to be on at least, six vellom beads a day, Melie thought to himself. He met Sparko's eye and the keeper winked at him and smiled coolly.

'You better get yourself ready early enough,' Dragonface continued, 'I shouldn't be the one to tell you of all people that your father is renowned across the empire for his punctuality.'

'Yes, sir,' Melie said promptly, darting away before the commandant could utter another word.

Tomorrow morning meant he had enough time to throw himself off the cliffs. Either that or he faced his father. The former seemed quite appealing at this point. Sleep eluded him that night and, in the morning, he could tell his father was present from the way the four other boys in his dormitory rushed to the windows facing the grounds. Melie peered through the boys' heads in front of him to confirm, and he found the sky was covered in a small fleet of armoured dragons. The midnight-dark frame of a gigantic dragon was unmissable. Luxor, his father's dragon, was at the front. Melie made out his father's tiny outline on top of the largest known dragon across the empire.

'*Whoa!* So cool,' exclaimed a fat boy everyone ironically called Mouse, as Luxor's great black belly flew over them.

There were channelled murmurs and looks cast Melie's way as he walked down the corridors headed for breakfast. Thankfully, he didn't have to meet his father until after the ranking ceremony and he did that only because he had been summoned. As expected, his father had more questions than he, Melie, had answers.

'Your alpha year should strictly be filled by perfecting your flying techniques and ground training,' his father said scathingly, 'and not searching for a dragon to tame.'

Modibo's moustache twitched in irritation as he peered down at his son. Austere and strikingly tall, with the perfect posture as always. The shoulders and front of his well-pressed black uniform were heavily decorated with gold medals, and his chest was draped with a smooth red sash. Peeking out from the scabbard at his side was his famous blade – the same one that had been forged with iron from the depths of a volcano and finished by the very smoke from his dragon. As a sign of importance, a fine black cape swept behind the general, clipped to the upper back of his standard uniform. Modibo dressed like this to all imperial functions and often complained about the cape's impracticality, but Melie suspected his father secretly relished the reiterated image of superiority that the extra cloth instilled upon everyone else.

Modibo was flanked by several other lords from the emperor's army, some of whom Melie recognised by face and knew by name, including Ramisk, a colonel on his father's inner squad. Ramisk was always courteous, even though Melie found him to be slightly aloof.

Dragon-shaped silvers, the size of coins, were pinned to the lapels of all the lords' jackets. They would have each received these at the ranking ceremony upon their own graduation from the academy.

Modibo then went on to recount the tale of Chidi the Great, a story Melie had heard a thousand times before, all from his father. As Modibo approached the end of the story, he brought his face lower, closer to his son so that the silver crested insignia pinned to his breast pocket caught some of the morning light and glistened. *Those frigid green eyes*, Melie thought with a shudder. He clenched his jaw and braced himself for the words that he was certain would follow.

'And even though Chidi is regarded as the greatest dragon lord our empire has ever known, no one hears his name except during a history lesson. And you know why that is?'

Melie's eyes shifted uneasily, and he caught Zayad's eyes far in the distance near a group of overly loud alpha boys. Zayad rolled his eyes into the back of his head and stuck out a lolled tongue as he drove an imaginary blade through his stomach. Melie struggled to stifle a laugh so he turned to stare at his father's shiny boots instead.

'Because, great as he was, even after his ultimate sacrifice on the battlefield, none of his nine sons tamed a dragon. His actions on the frontline ensured the continuity of our great empire, but unfortunately, not even a single son of his could ensure their surname was continued in dragon lordship. So shameful it was, that Chidi's widow invited her nine sons to dinner, fed them meat, and gave them wine to drink, before slitting their throats one by one with her own steak knife.'

Melie closed his eyes with his head still lowered.

'Some say it's because she couldn't bear the shame. Others say she was saving her children a life of ridicule that would have followed them across the empire.'

Melie looked up at his father now for his tone had changed. It became almost … desperate.

'A great name means nothing if there's no one to carry it forward.' Modibo looked at his son and sighed. 'Do not bring shame upon our family. Do not shame me, Melie. I refuse to be the last dragon lord.'

Melie didn't shift his gaze as he typically did because, for the first time, he saw something he had never seen in his father's eyes. Fear.

* * *

Their alpha year went by quickly, and even Maten now had his own tamed dragon in the keep. It was the smallest dragon Melie had ever seen, and several boys teased Maten and called him baby dragon to his face, but Maten seemed unfazed by this and appeared to bask in the fact that he, too, had a dragon, albeit a small one. Melie heard from some of the other boys that Maten's dragon barely had any fire strength; he also heard from someone else that the dragon was practically incapable of producing fire because that breed had extremely small lungs and short nostrils.

'How does one tame a baby dragon when it doesn't even know how to bow?' A boy said one day during class, in what was obviously a clear attempt to annoy Maten.

'I wouldn't know,' another said, chuckling mischievously. 'I have a *real* dragon.'

'Ruize is like that because he is from a breed of southern dragons that *are known* to be smaller on average,' said Maten acidly. 'Read a book for once, you idiots!'

'Oh?' teased the first boy. 'I'd like to see you run that sharp mouth of yours when mama dragon stomps in here any day now to take back her baby.'

And while Melie couldn't help but be envious of Maten, even with his baby dragon, he admired the unwavering pride Maten exhibited, regardless of all the taunting.

In all of this, his friendship with Zayad remained, and this alone kept his sanity.

'The boy with the largest dragon and the boy without,' Melie said one evening as they trooped into the forest after hours. 'At least that's one way for me to put myself into the history books, considering I can't find my dragon.'

'Heavens,' Zayad groaned. 'We've talked about this. Your father will just have to deal with it. Now shut up about dragons already and enjoy tonight, please.'

The moon was full and bright, and the boys were in high spirits, considering it was the eve of their ranking ceremony. To celebrate, Melie had agreed to sneak out of the academy with fourteen other boys from their cohort. There was no family reputation to protect at this point, considering he was already the failure, so he doubted very much that he could get into any more trouble than he already was.

They reached a part of the forest with several plants that glistened under the moonlight as if their petals had been sprinkled with diamonds. Several of the boys, including Zayad, cheered as they rushed to pluck the shiny leaves. Melie stared at them nonplussed.

'Don't tell me you haven't heard of moondust.' Zayad eyed him warily.

'I have,' Melie said truthfully. 'But I've never seen it before.'

Zayad handed him a freshly plucked leaf and explained how the sought-after plants were only available at full moon.

'It takes you on a trip.' Zayad smirked, eyes lusting after the large leaf he was holding. 'Lick it and you'll forget about all your worries, even if it's just for a bit.'

'Why though?' Melie asked.

Zayad gave him an exasperated look. 'Why not?' he asked as he placed his hand on the side of Melie's neck. 'As much as I'd love to hear some more whining about your father and the many ways you could further shame your family name, I'd appreciate going a few hours without actually hearing them. Now lick up.'

The soft drops touched Melie's tongue. It was sharp at first but surprisingly sweet and unlike anything he had ever tasted. Its effect was almost immediate. He felt the most relaxed he had ever been in all his life, and for the first time, nothing was troubling his mind. It was, quite frankly, just blank. He liked this feeling, so he reached down and plucked another plant, licking it just as fast as he had harvested it.

He heard Zayad's voice from somewhere behind him. 'Easy now. You don't want to take too much and go on a lengthy trip.'

But Melie ignored this. After all, what did it matter? He wasn't receiving a dragon lord's rank tomorrow anyway. This year, the emperor was coming to Bayelsa to issue the ranks himself, surrounded by his highest-ranking sky guards. Modibo would be at his right hand certainly, and Melie giggled as he pictured the look of disappointment that would be slapped across his father's face upon the emperor's discovery that the son of his most noble general couldn't even tame the smallest dragon.

But then Melie wept. Zayad rushed to him at once and held him close in his arms, and Melie continued to sob heavily into his chest. Tomorrow, the beta boys would round the alpha boys in the main courtyard and attack them with mud bombs, smearing their khaki uniforms and faces with the dark, filthy mass. An unofficial rite of passage. The alphas would take the public humiliation in stride, before washing up after and enjoying the biggest feast of the year later that evening. The emperor would be seated at the high table of the grand hall, raising his goblet to hearty cheers and the beaming faces of surrounding generals, overlords and proud new lords.

And the next morning, in more pomp and ceremony, Melie's former cohorts would fly out on dragon back to the capital, behind the emperor and his generals, several hours before the new betas start to arrive for their first day at Bayelsa. He'll remain here, while Zayad would fill out the paperwork at the ministry of defence, preparing for deployment to his new station, heart bursting with pride.

Melie was once again coming to grip the hard realisation that he would have none of those things. Two years here and he had failed, woefully. He felt sad now. Depressed. He allowed himself to sob harder, without shame.

'I told you to go easy on those,' Zayad said. 'It'll be alright, pal.'

As Zayad tightened his grip, Melie felt several more arms wrap around him. Some of the boys were now saying some things to him that he couldn't make out; he only felt their warm comforting breath down his neck.

* * *

He woke with a start. The moon was still bright and high up, but it seemed much larger than usual; he wondered if that was just the moondust effect. He looked around, and all the boys had fallen asleep on either side of him with their backs resting on tree trunks. Zayad was directly to his left, fast asleep and snoring lightly, his head bobbing slightly up and down on Melie's shoulder.

Pushing him away carefully, Melie stood and followed the moon. With each step through the thickness of the forest, the moon appeared to grow larger, shining even more brightly. And when the trees temporarily covered the moon, it was the dancing fireflies that seemed to guide him back to the lunar light.

The warm night air became increasingly cooler the further in he went, but he continued to walk until his ears and fingertips started to go numb, and every breath became as painful as inhaling tiny shards of broken glass. He must have walked for hours because when he reached the edge of the forest, he was greeted by the distant sounds of crashing waves.

And there it was.

Armed with an enormous pair of leather wings, and a half-spiked back, it was the most beautiful thing Melie had ever laid eyes upon. Even in its resting state, the silver-scaled creature towered several metres above him. His heart was racing so fast and his feet weighed a ton, so he trod carefully, inching forward with purpose, step by step.

The dragon must have smelled him because it lifted its massive horned head and peered down at the trespasser with fearsome blue eyes. What followed was a bone-chilling, low rumbling growl. The dragon thrashed a long spiky tail around and raised its thick neck to full length before unfurling a pair of great silver and black wings dangerously, blocking the light of the moon completely.

Uncertainty peaked inside Melie's stomach as beads of sweat gathered on his forehead and soaked the collar of his shirt despite the dragon's ice-cold breath that now surrounded him like fog. He pressed against his breast pocket and felt the tiny soft ball of vellom that he carried more out of habit than anything else. He placed it on his tongue and then, with the slightest hesitation, he swallowed. The familiar fire burned within him. There was no turning back now. He would have to ride on the dragon's back or end up in its stomach. Either way, he would not be bringing shame to his family come morning. Of that, he was certain.

MY HEART IS BROWN

I have no name, not because I choose not to but because it's the way things have been and the way things must continue to be. I've been a bounty hunter longer than I remember; actually, it's all I remember. You see, although I have no name, anyone who needs me can find me. That's how much of a reputation I've built. Ruthless, fearless, discreet or revered, it all depends on who you ask. I don't care for any of those labels though. All I care about is getting the job done.

As far as bounty hunting goes, I am the best on the continent and there has never been a doubt. It is neither up for contest nor debate. I always travel light, along with my companion, Toph. My tools are carefully wrapped inside my ageing satchel, which is strapped to Toph's side. My clothes are dark because it blends perfectly into the night, and my face is always half covered, never out of fear but because the only thing more unforgiving than me is the terrain through which I travel.

I have been travelling for nearly a fortnight now, travailing through villages and towns in my search. From the civilised gold-wealthy city of Bishopsmeade to the barbaric shanty town of Kaego-Dutsa. I sleep in different inns when night comes, provided it has an overnight stable to accommodate Toph.

I know what the girl looks like from the renders given to me by her seeker, and I show several people along the way, even in the villages far from the kingdom, but no one knows who she is or her whereabouts.

I stop at a chemist along the way to refill my medical supplies, and I ask him too; he is rather disgruntled when I don't give him any more coin than I owe. I suspect he is paltering with his tips for me to go east. And I am right because the lead turns out to be unhelpful.

While the girl seems to be sneakier than a stray cat, I finally track her down in a small, dingy tavern in Stone Town – one of the northernmost settlements. The inhabitants of this old mining town are geographically so far from the kingdom that they don't give a rat's ass about the monarchs. Impressive she even made it this far out; I give her that.

She has her hair cut short, typical. And her clothes are so raggedy she could pass for a common street boy. To any other person, she might have gone unnoticed. If this was an intentional disguise, it was rather amateurish to me, but still quite remarkable for someone such as her.

She is serving a pitcher of ale to two older men who are desperately attempting to grope her, clearly against her wishes. Whether they are trying to take her knowingly as a young man is what remains uncertain to me. A few punches and a kick later, I emerge from the tavern unscathed with the princess bundled and resisting on my shoulder. She kicks and screams, but it doesn't matter. I could take her out with just one arm if she tries any funny business. But I tie her wrists with a small rope for good measure. It's better this way to save both our time and protect her honour.

We begin our journey down south, back towards the princess's home. As we travel over a muddy path, my companion appears to be struggling at first, but then he becomes agitated.

'Toph, easy!' I yell as I pat him several times on the side of the head. 'Easy boy, that's it, good boy.' I go on calming my horse so he doesn't throw us off in this unusual fit.

When we are out of harm's way, she asks me my name.

'I have no name,' I tell her simply.

'Everyone has a name,' she says to me.

'I don't,' I say, stressing the last word in hopes that no further questions will follow.

'What, then,' she continues to ask, 'do people call you?'

'I have no business with *people*, so there is nothing for me to be called by them.'

She pauses for a bit as if she is pondering what I have just said before she speaks again. 'Well, you were obviously sent to capture me. So what name did the queen use in order to find you?'

'When you're the best at what you do, you don't need a name to be found.'

My words are greeted with silence after this, and I am quite thankful.

* * *

We are now about two days' ride from the palace after journeying for nearly a week. The mighty dark cloud above us is teasing rain and casting a great shadow. We take shelter in a public stable in a small riverine village because the weather has taken to misbehaviour in the last hour and Toph hates travelling in the rain. The princess tells me she needs to relieve herself. I hesitate, but because her request is polite, I tell her she can go around the back. But she simply stands there staring at me.

'Not a chance,' I tell her as she raises her tied wrists towards my face. 'And you better hurry.'

'How am I supposed to clean up?' she asks me, sounding flabbergasted.

'I don't care,' I say as I brush Toph's mane dry. 'Be creative. And be quick.'

She scoffs and disappears behind the stables. She is gone for some time, and I don't bother until she is nearly half an hour, and then I know something is amiss.

'I should have bound her feet,' I say through clenched teeth to an unbothered Toph before I walk behind the stables and into the village under the torrential rain.

I find her again in no time, soaking wet and hiding behind a fishmonger's cart. Anger mixed with irritation has welled up inside me, but I hold back my tongue and my fists. Her grimace is cut short by the deep look of impatience I give her. So, of her own accord, she walks back towards the stables, and I'm closely behind her.

'Do that again, miss, and I won't be so forgiving,' I tell her as I put her on Toph's back.

'My name is Ene.'

'I didn't ask,' I say to her sharply. 'I know who you are – Princess Ene of Gao.'

'I'm never going back to the palace, just so you know,' she declares. 'So you might as well just kill me right here ... right now.'

'The instruction is to bring *you* back to the palace. It didn't say you have to be alive,' I say to her truthfully.

She frowns at me, and I'm unsure if what's in her eye is fear or pure disdain.

* * *

We ride in silence for the rest of the day until we reach the foot of a hill, where trees are thick and plenty. I announce we are to make camp here; it's only a few miles from the palace gates. I am never one to ask too many questions, but I am curious.

'How did you manage to reach Stone Town?'

'I paid a travelling steel merchant to hide me inside his freight carriage,' she tells me. 'I was desperate, and he couldn't say no to the coin.'

'I see.'

'I suppose you're dying to know why I ran away, then?' she asks me later that evening as I am trying to start a fire.

'On the contrary,' I say out loud to her before muttering to myself, 'but something tells me you're going to say, regardless.'

'I ran away because I was miserable,' she starts. 'After the death of my mother, everything in my life spiralled, including my father, the king.'

— 90 —

I am still struggling with the fire because of the breeze, but I listen anyway.

'As the days went by, my father wouldn't even look at me. People closest to him told me it was because the loss of my mother was too painful for him. You see, I bear a striking resemblance to my mother, as if that were my fault.'

She stops and takes several deep breaths. 'And while my father was mourning his wife, he seemed to have forgotten I was in mourning also, for I had lost a mother. We grew so distant in the years that followed until one day he came to me and held me in his arms. He apologised and we laughed and cried all through the night. And just as we were rebuilding our lost relationship, his courtiers advised that he remarry.'

The fire is crackling and provides some background noise for the times when she pauses her story.

'You see, it's a long-known fact,' she continues slowly. 'Unmarried kings appear weak, both in front of their subjects and to their enemies. So along came my stepmother, the new queen that had been arranged for my father by the counsel. I never liked her from the start. Something about her spirit never sat well with me. I warned my father, of course, but he promised me nothing between us would ever change again. And, not that I blame him, he put his duty to the kingdom first, as would most kings.'

I eye her carefully now, knowing the story is approaching its end.

'But his duty and new marriage came first. He changed once more, and this time he would barely even speak to me. I had lost my father even as he lived. So I plotted my escape for a year, but it was difficult being under constant watch. Then the queen had a baby, and my father's only son became the apple of the king's eye.'

She pauses again and the fire crackles some more.

'A maid – a trusted friend – overheard the queen's plot to kill me and make it seem like an accident because she feared, as the first child of the king, I could still be next in line for the throne.'

And now I see her wipe her right eye.

'But I never wanted the throne, I didn't care for it. I just wanted a family. Anyway, knowing the king would never believe me, seeing the new man he had become and fearing for my life, I escaped with the help of my dear friend, the queen's maid.'

'Is this why you think queen sent me?' I ask her.

'She's the only one I know who wants me dead,' the princess says with a shrug. 'Who sent you after me?'

'I cannot say for I do not know,' I say to her truthfully. 'But you've said it yourself,' I continue. 'You have a friend in the palace who knows of this evil plot. I say you reveal it to the king and let him put an end to it, if all you've said is true.'

'Did you even listen to anything I just said?' she asks me with her mouth agape. 'My father doesn't exist inside the king anymore. You're delivering me right back to her, to be slaughtered.'

'I'm afraid this changes nothing,' I say to her as I rise to my feet. 'I have a job, and I always deliver.'

'Do you even have a heart?' she asks me now, and I can see her eyes are welling with tears.

'The wild boars this side are vicious, and I'm sure you've heard of the notorious bears and wolves too,' I say to her as I walk towards the trees. 'If you run and they get you, let's just say you won't be worrying about your stepmother ever again.'

I leave her with Toph and the fire to keep them both warm. Later, I return with a fat rabbit and cook it slowly by the fire. All the while, she doesn't speak to me and I don't to her. This is as it should be. Toph is munching on some of the pasture nearby while the princess and I share the smoking meat. If she hates it, her expression gives nothing away. She doesn't complain, neither does she ask for more. She never does. And when it's time to sleep, she lies on her side with her arm to her head like a pillow and her back turned to me. She is humming a tune quietly to herself until I hear her light snores.

* * *

As always, I am awake when she stirs from sleep in the morning. I am brushing Toph's coat with purpose, but I can sense she's about to speak to me.

'Do you ever sleep?' she asks.

'Of course,' I reply without taking my attention off my task. 'I am human.'

'Wow,' she says with emphasis. 'Who would have thought.'

I turn and stare at her gently. My scarf is loose on my neck these days since we arrived in the woodlands. She is frowning at me but, for a moment, her expression softens upon my gaze.

'Gather yourself,' I say to her abruptly. 'I have to deliver you before sundown.'

I turn to Toph to tighten his saddle, but I can see her eyes through my peripheral vision. And this time, I am certain it's full of loathing.

We ride under the cloudless sky towards Gao, and she is surprisingly quiet. I am almost fascinated. I realise she is deep in her own thoughts. In the distance, I can see the pointy spire of the cathedral, and people around the fertile cornfields stare at us as we ride by. Surely, word of the escaped princess would have gotten out by now and, even with her *guise*, the people here must recognise her.

The magnificent sandstone towers of the palace rise into view as we ride deeper into Gao, and scanty low buildings give way to taller, denser structures. I suspect that any moment now we could be met by guards from the citadel because this is officially royal territory. The roads are paved with cobbles here, and Toph's shoes strike them, adding to the sounds of the busy streets.

The smell of stale beer, sweat and rubbish is right under my nose. The air is still and smoky from all the burning coal. It's been years since I ventured into Gao, and it is definitely worse than I remember it.

I cannot wait for this to be over. I have been tasked with much tougher jobs in the past, but this one felt extra difficult for some weird reason. I am used to finding thieves, miscreants and scoundrels. Sometimes I am tasked with delivering people charged with treason and, on other occasions, I must find debtors for their lenders. But never have I been tasked to find a princess on the run – a girl escaping her own family, or so she claims.

I have met many liars and several dishonest people, and she does not seem to fit any of those descriptions. But this is not my problem. I am simply getting the job done, my job. I am eager now to get her off my hands, and so as we ride, I must confess that I even start to daydream about the money. It's a lot of money. And the most I will ever receive for a single job. It was offered to me before I could even decide on my fee, but there had been no need to bargain.

The princess still hasn't said a word, and I can hear her slow, deep breaths behind me. We are getting closer, and I can see the shiny metal helmets of several soldiers up on the fine stone battlements. A sharp contrast to the ugly, breathing beast that surrounds it. Like a single pretty rose growing out of a swamp. Disparity is something I always notice as I travel the world, but in the kingdoms of this continent, it seems even more stark.

Again, this is not my problem, so I continue to think about all the ways I will spend the money, but something strange builds inside me. I have heard of it but never experienced it myself. Guilt.

As we near the open gatehouse, two horse guards approach us. It appears they expected our arrival and are here to collect the princess. They don't appear to be armed, but one of them is holding a small, heavy-looking sack and the printed inscription on it looks freshly inked. I draw the reins and Toph comes to a stop. Only a few feet away now, I can see the glossy words on the black sack clearly. The Royal Mint.

That strange feeling from earlier has enveloped me. *I cannot do this.*

I tug at Toph's reins so quickly he jumps in fright with a loud neigh, but he knows the command. 'Hang on to me,' I yell behind me.

The princess doesn't hesitate. Even with her arms tied, she grasps my cloak for dear life as tightly as possible. The guards are confused. I'm sure the princess is too, but honestly, so am I. I try my best to avoid the pedestrians crisscrossing the streets and the wagons wheeling goods and passengers about. A woman gasps as we miss her by the whiskers, and one man points us out to another from the front of a tavern.

'What are you doing?' she asks me blankly.

'I don't know,' I say as we continue to gallop away. 'Saving your life – do you have a problem with that?'

I can feel her heart pounding behind me, but it could be mine in all the confusion.

'No,' she says. 'Not at all.'

I keep Toph at full speed in case the guards decide to follow. To my surprise, they do not. I am relieved, for even though I can take two guards easily, I fear what they might do to the princess for my actions. It is only now I realise how much danger I'd just put the princess in. If the archers had fired, it would've struck the princess on the back. And perhaps fatally too. *Reckless.*

'Why?' is all she asks after we slow down. 'I have no money to counteroffer you.'

I feel insulted, but I understand. Her incomprehension is valid. 'It's not about the money,' I tell her after I pull at Toph's reins to slow us down.

She lets out a harsh, derisive laugh. I tug at Toph again, and this time, he comes to a full stop, puffing uneasily.

'You couldn't do it, could you?'

I say nothing as I dismount, and I gently stroke Toph's forehead to relax him.

'So, you do have a heart.' She's staring at me in the strangest manner.

I withdraw a knife and cut the rope binding her wrists together. 'You're free to go.'

Her eyes widen, and she is looking at me as though I have gone insane.

'I don't understand.'

'You can go,' I say again, this time more slowly. 'You're free of me.'

'In the middle of nowhere, a few hours to sundown?' Her eyes are still open wide. 'And who told you I'm free? You think she won't send another bounty hunter after me?'

I shrug. 'That is no concern of mine,' I tell her with serious eyes.

The strange feeling from earlier has disappeared now. *Thank fuck.*

'If you leave me here, I'm as good as dead.' Her voice is sombre now. 'There's nothing around here for miles, and—'

'Alright.' I cut her short to rid myself of her whining that I know is bound to continue. 'I'll escort you to the nearest town, but that's it.'

She gives me a small smile, and it seems genuine.

'Thank you.'

We ride for a few more hours into the night until it's time to retire for the day. As I watch her lie on the ground, I toss her my satchel to use as a pillow. She lies on her side with her face turned to me for the first time. She starts to hum like she does every night, but tonight, it seems to carry more – melody. Her tempo is increasing now, and she breaks into a song. From the chorus, I gather it is a ballad, one about six deer and a woodpecker. Most of the words are in a language I don't understand, so I can't tell if it's a sad or happy tune, but still, her voice is lovely.

It's not very long until I can hear her snores. I expect it now really. I rest my back and head on the tree and say the traveller's prayer before I, too, drift off shortly after.

* * *

The next day, the ride is easier. She asks me random questions, like why I have a long scarf. I tell her it is to protect against the blistering sandstorms I often encounter. And then she asks many more questions. Way more than I would like, but I indulge her, mostly. She is shocked that I have no recollection of my childhood and that all I know of my life is bounty hunting. Her shock turns to pity when I tell her I have been in this trade since I was about nine. The only family I have is Toph. The only home I know are the golden-brown dunes of the desert.

'So, you've travelled a lot, I assume?' she asks me in what seems like a hopeful bid to travel vicariously through my words. 'And which is the most beautiful continent, in your opinion?'

'Yes, I've been everywhere,' I tell her frankly. 'From the continent of Lucia, past Mazeqaria and all the way to Dominga, but they're all mostly the same for me now. I never really go on leisure trips.'

'Wow, so four out of the five continents then!' she breathes excitedly.

Five out of five actually, but I keep this to myself.

'Oh, I'd love to see it all,' she continues, voice brimming with deepest longing. 'I've never left Lusaka. Until I ran away, I'd never been anywhere really. What's the landscape and weather like in Lucia, I wonder?'

'Very remote and too harsh for a princess, trust me.'

'And do the people of Dominga really eat their offspring?'

I cannot help but chuckle now. 'Not that I noticed,' I say calmly in contrast to her own overexcited tone. 'It's a beautiful continent alright, but I admit, they are a strange bunch, the Domingans.'

'So, do you ever, ever … kill people?'

Several images rush to my head at once but I say nothing, and with that, we ride in silence for another hour. I hear the gentle sounds of water now, a blessing after the last two days, so I steer us towards it. We all drink and the princess insists on having a bath since there is a warm spring here too. I am not certain that this is a good idea, but on second thought, I cannot see much harm coming from it, so I allow it.

'Nothing extravagant,' I tell her quickly. 'Azur is still quite the journey, and we must reach it by nightfall.'

'You'll be rid of me soon, don't you worry,' she says as she begins to undress.

I turn my face away towards the wildflowers competing for space with the trees, leaving her only to the mercy of Toph's stares. She is quick enough, and upon dressing, she comes to me and stares me right in the face until I can nearly taste her warm breath.

'I had no milk, scented oils or shampoo,' she says, biting her lower lip. 'There was nothing extravagant about that bath.'

As she stands before me, clean, with her short, wet hair and nice caramel skin, I can see now that she is truly a beautiful woman, with nice, large, almond-shaped eyes. I can count the freckles sprinkled on her nose, and we are locked in a dangerous gaze. She is smiling mischievously, and a hot tingling sensation is sweeping inside me. I know what it is. She leans forwards and up, and I place my hand on the nape of her neck and stoop down to kiss her. I wonder what her lips taste like, but then I hear a small crack nearby. Like the breaking of a small twig. I tilt my head to listen. It is faint this time, but I hear it again.

'We're in the middle of the woods,' she says, looking around. 'A rabbit or deer maybe.'

I shake my head and raise a finger to my lips to plead her silence. 'That's no animal,' I whisper softly.

I have a small dagger tucked inside my boot, another strapped to my shin, and I wear one short blade by the hip, but none of those will do. Slowly, I reach for the bigger, longer knives in the satchel hanging off Toph's saddle and, shortly after, four men have us surrounded. I know from the sounds they make even before I see their black cloaks – these men are bounty hunters. Stealth is our modus operandi. I suspected this would happen, but I was foolish to think we had a day or two more before anyone could catch up.

With eight knives reaching for us from all angles, I spin wildly on the spot. My eyes, darting around, search for the weakest of them. I can always tell, so I launch an attack on the man to the east. I try to invoke the code; I only aim to disarm him as all bounty hunters should with one another, but no. These men were not sent to capture, but to kill. So I fight to the death. Even with my experience and skill, it is quite difficult for me. However, I am less impressed by their skills than I am with the queen. Gathering four solid bounty hunters in two days is no easy feat. That is a skill in its own right.

All four men fall but I remain, barely up myself in all fairness. My chest and upper right arm are slashed, and I am bleeding profusely from the gashes. The last thing I hear is the sobbing princess dropping to her knees beside me, tears leaking from her eyes.

When I awaken, the princess is still here. Toph is too, towering near but over me. He can always sense when something is wrong. He has been my companion all thirteen years of this trade and shared in my pain far too many times for me to count. I can feel the princess's soft hands dab something cold and soothing on my wounds.

'I'm sorry,' she blurts. 'This is all because of me.'

She is no longer crying, but her large eyes are red and puffy. I can make out the gel leaking from the aloe vera leaf she is holding. There is a fire burning nearby too, and something is cooking on top of it. It smells terrible.

'What is that—' I start to ask, but I'm cut short when she speaks.

'Moss phlox roots.' She jerks her head towards the flames. 'Healing … It's the only thing I found interesting during my noble training as a child. I couldn't find everything I needed here, so I had to make the best of what I could. The cut around your chest was quite deep too, but thankfully, it missed your heart. Only narrowly, but at least you're alive. You'll have to take it easy though, you shouldn't be—'

'Thank you,' I say, gently forcing a small smile and resting her hand in mine.

That night, it is I who falls asleep first and, as we get up to leave in the morning, I wonder what she thought of my snoring.

'I don't think the queen will stop until you're dead,' I tell her as we ride towards Azur just around noon. We'd been travelling for hours now, having set out early in the morning, just as the last stars of night had began to fade.

She says nothing, so for the first time, it is I who continues to speak. 'You'll never be safe here,' I say to her honestly. 'I will take you to the harbour so you can take the boat to Brie. The grass is so green there it's surreal, and the weather is always right.'

I picture her now, vivacious. Running and leaving her footprints on the wet golden sands. Salt air pushes her hair back, and she is laughing as the turquoise waters kiss her feet.

'The beaches there stretch longer than your eyes can see, with lots and lots of coconut trees. It's the most beautiful of all the continents if you ask me. I think you'll like it there.' My voice drops a little. 'You'll be safe there … you'll be happy … you'll be free.'

Her grip around my waist tightens a bit more as I say this, and I feel her tenderness against my back. There is a strange feeling budding up in me again, but this one I do not recognise or have a name for. And while it's frightening, I admit it is not the worst feeling.

'If you weren't doing … this,' she says. 'What else do you reckon you'd have done?'

The question takes me unawares. I think long and hard, for such a thought has never crossed my mind. Not even once. *Bounty hunting, this is all I know.* I caution myself as my mind drifts. *Toph … my knives … the desert …*

'And baking bread,' I say under my breath. 'Perhaps I'd have been a baker.'

'What?'

I'm not sure if she barely heard me or my answer simply shocked her, so I speak again, in a clear voice.

'I'm good with my hands,' I say matter-of-factly. 'I could have been a baker.'

She instantly goes into a fit of giggles. I chuckle with her. As we continue in silence now, I can't help but think of kneading some dough. I allow my head to wander and my fingers stretch and massage the wet, sticky flour. *Peaceful.*

After what seems like an eternity, she speaks. 'I don't think you'll let me get on that boat alone,' is all she says.

I am silent again as we ride into the dense, tidy streets of the coastal town of Azur with its small colourful cottages, smoking chimneys, and charming rose bushes out front.

'Ene, the reason I have no name is simply because I've had no one to give me one.'

I feel another emotion, and this one is shame. The acceptance of my honesty makes my throat dry. And, for the first time in all my years, I feel naked ... vulnerable, but I suddenly feel much lighter than I have ever been.

'Yaro,' Ene says quietly, but just loud enough for me to hear. 'It means new dawn in my native tongue.'

I raise my head high and I am smiling now, but Ene is unable to see this from behind. I know she can feel my heart though. It is beating fast and warm with purpose, because things have changed.

KILLER ROBOT

'Palm trees,' came the monotonous voice from the flat, round speaker that was built into the robot's titanium chest.

Maja glanced at his friend, and it was obvious Gogo was daydreaming again. 'Someday soon, bud,' he said. 'Someday.'

The year was 2087 and most of Lagos, as it was previously known, had sunk and now lay submerged in the Atlantic Ocean. The city had grown faster than it could contain itself, and the corrupt government, in a desperate attempt to milk the real estate market, had embarked on a series of land reclamation projects in the last half century. Nearly all of them failed, except the Eko Archipelago, a group of man-made islands that housed less than one percent of Lagos's forty million inhabitants, leaving the millions of other people that already overpopulated the megacity to scramble for any habitable space that remained on the congested mainland.

The government never accepted this though; climate change sounded like an easier culprit. In terms of character, not much in Lagos had changed. Piles of litter dotted the streets, and cars never stop honking, even after midnight. The buildings had more than doubled in height, but they appeared to constantly be on the verge of tipping over. The lights that shone from them dazzled the metropolis at night, and they also revealed the heavy crime that lurked in the shadows.

Poverty was still rife, and crime was at an all-time high. Several people were homeless, and competition for makeshift bed spaces under the bridges quickly turned violent every night. Even the robots suffered these problems, and they, too, could be quite vicious.

After all, robots made up part of the census here and were well integrated. But whether they were liked by the humans was a constant debate every election season. Some people thought they had too much independence, and others thought it was playing God to have them as guards, nurses and chefs. One thing Lagosians agreed upon, though – these robots were incredibly smart.

The first batch of robots followed instructions to the letter. Their intelligence was limited, and they made decent mechanics, domestic cleaners and child entertainers and companions. Then the government began investing heavily in further research and their development; millions of them were created before humans in Lagos had any chance to debate. The government said they were created to make the lives of Lagosians easier.

'They are not here to take your jobs,' the governor at the time had announced during his re-election campaign to a multitude of applause. 'They are here to help and work side by side with us.'

And side by side they came to be.

Production of robots was ramped up, and their numbers on the streets increased until they became represented in every facet of society, from schools to the courts. There were all sorts of robots of different shapes and sizes. Some even showed an astonishing level of discernment. With time, their artificial intelligence progressed naturally. They grew emotional and conscious. There were good and bad robots, just like humans. Some people loved them, others despised them, and the rest – they feared what the robots could become. Many groups advocated for all robots to be destroyed. They cited ethical or religious reasons, but for every group against, there were more groups calling for even further protection of robots. It took protest after protest, a lot of them not so peaceful, and a riot that led to several arrests and a few deaths on both sides before a referendum was held.

The result: the robots were here to stay.

Today's Lagos now comprised of humans and robots. But acknowledging that difference was deemed discriminatory nowadays, so, *people* it was. Anything else would be considered unacceptable. The first robots had no gender. But as time went on, updated versions were assigned sexes during chip installations, by means of voices and personas, for equality's sake. Robots could also vote. They had rights, and they had free will.

In all of this, there was only one group of robots that still followed instructions. Some of the concerns from initial protests were that rogue robots might join the police and armed forces, so using a public opinion poll, an agreement was reached. Batch B, as they were officially called, would possess special chipsets, which meant their intelligence would always remain limited, and their operating systems, unlike the other robots, open property of the government, hence reassuring the citizens of Lagos of the government's dedication to their safety. But Lagosians called this new batch 'killer robots'; the reasoning behind this was in the name.

Gogo was not a conventional killer robot, and Maja still didn't understand why. His kind were famed for their frequent malfunctions, and horror stories of accidental discharges that ended in fatalities for petty crimes weren't unheard of. 'A bad batch,' the government's issued statement always said during their performative press statements. These mishaps never happened on the islands, though; the bad batch seemed to have landed only on the streets of the mainland, far away from the cabal.

On a rainy night eight years ago, a shopkeeper who was being robbed at gunpoint had raised an alarm to the patrol team. Within five minutes, a killer robot had been dispatched to handle this thief who had been described as no more than a little boy holding a gun. Killer robots had a firearm and a taser. Depending on the threat, the robot was to act instinctively – the only time their chipsets allowed them to.

To both Maja and the shopkeeper's dismay and utter confusion, this robot, upon its face-off with the intruder, had performed neither of its expected two actions; instead, it uttered two words. 'Palm trees.'

And thereafter began the peculiar friendship between an orphaned boy and a malfunctioning killer robot.

* * *

There was an air of urgency on the streets of Lagos that afternoon. People went about briskly with some sense of purpose. The public holiday meant offices and schools were closed, but that did nothing to stop the massive crowds that were already teeming the streets. Gogo walked behind a group of chatting young women just as Maja narrowly avoided getting hit by a yellow minibus that whizzed by. He cursed uselessly at the back of the rickety bus, and Gogo let out a dry chuckle.

'What's so funny? You won't survive one day without me on these streets,' Maja said to Gogo as they passed a busy intersection with several makeshift stalls teetering in the wind.

But Gogo seemed to ignore this; his focus was turned towards the pop-up food trucks. 'That smells really good,' he said without turning his head away from the sizzling ram meat on skewers that was being prepared on an open grill by a heavyset chef.

Maja rolled his eyes and shook his head in growing annoyance. 'Dude, we both know you can't smell that. And you can't eat either, so give it a rest, will you?'

'That doesn't stop me from appreciating it,' Gogo insisted. 'I'd also like to try some chocolate.'

Gogo explained that he'd noticed the way humans always had deep looks of satisfaction on their faces whenever they took bites of chocolate. 'I want that feeling too,' he continued, tilting his large oval head to follow a young child nibbling on a chocolate bar as she crossed the street with her mother.

'Focus, Gogo! We need to go through the plan again.'

'Someone is even crankier than usual,' Gogo said. 'It's Eyo Festival Day! Look around, you're the only one with an attitude.'

Maja frowned at him just as a group of young women rushed past them, giggling. One of them appeared to be staring at Gogo. She turned back with a grin, and Gogo waved his long-fingered hand enthusiastically at her.

'Gogo!'

'Relax,' Gogo said blithely. 'We've gone over it nine times already, and yes, I was counting.'

'There's no room for mistakes,' Maja continued in an even more serious tone. 'We have only a couple of hours so—'

'Exactly!' Gogo said quickly. 'We still have six hours until it's time, so please let's enjoy the festival like everyone else.'

And with that, Gogo hurried excitedly towards one stall that sold raffia hats before Maja had the chance to say another word. Maja trailed behind him, looking sullen.

The two friends were thieves. Their mornings were comprised of planning hits for the evenings, while their afternoons were typically spent going over the plans again. Maja mostly led this, since Gogo usually stopped listening after the morning lecture. They used to pick pockets on busy days like today, but two years ago, the government had phased out cash notes, and now everyone was forced to use drafts. These were digital currency preloaded onto cards with unique identifying numbers, which meant stealing became a bit more complicated.

At the start, Maja had tried searching for a job, but work was scarce in Lagos, especially for someone with no education and zero connections. It also paid much less than stealing, so Maja stuck with his vice. Gogo just went for the ride; it was fun running around Lagos, and he enjoyed spending time with his friend, even if the hours were criminal.

'I didn't know there was a planned rally today,' Gogo said. The lens of his eyes whirred and zoomed in at the organised crowd coming up the road. 'I would've liked to join in.'

Maja sucked his teeth impatiently. 'Gogo, we've spoken about this. You can't be seen marching for things like this. You have to keep a—'

'Low profile, yes, yes.'

The pack of demonstrators continued their march upwards. Many people cheered them on while others booed as the large group, who were a mix of humans and robots, passed by. The demonstrators remained peaceful, chanting 'amend the amended constitution!' and holding up banners and placards. There were all kinds of robots present, with the exception of killer robots. A couple at the forefront, a human male and a robot female, held hands tightly and raised each end of a short banner with their other hand.

'Support the marriage referendum. Society shouldn't tell us who to love.'

Maja and Gogo wove their way onto Allen Avenue. It was bursting at the seams with its old medium-rise buildings covered in murals that depicted humans and robots living together in harmony. Here, a preacher was shouting about Jesus Christ into a megaphone. 'Change your evil ways,' the man yelled as they approached. 'Repent, for the kingdom of God is nigh. He is coming again to judge the wicked.'

The man offered flyers from the stack on his small table to passers-by, but no one bothered to collect them. When Maja reached him, the man shoved the flyers in his face and screamed at the top of his lungs. 'Repent, for the Lord sees all, even the deeds we do in the dark! Repent now or burn in hell later!'

Maja ignored the man and continued walking without a care. It was Gogo who stopped to collect a flyer before thanking the preacher.

'Robots are an abomination!' the preacher yelled after Gogo. 'Machines that can think for themselves shouldn't be allowed to coexist with us, walk our streets or tend to our children. It is unnatural. We have lost our way, and God frowns at this. He frowns at us. Robots are evil, yet many of you choose to befriend them. Some of you even lay with them! Away with the machines or we shall all perish. Repent or burn!'

'What a prick,' Gogo said in his monotone voice immediately after, but not before squeezing the flyer and chucking it into the nearby bin.

'Can robots end up in hell?' Gogo asked Maja out of the blue. 'Considering God didn't create us, I mean.'

'I wouldn't worry about that, buddy. It's all bullshit, anyway. Lagos is already hell for broke rejects like you and me. The life here is hell, but all that will change soon.'

Gogo tilted his head from side to side as they walked. A robotic display of sympathy. Maja frowned as he found the receivers of his friend's pity. Beggars crouched on the side of the road with their sun-darkened faces low but arms outstretched, holding draft terminals up in the air. Their desperate voices, hopeful, but dampened by the heavy activities around the streets.

As the light began to fade, Maja stopped at one of the stands to try some of the food while Gogo stood beside him, at least one foot taller than his human friend. Several passing people stared at the duo. Even the robot serving stir-fried noodles to Maja at the front of the booth kept throwing both of them glances. And even though she had no facial expression, Maja and Gogo knew what she was thinking even before she spoke.

'Shouldn't you be on patrol on a busy night such as this?' the robot asked Gogo.

Maja opened his mouth to speak but, as usual, Gogo was faster. 'You should be more worried about making better food.'

Maja nearly choked on his noodles while the robot's rectangular head recoiled suddenly. She had clearly been taken aback by Gogo's sharp response.

'Because other than my friend here, I don't see anyone else queueing up to try your food,' Gogo added without pause.

They continued their walk later, but Maja was worried. He chastised Gogo. 'Gogo, you can't keep telling people we're friends. We've talked about this.'

'But everyone sees us together already, and we are friends,' Gogo told him pointedly.

'Which is why we constantly have to change locations, so no one has that impression. But if you're just going to keep telling people anyway, we might as well turn ourselves in now.'

'I really don't understand why we must hide. I see other humans and robots hanging out all the time.'

'The difference is they aren't seven-foot killer robots!' Maja said with a sigh. 'We've been over this a hundred times. If anyone suspects you've malfunctioned, they could report you and you'll be disintegrated,' Maja added grimly. 'Or even worse.'

'I'll be reset,' said Gogo.

'Exactly,' Maja said out loud before reducing his voice to a whisper. 'And I won't be spared either.'

'You could also go to jail or be executed,' Gogo said.

'Thanks for reminding me of the options,' Maja said with a scoff. 'Now, let's go over the plan one more time.'

Standing behind the statue of a giant catfish, they went through the details again. In the distance, tall, white-cloaked masqueraders wearing large hats emerged in a small group. They were holding long wooden staffs and were greeted by loud cheers on both sides of the road. Scantily dressed women followed them closely behind, colourful feathers adorning small parts of their glossy skin. Several men wolf-whistled as they passed. As Maja and Gogo made their way towards the front of the metro station, whose walls were covered in graffiti, Gogo stopped to watch the shirtless men that were now blowing long streaks of fire out of their mouths.

'Oh, I love this,' he said to Maja, who was growing impatient.

Gogo clapped as the crowd erupted into more cheers. The peacock ladies were now dancing around the shirtless blazing men while the masqueraders hit their sticks on the ground, sending up shiny sparks.

'Let's go, buddy!' Maja grabbed Gogo's cold metal arm, and the both of them hurried down the steps.

They rode on the noisy underground train and discussed what they would do with their prospective loot. Maja wanted to live in one of the white mansions that dotted the new Eko islands. 'You know, the ones with the big glass windows,' he said. 'Right in front of the ocean with a very large pool in the backyard.'

'Why would you want a pool in your backyard when you live by the waterfront?'

Maja stared at him in disbelief. 'Why do we want anything, Gogo? I don't know.' He shrugged.

'I'd just like to go anywhere with palm trees,' Gogo said.

'Right, of course,' said Maja scathingly.

Pickpockets might be operating on this line, the automated announcement rang out. *Please watch your belongings at all times.*

As they approached their stop, it became obvious that people aboard the train had been staring at them the entire time. Maja, who was slightly embarrassed, looked to the floor, but Gogo was oblivious and continued with his chatter. He was explaining lesser-known facts about butterflies to Maja.

Then came an electronic chime. *We are now approaching Ocean Parade Station. Alight for Palm Grove Amusement Park, Banana Island and regional ferry services.*

When the train doors opened, Maja tugged at Gogo and rushed off. Overground once again and down a road with dull streetlights, a group of mostly young women in tight, skimpy clothing lined both sides of the street here. Some escort robots stood amongst them.

'Fine boy,' called one woman. She was curvy, with colourful geometric cobra tattoos on her right thigh, and she called to Maja with a smile as they passed hurriedly in front of her. Her glass-heeled shoes were so high her ability to stand and strike a pose in them was a respectable art form. She stuck out her tongue to reveal the pink bubble gum she had been chewing before winking and smacking her lips noisily. 'I just need five minutes to give you the best time of your life. Your friend can join too. I'm feeling very festive today, so half price for him … or *her*.'

Gogo whirred his head around to study the woman who was still smiling seductively as the others cornered them now. Each woman and robot seemed to offer a different discount, each apparently more generous than the other. Maja waved them all away with a gentle, yet dismissive hand as they weaved their way out of the hold.

Two of the women became engaged in a shouting match with one robot. Probably one over territory. Encroaching even by a few feet was a big deal here, and arguments like these were common. It wasn't out of place for scuffles to break out between the night sisters, as they were called around here for decency's sake.

'It's a tough city,' said Gogo after a minute or two.

'Indeed, eat or get eaten,' Maja murmured in agreement.

They passed the lit up but empty park with its dazzling Ferris wheel and only had to walk briefly after that before reaching the quiet waterfront.

'This is it,' Gogo said.

Maja beamed and rubbed his palms together. 'Well, you know what to do.'

He watched as Gogo carefully rewired one of the jet skis docked at the pier. Maja took the handlebars with Gogo behind him. As they rode the small waves, several loud cracking sounds could be heard from behind. The sky in front of them was lit in quick flashes by fireworks coming from the mainland.

'There are palm trees here.' Gogo pointed wildly to the trees leaning lazily into the lagoon the moment they set foot on land. 'There are trees everywhere – look, Maja. Palm trees.'

There was, of course, no change in the tone of his voice, but Maja knew Gogo was excited whenever he repeated something.

'I know,' Maja said without as much as a glance. 'I lived here as a kid.'

Maja heard the mechanical sound of Gogo's neck turn at this.

'Your parents – they were part of the cabal?'

'Yes,' Maja said. 'The lovely, selfless one percent.'

The houses here were mostly white, with nice, open lawns and flashy cars parked out front. Unlike the mainland, there were no robots on patrol here, only humans. They stood facing a grand white building with black wrought-iron gates and ornate points at the top. Two uniformed guards sat holding small bottles of what looked like beer. They were singing at the top of their lungs with their free arms across each other.

'Don't forget the plan. I will distract, and you will tase them. If—'

'Maja,' Gogo said in his usual calm tone, 'I know the plan.'

'Alright, alright. We can't mess this up, otherwise we're fucked,' Maja said. The nervousness wrapped his voice like a blanket.

Gogo went ahead of him, tasing the men within seconds, just as another stream of fireworks shot into the night sky. Maja was now following Gogo's lead.

'You know, I don't even enjoy stealing,' Gogo said from ahead, walking noiselessly but at his usual pace.

'What?' Maja exclaimed, trying to tread as carefully as was humanly possible.

'I don't particularly like stealing is what I'm saying, or hurting others either.'

'Dude, I heard you the first time,' Maja snapped. 'Why the hell are we talking about this now?'

'I just thought I should let you know.'

'Now's not the time, Gogo. Remember why we're here and focus your thoughts on the damn plan,' Maja hissed through gritted teeth. 'We can revisit this after we *leave* here with the freaking drafts.'

Gogo blasted the pin pad at the front entrance, forcing the door to slide open and reveal a large opulent living room with decorated marble floors. A large version of a flag with the familiar symbol of Lagos, a fisherman on a boat, was spread across the wall above the stairs. This was the house of the governor, and it was the only time of the year when he, as well as the domestic staff, would be on the mainland enjoying the festivities like the other citizens of Lagos.

'Nothing to feel bad about here – this is a very corrupt man,' Maja said as they went up the winding staircase. 'Why should the governor have drafts stashed away in his house if he isn't in cahoots with the central bank director? This government is one of deceit and propaganda. They don't care about us, humans or robots. They keep telling us that all is well, but they're tucked away here, in their nice little islands, while we suffer and beg for crumbs on the cramped mainland. They're all the same man, and look, all the drafts in here belong to us, we … the people!'

'I know this, Maja, but not everyone we've robbed was always corrupt,' Gogo reminded him as they reached the first floor. A large, framed picture of the current governor and those of his predecessors lined the wall.

Maja stopped in his tracks now, clearly irritated by Gogo's new-found piety. 'Tell me when we've ever stolen from someone who didn't deserve it.'

Gogo, too, had stopped now. He faced Maja squarely. Even though he towered over Maja, Maja stood there, unflinching, apart from a muscle twitching heavily at the side of his temple.

'The shopkeeper at the marina,' Gogo said. 'He was an old man and even had a bad leg.'

'I was a child!' Maja lost his temper. 'For God's sake, I was struggling to survive and hadn't eaten in days.'

'Hey, you asked and I'm just telling you,' Gogo said and turned to continue walking. 'Still doesn't make it right, does it?'

'If you hated it so much, why did you go along with it then?' Maja's voice was rising now.

'I-I don't know.'

'Oh, I'll tell you,' Maja said, spitting furiously. 'Because you're a weird, lonely robot that can't even fit in with your own kind.'

If Gogo had an actual face, it might have shown hurt, but other than the blue lights of his eyes that dimmed slightly now, his smooth metal head remained void of expression.

'And I think, deep down, you're just as bad as me,' Maja added. 'If you are sick of it, you can just leave. In case you haven't noticed, not all of us can do without food and water. I'm human and I need to survive.'

'We can leave together now, it's not too late.' Gogo turned to him again. 'We can move to another state and find employment, no matter how small. We will be happy regardless.'

'*You* will be happy!' Maja corrected him. 'Aren't you sick and tired of living in a rat-infested shithole? I refuse to settle for crumbs when the prize is right here! Blast that door open for me and then you can fuck off to wherever! You need me to survive, I don't need you!'

Gogo stood there as if considering his next plan of action for a minute. 'Alright, then.' He turned towards the heavy metal door. As he inched towards it, a series of red lights flashed from tiny sensors on the walls.

'Blast it, just blast it!' Maja yelled frantically.

A loud alarm went off after Gogo raised his firearm, but instead of the door swinging open, metal bars rose from the floors and locked into the ceiling. They were trapped.

'Shit!' Maja cursed. 'We're screwed.'

Gogo attempted to blast the metal bars, but the effort was useless.

'Yo!' Maja called to him with wide eyes as the bullets ricocheted off the long metal rails. 'Unlike you – my skin isn't bulletproof.'

They stood in silence afterwards for about half an hour until they heard voices, followed by heavy rushing footsteps. As the sounds drew nearer, Maja continued to curse with his face buried in his hands. Gogo stood there, incapable of panic. Instead, he rested his metal arm on Maja's shoulder.

'It'll be alright, Majaro,' he told him.

'No, it won't,' Maja lamented. 'We're done for.'

At least a dozen policemen came rushing towards them. They were accompanied by four killer robots at their side, and when they stopped, a portly coal-skinned man came into view. He was panting and had a severe look on his face as if he had just been stung by multiple bees. A sharp contrast from the smiling picture of him that was hanging only inches away. A young spectacled man carrying a tablet that seemed nearly as heavy as he was hid behind the governor's massive build. There was a zesty scent in the air, like a bunch of citrus fruits squashed together. The governor spun rapidly on the spot, an impressive feat for a man his size.

He was looking at no one in particular when he asked, 'How?'

Dissatisfied by the silence, he turned forward and shouted again, this time at the two people behind the bars.

'Who are you and how did you get in here?' demanded the governor.

They had barely had the chance to speak when he asked again. His voice was rising now. 'Why are you here and what do you want?'

One of the officers drew closer to the governor and leaned down to whisper something into his ear.

But the infuriated governor only seemed to have more questions. 'How does a killer robot break into my residence with a human? I want them to answer me!'

When neither Maja nor Gogo would speak, the governor ordered they be brought out of the cage. He started by asking Maja a series of questions directly, but Maja, although trembling in fear, peered down and said nothing.

The governor slapped Maja hard across both sides of his face so that the thick-cut gold ring on his stubby finger instantly became stained with blood. Maja sniffled and wiped his nose as it dripped scarlet.

The governor turned his attention to Gogo with his head lifted so high the warm golden lights from the ceiling exposed his clenched jaw and throbbing moustache. He had even more questions for the robot. 'This shouldn't be possible! Even if you malfunctioned,' he started. 'How can you have this level of intelligence?'

But Gogo, just like his friend, remained silent.

'Very well, then,' the governor said, twirling another fat finger in the air.

His killer robots raised their firearms at once, and half of the policemen rushed forward. Two of them held Maja, who was straining as hard as he could, by both arms. The remaining four men pressed themselves on Gogo, who still remained calm.

'Bloody thieves, I'll deal with you as such.'

'Maybe we are thieves, but we are only taking what rightfully belongs to us,' Maja said with a slight tremble in his voice. 'You – you and your cronies feed fat off state treasury while the likes of us suffer out there.' He tilted his head towards Gogo.

'*Us?*' the governor asked and turned around to his men, half-amused. 'Us, he says. The rascal believes robots actually have rights too.' He laughed maniacally. 'You're completely deranged, boy. You're a child, you know nothing about politics.'

'When was the last time you actually walked the streets of the mainland? *Your Excellency,*' Maja asked, the fear momentarily leaving his voice and being replaced by bitterness.

The governor's eyes widened to the size of small coins. 'How dare you speak to me in such a manner, little boy. I am the governor of Lagos! *Your* governor, you shall accord me the respect—'

'Respect is earned, Mister Governor,' Gogo finally broke his silence. 'Only then can it be given. You've failed the citizens of Lagos, all of us, so we won't be according you anything today.'

Gogo's words seemed to be the last straw. The governor stood there, dumbstruck. It was as if someone had knocked the wind out of him. He was looking at Gogo and there was no masking it, he was completely terrified.

'H-how?' he eventually managed to mumble. 'How!' he shrieked and turned to the man standing nearest to him. 'Okopi, tell me how this is remotely possible!'

The scrawny man the governor had called Okopi gently pushed his thick horn-rimmed glasses deeper into his bony face and took a few calculated steps forward, like a cat gracing a short runway, towards Gogo. Maja's nostrils took in an abundance of lemons and oranges as Okopi passed by him. Okopi raised the massive tablet and aimed it directly at Gogo before resting the device on his skinny arm. He poked the screen with his long magenta-coloured fingernails as the room fell silent. Only the laboured breathing of the governor could still be heard. He pulled up a picture of what appeared at first to be Gogo, and with a soft flick of his finger, the still image became a slowly revolving three-dimensional rendition of a killer robot so that everyone in the room could now see. He pinched the air above his screen and zoomed into the miniature-sized hologram as he peered from it to Gogo and then to the four killer robots behind him.

His mannerisms became even more effete when he smacked his big glossy lips together and found a clear tenor voice. 'On the surface, sir, it appears to be exactly the same as the other P1260 models. It must be a glitch—'

'I know it's a fucking glitch, you fool!' the governor shrieked. 'Still doesn't answer my bloody question, does it?'

Okopi nodded several times and swallowed. 'Definitely a bad batch, Your Excellency. The worst of the worst. Perhaps – perhaps, a faulty chipset during the installation process. But even in that case, intelligence … consciousness shouldn't be this profound.' Okopi reduced his voice to a mere whisper. 'Shouldn't be … possible.'

'Lock the stupid boy up in the pit.' The governor's eyes twinkled with pure malice now. 'And reset this damn abomination of a robot!'

'Ah no! Please, please don't reset him. I'll talk. We only wanted to steal a few drafts, nothing else,' Maja pleaded.

'Too late.' The governor grinned, eyes cold. 'You'll rot in my jail where no one will ever find you. That's if anyone bothers to even look for a street miscreant like you.'

'That's the truth,' Maja declared. 'I'll leave Lagos. We'll both leave the city and never return. Please, please!'

'*Oh oh*, look at that,' jeered the governor. 'The boy made friends with a twisted killer robot and thinks he's found himself a sidekick.'

The policemen sniggered now as they pulled Maja near the open elevator.

'I promise we won't tell anyone what we've seen if you just let us go,' Maja called back to the governor.

'You've seen nothing here, boy.'

A hard hand shoved Maja into the elevator now, and two of the men followed him inside. 'Please, it's all my fault. I'm sorry,' he cried as the elevator bell dinged.

'You, Okopi!' the governor barked again. 'You know what to do with this thing … we can't have a killer robot from a bad batch running around,' the governor concluded as Maja's cries filled the large room one last time before they were drowned out by the closing metal doors. And all the while, Gogo had remained as silent as ever.

* * *

Two weeks had passed since Maja had lost his only friend. He sat there, forlorn, in a tight prison cell that smelled strongly of kerosene. The shallow hole he used as a toilet was right next to him too. Every breath he took was tough, and staying awake was a pain, but sleeping was also torture, for the floor was cold, hard, and bare. There seemed to be some sort of major construction work being carried out on the floor above.

It was always the sound of heavy drilling and the rushing of water through pipes. It stopped after a few hours, but it woke him with a start every morning. Every morning, he woke, hoping that all that had transpired was a nightmare and his friend would be there to greet him in that monotonous yet quirky tone, but it wasn't a bad dream. It had all truly happened.

A dull flickering fluorescent tube hanging down the corridor provided the faintest source of light to the otherwise empty floor. And the only sounds that he could hear the rest of the day were the intermittent drops of water leaking from the ceiling to the stone floor.

Tap … tap.

Once a day, he would hear the light clanking of metal as one of the domestic robots approached with a tray.

'The governor is truly a generous man,' one of the service robots had told him a few days ago. 'Even with your unforgivable crimes, he still provides you sustenance.'

The food was the same every day; a brownish broth that contained miserly bits of broccoli and floating beans that Maja could always count on one hand. He never received water. So he was forced to open his mouth and aim his tongue properly if he was to catch any of the intermittent drips from the cracked, algae-covered ceiling. In the days that passed, he had tried to distract himself by watching the spider in the corner spin her thread, but after a few hours, his mind would wander back to his current predicament.

He thought of Gogo and wiped his tears every time. He had treated him terribly over the years, and despite this, Gogo had always stayed. The compact studio they both shared in the ghetto of Ebute-Metta flashed in his head now. It was far from perfect, but Gogo had never once complained about the state of it. Maja's head was reeling in regret. He knew that at the very core, Gogo was good, with more *heart* than anyone he'd ever met. Malfunctioning, yes, but far from corrupt. It was he, Maja, who had done that to him. He had made him that way, and now they had both lost their friendship and their future as a result.

It was he who needed the robot and not the other way around. Gogo's silence on the day he was dragged to the pit still haunted him. Not a single farewell after their many years together. Gogo must have been angry, and Maja now understood this. Maybe he deserved this ill fate after all. If only he had listened to his dear friend, even just for once.

He'd always assumed he'd do fine all by himself. Why then, did he feel so empty now? It suddenly hit him, hard. Gogo hadn't just been his best friend. He'd been his brother. His family. Maja couldn't even remember the last time he cried. But now he felt his eyes sting and start to water. They could have gone to another state and found the simplest of jobs. They would have been happy. He would have been happy, as long as he had Gogo.

He heard the soft thuds of metal hitting the floor. As the robot approached, Maja decided he wasn't even hungry. Today, all he wanted was to wallow in his misery and feed himself with it. When the puny robot reached him, it simply stood there. Stainless steel with bits of cheap-looking plastic – definitely a cleaning robot. Unusual, because they always sent the ones from the kitchen who were slightly taller and sturdier. Maja stared at it, and it stared back. It raised one of its arms and dangled a bunch of keys; Maja frowned in confusion.

'Palm trees,' it spoke in a monotonous female voice.

Only this time, Maja understood perfectly.

The Fifth Day

Ekele wasn't particularly handsome, but all the young women in the village fancied him. He was tall and quite lean, and yet he never wore a shirt, so his sweaty, toned muscles gleamed under the sun as he tugged at the chestnut-brown leather reins of his snow-white stallion, Akor.

There was something extremely attractive about his confidence, the way he carried himself and the manner in which he spoke. That bass voice, those deep-set brown eyes and his smile. Oh, that smile. Charming ... knowing ... dangerous.

He followed the same path to his cocoa farm every day, except on the fifth day of the week. He was always on time too, and Onyaole knew his schedule. She knew it very well because she had watched him daily, unfailingly, for the last three years, except for the fifth days. It troubled her greatly that she didn't know what he got up to on those days, but that didn't stop her from dissecting his day and piecing it all together again inside her head. Perhaps he prayed to Owoicho for more blessings or poured a sacrifice of drink on the ground to his ancestors for them to grant him protection. Or was it the day he met other women? *No, no.* She banished that thought instantly. Maybe he just slept all day, wearing no clothes at all.

Onyaole saw it imprinted in her mind now – the shiny, nearly perfect cross-shaped scar under his navel. She would know soon enough, though, because she was going to be his wife. She had dreamed it on two separate occasions, so surely it was bound to happen.

'You are daydreaming again,' Ochanya's voice came from beside Onyaole.

'I'm manifesting,' Onyaole corrected her.

'Same thing. It's all a fantasy. He doesn't even know you exist.'

'You're wrong,' Onyaole started defensively. 'He smiled at me last week.'

Ochanya laughed viciously. 'Wow! You truly are delusional. He nodded at all six of us. You know, like he sometimes does … because he is being courteous. You didn't even see his teeth.'

This was true. Onyaole, Ochanya and four other girls had been filling their pots with water from the river that afternoon when Ekele rode past and glanced at them. It was brief and ended with a sharp nod. But at that moment, Onyaole felt like the only girl in the world. The most beautiful too. And the only one worthy enough to catch the attention of the former war hero turned farmer.

'You're too fat,' Ochanya continued unkindly. 'And let's be honest, he'll never look at you that way.'

'But I barely weigh sixty kilos!' Onyaole protested.

'I hear he only likes beautiful, skinny girls … like Jonchi.'

Onyejonchi. The one Owoicho had been partial with and endowed with tremendous beauty. Nearly all the young men in the village wanted her hand. She wore her long black hair in a unique style each week, and her nose was always up in the air. And because her lips had a certain permanent pout, it always appeared as though there was a bad smell prevalent in her surroundings. Her skin carried no blemish. And when she walked on the balls of her feet, the dozen coral beads on her small waist always jingled with every step. Apparently, all her friends fawned over her because they were afraid she could end their relationships by taking their men, if she pleased.

So yes, Jonchi was pretty, the stuff of dreams for several men and the source of many women's nightmares, but this had never deterred Onyaole.

'Jonchi has a terrible attitude, and she's arrogant. I also heard one girl say she's a terrible cook,' Onyaole said as she drew out her full pot from the river.

'Men don't care about things like that when the girl looks like Jonchi. As long as she has a pretty face and excellent skills in the bedroom, they'll find a housemaid for the cooking and cleaning, if that's what it takes to keep her.'

Onyaole was so annoyed by Ochanya's harsh revelation that she kept quiet after that. She placed her pot so it sat flat on top of her head and announced to her friend that she'd be walking home alone.

She enjoyed the silence. Ochanya never stopped talking anyway, and Onyaole's mother had never liked her. 'There's something off about that girl, but I can't quite place my finger on it,' she would say. So she used the time to clear her head, to think of nothing, not even Ekele. She'd just enjoy the silence and be present in her environment. Because no one was watching her, she practised her catwalk. She positioned her neck straight so the pot of water remained balanced on her head and set her eyes straight, focusing on the path ahead of her.

She swung her hips intentionally. *This is what men found attractive?* she asked herself with a chuckle. *It's not even that difficult.* She wondered if she could make these steps a habit from now on, without ever pissing herself with laughter.

The path was wide, with shin-level bushes on both sides, and the cherry trees with their ripe golden fruits called to her tantalisingly on her right. Her eyes followed the butterflies fluttering around the burst fallen cashews to her left and the blue and orange agama lizard climbing up the bark of the tree. Onyaole dropped her gaze and saw her own shadow occupying some of the ground beneath her as she went along the reddish soil that could be found all over Otukpa. Opening up her senses to it all, she heard the scratching noises of bats stirring from sleep in the trees as the warm, gentle breeze swept past her face while she allowed the soft sands to tickle her bare feet as she continued her strut.

Her eyes found the hoof marks that lined the path. *Ekele was here,* she thought, and smiled to herself.

'My sweet! You're always as gracious as a swan.'

Onyaole screamed and jumped, nearly twisting her ankle. The pot fell from her head and shattered into a dozen pieces.

'*Owoicho Kum!*' she cried. 'Look what you've done now.'

She scanned the ground to assess the damage. It seemed the man responsible had been expecting her to pass by before he jumped out from behind the bushes. He dropped to his knees now and tried to gather the pieces of the pot in what was clearly a useless attempt.

That was her favourite water pot, smashed to bits now because of this clown, Omale.

'Sorry, my sweet—'

Onyaole's skin crawled. 'Stop calling me that!'

'I'm sorry, Onya. I will fix it for you, don't worry.'

Omale continued to stack parts of the broken clay together.

Onyaole clicked her tongue impatiently. 'Leave it. You can't repair it. It's useless now.'

'I'm-I'm sorry, my sweet. I'll buy you a brand new one.' He was rushing after her now.

'Leave me alone, Omale.'

He caught up with her easily. 'My sweet – Onyaole,' he corrected himself as soon as he noticed her eyes flash. 'Why do you keep hiding from me?'

'I'm not. And even if I were, you always spring up on me anyway, don't you?'

'So why won't you give me a date to come and pay your bride price to your parents?' His voice carried great sadness now. 'My people are ready. I've been ready. Please give me a date and I will come.'

'I've told you. I'm not interested.'

'But your mother adores me, and even your father has technically given me his approval. I just need you to confirm a date so I can come and perform the rites.'

Onyaole's eyes became slits as she laughed derisively, while Omale simply frowned as though puzzled.

'Oh, is that so? Well, in that case, you don't need my permission, then. You can marry my father … or my mother. Maybe even both of them, since the three of you get along so well.'

She walked off, but Omale held her by the wrist, forcing her to stop in her tracks. Then he pulled her close to him until her breasts became one with his powerful chest muscles. So close that she could almost taste the sweet basil on his tongue.

'Don't speak like that. You know how much I love you,' he cooed. 'What exactly is the problem? Are you worried I won't be able to provide for you? Because let me assure you, I can. I have a massive farm and three enormous barns that hold different crops all year round. There are over forty N'dama cows on my ranch that are the envy of other herders, and my palm oil plantation is so vast it'll take you several hours to walk from one side to the other.'

There was no arrogance in Omale's voice, though. Onyaole could only hear the plea of a man desperate to prove himself. The look on his face was so intense she had to turn her attention to the hen that was scurrying past them along with her chicks.

Omale stretched out his veiny sunburnt arms for her to see. 'Look at my hands. I am fit, healthy, and I work very hard. I built my hut all by myself and renovated my parents' hut with these bare hands.' Omale's eyes were tearing up now, and his voice changed. It became raspy. 'Onya, I promise … I will dedicate the rest of my life to making you happy.'

Omale was the perfect man on paper. Even Onyaole had to admit that to herself now. She tilted her head to the side, and her eyes softened.

'Look, Omale.' Her voice was gentler now. 'I know you're a good man, and I believe your heart is in the right place. It's just … it's just not for me. And I'm certain you'll find a woman who deserves all *this*. A woman who'll be so lucky to have you, but—'

'That woman isn't you.' Omale swallowed painfully.

He forced a severely hurt smile, and in that moment, Onyaole despised herself. He didn't deserve this, but unfortunately, her heart was already beating for another. Omale nodded his understanding and gave her a small bow before turning his back to her. She saw he was still clutching small fragments of her pot as he walked away.

She reached her father's compound. It was about a quarter of a hectare, with an open front yard and behind that, five huts varying in size. One for the head of the family and three for each of his wives and their individual children. They all used the smallest of the huts as a general kitchen, and it also served as a mini silo for storing yams and grains.

There were several peafowl strolling around the premises. One peacock was piercing the afternoon air with a shrill call, and his extravagant blue plumage was on full display, while another two were frolicking on top of the thatched roof of her mother's hut in what appeared to be a courtship ritual.

Her father had always associated these birds with noble status and had purchased them for next to nothing, years ago, from a stranded travelling trader who had been passing by their village from a faraway exotic land.

Perhaps he'd seen the peafowl as an extension of himself and his family, since he was always talking to them about class. 'You should hold yourself in public as you would in private. They will regard the reputation you garner outside as a reflection of me.'

He was chief of Olachagbaha, the smallest of the twelve districts in Otukpa.

Onyaole's mother rushed out of the hut. The new jade-green cloth she had wrapped around her body threatened to slip down from her chest. She had a severe look on her face.

'What have you done now, Onyaole?' she demanded. 'I hope you didn't postpone Omale's introduction again.'

'Postpone would mean I had chosen a date in the first place, Mama.'

'Don't you dare take that snide tone with me, young lady. Whatever that was, it didn't look good. What did you say to him now?'

'You were watching us the entire time?'

'I heard someone scream, so I – oh, never mind that. Answer me!'

'I ended things,' Onyaole said flatly. 'Not like anything had begun, anyway.'

Her mother looked windswept. 'Onyaole!'

'You know I don't have feelings for him.'

'Feelings? Feelings!' her mother said, eyeing her up and down. 'You think feelings are what will put food on your table? Feelings won't place a roof over your head either. And where's the water that took you over an hour to fetch? Where is your pot? You know I need that water to make dinner.'

Onyaole sighed. 'My pot broke. Did you miss that part when you were spying on us?'

'You had one task for the day, just one,' said her mother. 'Your father and brothers will return from the farm soon, and they'll be hungry.' Her mother shook her head slowly. 'You know it's my turn to cook today and yet you want to shame me.' She reduced her voice to a whisper as she stared wildly towards the other huts. 'Onyaole, you want my co-wives to mock me? What will you tell everyone after you've killed me, eh?' She started sobbing lightly. 'Your father will get a heart attack from the shame.'

'What shame?' asked Onyaole hotly. Every day, it seemed her mother found new ways to be more dramatic.

'The shame you'll bring upon us since you've refused to marry. You want me to be the laughingstock of Otukpa!'

Onyaole opened her mouth to speak, but she closed it at once because her mother was sobbing some more now. She stood there, watching in confusion, before deciding it was best to go into the small hut and take one of the empty water pots. She'd rather be back at the river anyway than stay here as her mother emotionally blackmailed her. When Onyaole emerged from the hut, her mother was patting her cheeks dry with the edge of her cloth and was ready to continue.

'You can't even complete a simple household chore and yet you're picky towards the only man in the twelve districts who's asked for your hand.'

Onyaole ignored her mother as she made her way out of the compound and back onto the path.

Her mother's voice rang from behind. 'You haven't even birthed your first child but look at your increasing waistline. Who will marry you now like this?'

Onyaole was glad her mother couldn't see her teary face because the words pierced her heart much deeper than Ochanya's had done earlier.

* * *

Today was the fifth day of the week, and Ekele wouldn't pass the trail. This meant that Onyaole could be more carefree about her looks. She didn't polish her nails or tie her hair in neat knots. Her cheeks were powder-free, and she had even forgotten to put gloss on her lips. It was also the day she undertook the embarrassing chore of washing her family's clothes in the river. Even the cloth she had wrapped around her body was her oldest – faded all over and frayed at the hem.

Onyaole and some of the other girls from her district chatted away as they did their laundry in the shallows of the river. It was the same theme of gossip every week amongst the girls – who this girl was seeing now or who that girl had caught her man cheating with. Onyaole found it tiring because it was so much work to keep up and nothing new shocked her anyway. The gist got boring quickly, except that time Iyono got pregnant and couldn't say for sure who the father of her unborn child was. *Now that was a real scandal.*

'Word on the street is you rejected Omale's marriage proposal,' a short girl called Elameyi said with no preamble.

Today's prattle had been slow and dry, so Onyaole knew the girls were dying for a juicy bone to nibble on. She continued her washing in silence, aware that the eyes of all the girls were on her. Their ears waited too.

'Yes, and so what if I did?' she said uncomfortably.

Elameyi gasped ludicrously. 'But he's such a catch!'

From the sound the other girls made, they were all in agreement.

One of them, Ebowo, gushed uncontrollably. 'Not to mention, he's very handsome, and he makes a lot of money too, I've heard.'

'Well, I don't love him,' Onyaole said mechanically.

'Love?' Ebowo asked. 'My mother says love doesn't put food on the table. I think one can always learn to love a man.'

'Especially if he is rich,' the twins, Aladi and Alache chorused, and both of them roared with laughter.

'I will only marry a man I love,' Onyaole insisted as she placed a washed cloth into her basket that rested on the smooth flat rock that jutted out of the river. 'I'm not ashamed to say I want a burning, passionate love. The kind that keeps me up at night and makes my heart race during the day.'

All the girls paused their laundry to stare at her. Onyaole picked a dry cloth from the small heap of unwashed clothes near her. She dipped it into the river.

'I guess what I'm saying is I'd rather remain single forever than marry a man only because of his looks or to guarantee my financial security.'

Some girls stared at her bewildered, others in wild fascination. It was impossible to tell exactly what any of them were thinking.

'Pay her no mind. She doesn't appreciate what she has in the present,' Ochanya quipped. Before now, she'd been the only one among the girls who hadn't chipped into the discussion. 'She'd rather head towards a *very* uncertain future.'

Onyaole thought she sensed resentment embedded in Ochanya's voice.

'Well, if you want Omale, you can have him. He's single, and last time I checked, no man has asked for your hand yet.'

Ochanya glowered at Onyaole before gathering her things and storming off without another word. Onyaole watched her go down the path, unsure of what to make of what had just transpired.

'Hmm, sis, you better watch your back with that one,' Elameyi said and jerked her head towards the path.

Laundry continued after this. The girls didn't pester Onyaole further since they'd had their fill of drama for the day. Another group of girls came towards the river now, each carrying empty water pots. Six of them were walking behind a beautiful girl, almost as if they were too scared to overtake her. Jonchi, aware of the aura of authority she commanded, seemed to take her time as she purposefully counted her steps to the river's edge. She dipped her pot lazily and scooped the flowing water.

She came and went without interacting or casting the girls in the river as much as a second glance. The six girls filled their pots too, then dallied quietly behind Jonchi again like lackeys. The scene could have easily passed for a solemn funeral procession.

There was a distant rumble as the clouds connected and darkened. Onyaole still had a few clothes left for washing as the others hurriedly packed their things. By the time the fat, heavy drops of rain came pouring down, she was all alone. *Only three pieces of clothing left,* she thought. So, stubbornly, she carried on with the washing as lightning struck and the rain increased in intensity. The rain continued ferociously and came down much harder and faster than she had expected.

Screw this! She'd have to finish tomorrow. Onyaole grabbed her basket of wet clothes from the rock and waded through the water with great difficulty. The water level had risen significantly. She slipped on a small, smooth stone and fell face front into the chilly waters. She glimpsed her laundry basket and scattered clothes drifting away with the rushing river. Onyaole, distressed, instinctively swam after her items to recover whatever she could, but the water was flowing too fast and the lashing rain made it nearly impossible to see anything.

Suddenly, a torrent swept her off her feet. She tried to find the riverbed with her toes, but all they met was more water. She tried to save herself by swimming to the riverbank, but moving her arms and legs was futile. She was stuck, caught in a current and struggling now to keep her head above the surface. Next thing, she was gulping a lot of water.

The once mostly clear river had become so unsettled and murky that now she had zero visibility underneath. And not long after, she started sinking … giving up … drowning.

* * *

A firm hand pulled her from under her arms. If it was a water spirit, Onyaole didn't even bother to protest. *Death is near anyway.* The hand pressed against the middle of her chest in firm, rapid succession, and she felt the liquid as it rose from her throat and spilled out of her mouth in a rush.

'Hey, are you alright?' a man asked in a pleasant bass tone.

Ekele. She'd be able to recognise that voice even if she were in her grave. *Why today of all days?* The one day he had broken his routine was the same day death had tried to prove itself. She coughed and opened her eyes slowly. The rain was but a drizzle now, or had it stopped and that was just the water dripping from his face?

'*Owoicho Kum,*' Onyaole said slowly, still slightly dazed. 'I thought I'd died.'

His clean-shaven face was still leaning close above hers, and his voice came out warm and steady. 'How, then, would I ever be able to pay your bride price if you die?'

The wet, shirtless man grinned at her now, showing off a full set of teeth, and his snow-white stallion neighed on the other side of the river.

KOKOUVI

My name is Shogok, and my best friend's name is Kokouvi. We both enjoy Bollywood movies, white chocolate, and long walks along the grand canal in the evenings. I love to eat spicy jollof rice and drink an unhealthy amount of Dr Pepper. Kokouvi enjoys exactly the same. He only wears bright-coloured pinstriped socks, and I always add colourful strings to my hair extensions. We are birds of a feather with different physical traits.

Kokouvi is hefty with skin the colour of roasted coffee. The complete opposite of me. I grew frail in my early teens, so I've been on some much-needed multivitamins ever since. Mummy drives all the way to my school to drop me a fresh bottle every month.

I hate medicine, but Kokouvi always reminds me to take it. If I'm being honest, there've been a lot of times I'd just pretended to take the pill, like when I visited my family on the weekends or when I was back home during the holidays. Because Mummy and my elder sister, Asabe, insisted I take the vitamins daily, I'd pop one of the hard, coloured capsules inside my mouth when I was in front of them. But I'd spit it right into the toilet bowl after. I don't understand why everyone makes such a fuss about it. *I'll be fine.*

* * *

I am a final-year student of financial accounting at the University of Jos. Kokouvi is in my year too, but he's majoring in geology. Rocks always fascinated him, even when we were kids, the way they sat in mysterious formations all around our former neighbourhood of Sabon Gari. Kokouvi is definitely the smarter one between us.

* * *

We share so much together, and he knows everything about me. I've told him every single thing … all my secrets. He knew the first time I kissed a boy and that time when I'd accidentally set fire to Mrs Deborah's shop.

As children, we'd go swimming together at Zaramaganda Country Club every Saturday morning, until one day when both of us nearly drowned in the deep end of the large outdoor pool. That was the last time either of us went near any swimming pool and the last time we went to the country club.

I told him the first time I made out with a boy, and I explained to him in vivid detail how I'd allowed Matthew to put his hand under my blouse in the cinema. And the day before my sixteenth birthday, after Tijani broke my heart, Kokouvi had been there to hold my hand and comfort me. He'd said everything would be alright as he cursed Tijani and called him ugly.

He cracked so many jokes that night until I laughed again. Kokouvi was always by my side through thick and thin.

The only period he was absent was during the most trying time of my life. My father's funeral. Daddy passed away in the second semester of our first year at university.

Grief, if not managed properly, can lead to insanity and, unfortunately, the worst of it had struck me. If it wasn't for Kokouvi, I'm certain I'd have lost my mind.

He'd been there to console me right after I'd received the news, refusing to leave my side until I got a call via the hostel phone that

Uncle Ben, Mummy's younger brother, was waiting outside to take me home. Kokouvi only missed the funeral because he'd fallen ill for a couple of days after contracting a bad bout of malaria.

* * *

But no relationship is perfect, not even the most solid of friendships. Sometimes we fight and go for a few days without speaking or seeing. We are both very proud, but he is usually the first to crack, even when we know I'm in the wrong. Kokouvi cares for me like that. He always took care of me even though we were age mates. As children, we rode our bikes into ditches together and skinned our knees. We played hopscotch and skipped rope until we were gasping for breath. And on my first driving lesson, he sat in the back of the car as the grumpy instructor led the way because he knew I was super nervous. I'd be completely lost without him.

'Your beard is too bushy,' I said to him as I adjusted the falling lilac scarf that was wrapped loosely around my head. 'You should cut it – you'd easily look three years younger.'

'Err, sure. Thanks, mom,' he said with a friendly snort.

I'd just met him in front of the faculty of business and arts where he'd been waiting for me to finish my quantitative methods exam. Four students in a Peugeot 505 drove by. At first I thought they were final-year students like Kokouvi and I and were celebrating the end of their exams, but I noticed they were waving small green-white-green flags and singing at the top of their lungs to the nationalist music blasting from the car's speakers.

I'd been so consumed with studying for my finals that I'd forgotten. Today, Nigeria was celebrating its twenty-fifth anniversary of independence from British rule. I waved enthusiastically at them, and Kokouvi gave them a thumbs-up.

'You have the potential to be very handsome, but you look more like one of the homeless men at Dadin Kowa junction,' I said to him again after the revellers were some distance away from us.

He gasped comically and shrugged his beefy shoulders. 'Well, if I were to be homeless, I'd definitely be the coolest. Everyone would give me alms at the first glimpse of me.'

Kokouvi's face smouldered, and he changed poses for the imaginary camera flashing at him from all angles.

'Oh stop, I'm shy. More money please, less pictures.'

We both laughed at the silliness of it all.

* * *

Kokouvi doesn't have any other friends besides me. According to him, friends are a distraction. I have no friends either, really, so this arrangement works for me. He's never been in a relationship, and he doesn't even go on dates. And even though our relationship is platonic, he only wants to dedicate his time to me. There's no other way to put it; I am the luckiest girl on the planet.

Sometimes I feel like people are envious of the dynamics of our relationship. They want what Kokouvi and I have. People constantly stare at us anytime we walk by, even when we are only talking. I know we are both loud talkers, but staring is just rude. You'd think people would keep up with the times instead of eavesdropping and acting shocked that a boy and a girl can be best friends with no strings attached. I mean, it's freaking 1985!

Last Saturday, the weather was wonderful, so we went picnicking at Rayfield Resort. We'd done this maybe a hundred times, but in his usual spontaneity, Kokouvi suggested we try the speed boat ride for the first time. I bit my nails, considering our shared experience many years ago at the swimming pool, but my fear soon dissipated because when I was with him, I had no valid reason to be afraid. He had that calming effect on me.

Kokouvi's parents, for lack of a better word, are poor and came to Nigeria in the early sixties as economic migrants. He is only able to be in university thanks to the state government scholarship. He has a part-time job as a plumber, but it pays peanuts.

It's sad how he spends so many hours unclogging toilets and still makes very little.

Thankfully, I receive a generous amount of pocket money monthly from Mummy. She has a fantastic job at the Ministry of Internal Affairs. My sister is a secretary at Jos International Breweries and she helps a lot too. I address her as 'Asabe the Munificent' whenever I need some extra cash.

So it's no surprise that I do the heavy lifting when Kokouvi and I hang out. Bus fares, cinema tickets, that sort of thing. After all, what's mine is also his.

When I brought out cash to pay for two tickets at the resort that day, the old man at the ticket booth peered at me strangely.

'Why are you paying for two tickets?' he demanded sharply after I handed him a crisp ten-naira note.

'One for me and one for my friend, of course!' I snapped.

The man simply shook his head as he handed me two small paper tickets and my correct change.

'Stupid sexist pig!' I hissed when we joined the four already seated passengers on the boat.

Kokouvi sat beside me. He was smiling as usual and seemed to have taken the whole thing in stride.

'Ah, don't blame him,' he said calmly. 'Most people from his generation can't fathom why a woman would sort out a man's bill.'

Our ideologies aligned. Nevertheless, we bantered lightly on some occasions or disagreed heavily on touchy subjects, like politics and religion. We also debated a lot too.

But yesterday was bad. We got into a heated argument, and it ended in a nasty fight. Even as close as we were, Kokouvi had never invited me to his new house. We used to live on the same street, but shortly after the incident at the pool, he and his parents moved to Vom. And while it was far from my house, I was still willing to travel all the way. So naturally, I wasn't happy that Kokouvi seemed to find one new excuse after the other.

'Shogok, not this again,' he said in that extra low tone he took whenever he was getting irritated. 'I already told you, there's a lot going on at home at the moment. Now's a bad time.'

'It's always a bad time,' I fumed. 'I've also told you, I literally don't care if bombs are going off in your front yard. It's ridiculous you won't let me visit you during the holidays.'

'We spend so much time together at school already,' he added, and I opened my mouth to retort, but he held up his finger to stop me. 'I'm always in your room, and we still meet virtually every day during the holidays, anyway.'

'In the park, yes, but that doesn't explain why you refuse my visits,' I said crankily. 'I already know your situation. There's nothing to be ashamed of.'

I saw the worried look in his eyes and knew I finally had him backed into a corner.

'You've said it yourself. Your mom is getting so pushy about you meeting someone to get serious with. I worry they could misinterpret our relationship.'

'What about your dorm room here, then? You won't even let me come in there.'

Kokouvi sighed exasperatedly. 'We've been over this only a thousand times. Unlike you, I share a dorm room. We're six guys with distinct characters in a small space. Even if you didn't mind coming to hang on my bunk bed, do you think it's fair to them? Surely you can understand the discomfort that'll bring them.'

His reply irked me. Why did he have to be so logical and reasonable all the time?

'You're lying. I think you're hiding something from me.'

I don't know why I said that. I didn't even believe dishonesty was at play here. Maybe he was ashamed of something, yes. But Kokouvi had never given me a reason to doubt him, no.

He flipped in that moment and his face became monstrous. If there was one thing Kokouvi loathed, it was being called a liar. He shouted at me, and I yelled back. Several students passed us with quizzical looks on their faces, but I ignored them. Kokouvi, too, didn't seem to care about them. Even when he was mad at me, I was still the only thing that mattered. Instead, we raised our voices higher, each of us trying to drown the other with counterpoints.

It wasn't going my way. He was adamant that nothing could change for now. I couldn't visit him, and he wouldn't be visiting me. We were only to hang around campus or in the parks or resort during the holidays. So I told him never to talk to me again, and I stormed off, leaving him in front of the sports complex and under the rain that had come out of nowhere.

* * *

We didn't talk for several days after that, and soon the days stretched into weeks. I was home for the holidays at the time, and when the phone rang, I'd hurry to answer, secretly hoping it was Kokouvi, calling to apologise and laugh at how absurd the whole thing was. But he never called, and I became miserable, missing several doses of my multivitamins. I lost so much weight too. It was the worst period of my life.

They released our exam results a month later. I finished with an upper. A decent enough feat considering how much I'd struggled in the semester that followed Daddy's demise. And my grades would have suffered more if it hadn't been for Kokouvi, who'd come to my room to study just so he could be sure I was studying too. I missed him so much, but my ego didn't let me reach out to him, so painfully, I went on without him.

* * *

The University of Jos held its convocation ceremony three days into the new year, on the first Friday of January. As we thronged into the jubilee hall, I saw Kokouvi near the front of the line with his classmates. As usual, he wasn't engaging or chatting with anyone. He just marched quietly inside and disappeared into the sea of people. As the registrar made her way to the stage, I fought back the strongest urge to disrupt the proceedings so I could find him and give him the warmest hug.

After the ceremony and outside the hall, just as I was about to have my picture taken with my family, I noticed Kokouvi watching us from the foot of the steps. His amaranth gown with its loose oblong sleeves flowed gently with the harmattan breeze.

At first, I pretended not to notice him, but I missed him too much already, so I looked back eventually. When our eyes met, we both softened and smiled. He waved to me, and I yelled out his name.

'Come and join us, hurry! I want you in the picture.'

Mummy had a concerned look on her face, and Asabe looked uncertain, but neither of them said anything as Kokouvi raced up the wide concrete steps to stand by my side. I felt his grip on my waist as the photographer clicked his shutter and the light flashed rapidly in front of our smiling faces.

Chuckling loudly, Kokouvi eagerly dragged me to a corner. He apologised for everything, and I told him I was sorry too. We agreed that the whole thing had been so silly. Kokouvi told me he liked my perm as he used a finger to brush a lock of hair away from my face. I could see my mother and sister casting us questioning looks as they whispered to themselves. Then Mummy smiled at me as if she thought the moment was cute, or perhaps she pitied me. It was a strange look, so I couldn't say for sure.

'You see that?' Kokouvi asked me quietly. 'They're already misinterpreting us.'

He promised he'd see me in a week. 'We're off to Pankshin for five days from tomorrow. My father insists we go visit my grandma, but I'll come to your house once I'm back.'

'My house?' I perked up as I asked hastily.

Kokouvi laughed heartily. 'Yes, your house. We'll drink lots of Dr Pepper and see who can finish the most bottles first.'

'Deal! Prepare to get your ass whooped,' I told him squarely.

We hugged, and I hurried down the steps, giggling madly but careful not to trip over the bottom of my robe and the new pair of high heels I was wearing. Mummy and Asabe were waiting for me near the car. They still had that weird look sewn into their faces. I was curious for a moment, but I was too happy and unconcerned to ask them why.

* * *

It's been exactly a week since the convocation ceremony, and I am expecting Kokouvi to knock at the door any second now. I'm a decent cook even if I don't do it often. The jollof rice I just finished cooking is in the pot on top of the electric stove. Piping hot, just how Kokouvi likes it. There is a knock on the door, and my sister answers it. Mummy and Asabe aren't aware Kokouvi is coming over, but they're wondering why I'm in such a cheerful mood.

But it was the postman who'd come, because Asabe runs into the kitchen with a smile on her face and Mummy hurries along behind her.

Asabe hands me the white envelope that has the bold label of the photography studio. It has my full name written in black ink, and I rip the paper in excitement. I pull out two similar pictures with slightly different poses.

'Mummy,' I call out loudly, even though my mother is just beside me now. 'These are the convocation pictures.' My voice drops now. 'Kokouvi isn't in any of them … how strange.'

Mummy looks at Asabe, and they both share a worried expression. The same one they had last week on campus.

'Shogok, you've gone off your meds again …' Asabe falters and her voice breaks. It looks like she is fighting away tears, so Mummy takes over, choosing her words carefully.

'It was just your sister and I present, dear. Kokouvi wasn't in any of the pictures. He couldn't be. He's been dead for eleven years now.'

I stare at both of them, perplexed. Asabe is sobbing. I wish she would stop and tell me it's all a joke, but she doesn't. She's just crying harder. So I turn to Mummy to see if she'll laugh, but her eyes are sad … scared … tormented.

'He drowned in the pool. You were there too – you saw it happen. That Saturday morning at Zaramaganda Country Club.'

THE MASKED ONE

Not that long ago, in one tiny village, the people were reputable for their peaceful nature. The village had survived this way, hidden, since the red gods themselves roamed their lands. One tributary of the great Niger River snaked through it, and several mud houses lay nestled behind its majestic mountains. This ancient settlement was just north of the uneven terrains of the Sahel region. So peaceful were the people here that they hadn't needed a leader or a protector in over a century. It was tight knit enough, the sort of place where everyone knew everything about everyone else.

In all this land, their most sacred area was located in the centre of the forest, the only place in the village where the redwood trees grew to staggering heights. The soil on the ground here had a distinct reddish hue that no one truly understood. It was said that the gods made it so for nourishment and that, together with the red-barked trees, established a much-needed balance in the world. After all, the crops here ripened faster, and the food tasted better too. It was also said that the soil should never be excavated further than what was needed to seed it or bury the dead. For if that was ever to happen, calamity would follow.

And so no one dug further down. There was nothing to fear anyway, because they mostly lived in isolation, avoiding any exposure to the other faraway towns.

Until one day, six years ago, when massive vehicles the size of the largest houses in the village drove into the land and started drilling the red earth.

Akufa himself was barely a teenager at the time. But he remembered it was the day that everything changed. At first, the villagers were too taken aback to act against their foreign invaders, but, as time went on, the quality of the crops worsened and the food lost its usual taste. People also reported strange ailments, something that had never happened before the invasion. So, naturally, the villagers grew frustrated and angry. But since they had no leader or protector, they had no voice.

The closest thing to an army in this village were the masked men – adult males that wore wooden masks, known by the local people as kenga. A kenga was carved from the thick bark of the giant sacred redwood trees, and each kenga was as unique in looks as it was in power. The men of this village received their kenga upon turning eighteen and gained a new power at their masking ceremony surrounded by the entire village.

The masking ceremony was one of the three most important periods of a man's life, alongside birth and death, in no particular order. At every masking ceremony, the red gods blessed the male celebrant with a new gift that equipped him to protect the women and children in his life for as long as he lived. Upon the masked man's death, his kenga was broken into equal pieces. A piece was buried with him, and the others distributed among his immediate family, ensuring his protection remained with those he left behind, at least in spirit.

Akufa was just about to turn eighteen, but he wanted no part in any of this. Not the gift that every other young man yearned for, nor the responsibility of protecting his future family. In fact, the very thought of committing to a woman and the children she would bear for him frightened him.

'I don't want any of that. You already know this,' Akufa told his twin sister when she brought up the highly anticipated masking ceremony that was less than a fortnight away. Akufa frowned at her.

He suspected she had intentionally brought this subject up, knowing it would upset him.

'Oh, I know your thoughts on the matter,' Talatu said with a mischievous grin that confirmed Akufa's suspicions. 'But don't let Father or Mother hear.'

'What shouldn't I hear?' their mother asked as she came into the house.

She had just returned from drawing water from the well, but she was clutching a small stack of fabrics under her arm too. As Mother emptied the full bucket into the barrel in the corner, Akufa eyed his sister warily, shaking his head at her as she opened her mouth to speak.

'Akufa doesn't want to attend his masking ceremony,' Talatu said to their mother.

'Makir! Not this nonsense again,' Mother blurted out as she dumped the newly woven textiles she was carrying in one big heap on the mat. 'He doesn't have a choice. How else would he get his kenga if he doesn't attend his own ceremony?'

'Oho!' Talatu piped.

'And how can you receive your gift?' Mother said, turning to face him with a look of concern.

'Mother, I don't want it,' Akufa said, trying not to sigh or roll his eyes.

His mother hated when he did that; she said it was a sign of disrespect towards one's elders.

'Not the kenga, not the gift.'

'Please stop this foolishness at once. What else will you do?' Mother asked, mouth wide open.

'I want to travel the world,' Akufa said, eyes lighting up. 'Past the Sahara and towards the Mediterranean coasts. Maybe I'll even reach the Arctic plains one day.'

'Enough of this wanderlust, Akufa!' Mother sounded cross and she looked it. Mother never got angry. Her face softened within seconds and she spoke again. 'Your father can never hear of this.'

'And what mustn't I hear?'

The unmistakable sound of Father's booming voice filled the small hut. Akufa scowled at Talatu, and even with her facial expression, the opposite of his, their striking resemblance was uncanny. Mother shook her head at Talatu, but there was no stopping her.

'Your *only* son doesn't want the kenga or its gift,' Talatu said, without mincing her words. 'He'd rather travel the world instead of partaking in outdated customary traditions.'

'Talatu!' Mother scolded.

'What? Those were his exact words, not mine,' Talatu said unapologetically.

'Is this true?' Father asked, his bushy moustache twitching. 'You'd rather gallivant than uphold generations of our most sacred way.'

It always took Father very little time to get vexed. Mother said that was his worst trait. Akufa blinked several times at the red wall; he avoided Father's eyes and said nothing.

'Is this true, boy?' Father boomed.

Mother drew in a sharp breath, and Talatu bolted out of the hut. Akufa looked at his father, whose chest was heaving rapidly.

'I understand it's important to you—' Akufa started.

'Important to *me*?'

'I know it's important, I just—'

'Stop right there, young man,' Father said, lowering his voice only after looking at Mother, who was clutching her chest tightly and had her mouth open. 'I have my kenga, and all I have done is protect my family. Without your kenga, how do you plan to protect yours?'

'What have you protected us from?' Akufa asked, finding the courage despite the extremely sour look on Father's face. 'We've lived in peace all our lives and are told to take on a mantle for a possible threat. Well, thank you for your protection, but I won't be needing it anymore when I leave this stupid village.'

Mother gasped, her eyes and mouth widening with horror. Father, who was usually quick with his words, fell silent too. He looked as though he has just been slapped in the face in the middle of the public square.

Heart thumping, Akufa walked out of the hut, nearly bumping head-on into Talatu, who appeared to have been listening through the cracked walls the entire time.

Ignoring her, he made his way through the village and towards the oasis, passing the drilling trucks of the invaders on the way. He sat quietly for what must have been hours, throwing small rocks into the water and counting their skips in his head. He was lost in his own thoughts until a hand rested on his shoulder. It was Talatu.

'What do you want?' he asked without turning his face from the water.

'Not this,' Talatu said as she went to sit beside him.

'You caused this, and now you want to gloat,' said Akufa, concentrating hard on the rock he had just thrown. He was fuming again. For a twin he had always looked out for, she was becoming a sharp thorn in his flesh.

'I'm sorry,' she said, picking up a small pile of rocks. 'I don't enjoy seeing Father mad, and I never meant to make you upset.'

'And yet you did it anyway.'

Talatu sat there quietly too, now skipping her own rocks alongside her brother's as if in silent competition. 'I'm jealous,' she said plainly.

Akufa dropped his arm to look at her. 'Jealous?'

'Yes.' She shrugged sadly before throwing another rock so it made several skips.

'Jealous of what?' Akufa asked, perplexed.

'Of you, idiot.'

'W-why?' Akufa asked slowly.

'You're a *man*,' Talatu said with a heavy sigh. 'You get a kenga and I don't. Soon I'll be expected to find a man to marry me so that I can be *protected*. And guess the most painful part.'

Akufa said nothing but kept his focus on her. Talatu kept talking but didn't turn her face to him. 'You don't even want it. I do, I really do. I'd love to be able to protect my own children too … my own family.'

'But—'

'I'm a woman, I know. Protection is the man's duty.'

'That's the way things have always been,' Akufa said gently. 'That's our tradition.'

Talatu skipped another rock. 'It's a stupid tradition.'

'Oh, I agree.'

Talatu turned to him, and both of them laughed.

'How long have you felt like this?' her brother asked.

'As long as I can remember.' She shrugged again. 'I am really sorry about today. It's just so hard, and I guess I've been lashing out more as your masking day approaches.'

'I wish there was something I could do.'

'As Mother would say—'

'If wishes were horses,' they chorused, 'we'd all ride them into town.'

They laughed yet again, but the gravity of his sister's pain was not lost on him. He wanted to reach out and hold her hand, tell her he understood how she felt, but he didn't. So he kept his hands to himself. Instead, they both skipped their rocks, enjoying the silence of each other's company.

'Deep down, Father means well,' Talatu told him after some time.

Akufa grunted and gave what seemed like a half-nodded agreement.

'And he has protected us,' Talatu said again. 'In his own capacity.'

Akufa nodded fully this time. 'I know and I'm sorry, but I refuse to be trapped here in this village,' he said. 'I'll be so … miserable.'

Talatu gasped and clutched her chest, causing Akufa to chuckle lightly.

'It's the invaders that have them so worried,' said Talatu, and she sounded concerned now. 'Things have gotten worse with them here the past few years.'

'Our village hasn't been marauded in nearly two centuries.'

'Well, look at what's happening right before our eyes. That's what happens when we let our guard down. Invaders come in and grab whatever they want.'

'Talatu, they're only digging, taking a part of the earth we have in abundance. Plus, they always leave anyway, right? Why are we trying to start a war when we don't have to?'

'Because it's our land,' said Talatu indignantly. 'And it's our duty to protect it no matter what. I know you don't think the new diseases are linked to their exploits in the ground, but I really think they are.'

They sat in silence again.

'And because they are yet to strike us physically doesn't mean they won't eventually,' she added. 'They already trespassed by entering our village six years ago. We can't just fold our arms and watch. It's why Father and all the others are so uneasy.'

'I could take the mask and give it to you,' Akufa teased.

'Right, I'm sure that'll work,' Talatu said, stroking her chin.

'Aren't you the least bit curious though?' she asked him flatly.

Akufa stared at her blankly.

'About your masking gift? What it could be. Surely, you think about it sometimes.'

Akufa shook his head slowly. 'Not really, no.'

'You really don't care about it, do you?'

He shook his head once more. 'Honestly, not even in the slightest,' he answered with all sincerity.

'That's a shame,' said Talatu, biting her lower lip and staring at the lake. 'Well, I hope for your sake that the red gods grant you the gift of having no gift at all.'

'Oh, I'd love that. An empty kenga to mask my shame.'

Their heavy laughter was drowned by the renewed sounds of drilling not too far away.

* * *

It was exactly two days to Akufa's masking ceremony when Mother rushed into the hut. Talatu ran closely behind her, holding several unfinished textiles. Father and Akufa had tilled the soil earlier that day and had returned home to rest for a few hours. The women told the men how the invaders had brought several new trucks into the village today, nearly triple the number they usually came with.

'Some of those trucks have been here since yesterday. I saw them,' Father told them. 'They must have drilled all through last night too.'

'The masked men are gathering near the abattoir. We saw them on our way home,' Talatu told Father, who sprang up dramatically.

Father went into the inner room briefly and returned with his kenga. Mother bade him farewell as he rushed out of the house. The three of them talked in hushed tones until their neighbour came into their hut unannounced. Her name was Jola. She popped by regularly, and Mother didn't like her one bit. She gossiped a lot and bragged about everything, but as usual, Mother smiled and offered her soup as she sat down on their mat.

'We pray to the red gods to protect our brave men,' Jola said after she took the first sip of her soup. 'My husband and three boys were among the first men to act.'

'Hmm,' said Mother. 'They are brave men indeed.'

Akufa caught Talatu's eye, and the siblings stifled a laugh.

'Soon Akufa can join them,' Jola continued. 'There is no greater service to our village than this.' She took another sip from the small bowl cupped in her hands. 'Akufa, are you looking forward to your masking?'

'It's all I yearn for,' said Akufa.

This time it was Mother who eyed him. It was difficult to tell what was going through her head.

Jola pressed on. 'What do you think your gift will be?' She looked at Akufa briefly before turning to face Mother. 'Two of my boys got the gift of mind reading. They say it's the chosen gift of the red gods, truly nothing greater, except being the protector, of course, but as we all know, that's a virtually impossible chance.'

Her loud laughter filled the hut, and Akufa was quickly put in mind of a horse being strangled.

'My youngest got the gift of jumping. I should have known, the boy could nearly touch the sky even as a child.'

'The gods have blessed you more than most,' Mother said to her.

'That's true, that's true, but don't say that. I'm sure Akufa will get something decent.' She slurped the final contents of her bowl and turned to face Mother again. The look on her face now was deadly serious. 'I hope you and Sanusi have started searching for a bride for him.' She laughed even louder than the first time. 'Nearly all the good girls are now taken, I must warn you. You'd be shocked at the things young girls are doing these days. My boys were so lucky to land virtuous women, may the gods help us.'

Akufa sought his sister's eyes again, but she was staring at the thatched ceiling with her lips pursed tightly. A clear attempt to prevent herself from cackling out loud. They had to endure Jola's rambling over the next hour. She was going on about how her family's farm still yielded fresh crops despite the soil troubles when they heard a loud bang.

Mother clutched her chest as she did whenever she was frightened while Jola screamed and threw aside her empty bowl with a clatter. Talatu pressed her ear to the walls keenly, and Akufa got to his feet and rushed towards the hut's door.

'Akufa!' Mother called with an alarmed look on her face. 'Akufa, sit down this instant! I forbid you to go out …'

But Akufa was outside already. In the distance, he could make out several shiny trucks. They were definitely twice as large as the usual ones, and that was saying a lot. In front of the intimidating machines, shirtless masked men had formed a wall. They were preventing the trucks from coming any further. Squinting both eyes, Akufa noticed that one of the trucks in front had a huge dent on its side and a brownish-red liquid was leaking from it. There appeared to be a couple of men in the trees and a man floating several feet in the air. Even from so far away, Akufa could make out his father. His distinct broad shoulders and shiny black skin glistened under the sun. The blue and yellow frills on his kenga swayed gently in the wind as he bobbed up and down.

'Akufa, tell me what you see.'

It was Talatu; she was tugging lightly at his linen skirt from inside the hut. Akufa returned inside and narrated what he had just seen. Jola told them about the rumour going around, and this time she had their full attention, especially Mother's.

'They come from the big city near the grasslands,' she said. 'Their trucks are heavy but move quite fast – that's how they travel back and forth within a few hours.' Jola went on to tell them that the leader of the savannah region in the east had taken over all the towns surrounding his own, along with their resources.

'He first sent his trucks south to the prairies, and now he has supporters from there to the western mangrove bay. Whether it is out of fear or true loyalty, I cannot tell you. They call him the conqueror, and any town or village that resists him is dealt with precisely.'

'What do you mean, *dealt with*?' Mother asked Jola with wide eyes. 'And how come we've never heard this before?'

'Because there are barely any survivors to tell the tale,' Jola told them, clapping her hands together so loud that it startled Mother. 'I heard it from another, so I cannot tell you for a fact.'

Ironically, it was the first time Akufa found himself taking Jola's words seriously.

'Makir! What does this *conqueror* want with our soil, do you know?' Mother asked Jola again.

'They've been tapping the very essence of our soil for yaji.'

'Yaji?' This time it was Talatu who had asked, and Jola nodded as Mother clutched her chest.

Akufa frowned now. He was of the opinion that the interest of the invaders, though unspoken, was widely known. 'I thought everyone already knew this,' he said, turning to look at all three women.

'Yes,' Mother said impatiently. 'But they were only suspicions, and now that it's been confirmed – it's different.'

Her hands remained on her chest as she shook her head from side to side. Akufa only had one burning question, but it was Talatu who asked it first.

'But what could he possibly want with that amount of cooking spice? Is he trading it for money?'

Jola let out a small laugh. 'They are saying he uses the yaji powder to build powerful explosives.' Jola's tone was grave, and she was rocking back and forth on the spot now, perhaps out of anxiety or simply for a more dramatic effect, Akufa wasn't sure. He ignored this and asked his own question, one Mother and Talatu were probably too terrified to ask.

'And what does he need explosives for?'

'Well, he's a conqueror, what else?'

* * *

Father returned that evening with a dusty kenga and a toothy grin on his face. He announced to his family that the invaders had retreated and that there was a bonfire celebration going on in the village square.

'They just left?' Mother asked him with hands on her cheeks.

'We stood our ground, crushed some of their trucks and, after some time, it seems they received an order from above, so yes, they just left.' He was still beaming. 'Took all their trucks and pipes too, everything.'

'The gods are indeed faithful!' Mother said, jumping for joy.

'It's what we should have done earlier,' Father said, with regret etched in his thick voice, 'instead of remaining silent in the name of peace as they bled our land dry. We should have protected our village long ago.'

'Better late than never, Father,' said Talatu.

'Right, right,' said Father. 'After tomorrow, you'll be able to join the real men at the front, Akufa.'

'Well, now there's even more reasons I can give you as to why I don't need the kenga,' said Akufa. 'You said it yourself – the invaders are finally gone, and all it took was a few super punches from one or two people …'

Father's eyes were flashing dangerously, and Mother looked at her son with pleading eyes from behind him, but this was the only chance he might ever have to make them see reason, so he soldiered on. 'Talatu wants the kenga.'

And now he saw Talatu shaking her head vigorously with a quizzical look on her face; it seemed she was struggling to understand the rationale for his continuous foolishness.

'And I think she deserves it. Can't we just pray to the red gods to give it to her instead? At least that way I get to do all my travelling in peace.'

Mother gasped loudly and clutched her chest so tight she had to open her mouth to breathe. Talatu rested her forehead on her palm just as a hard hand struck Akufa across the face. Akufa, though momentarily taken aback by the slap, rushed forward intending to strike Father back, but he lowered his hand quickly when he saw the aghast look on Mother's face.

'If you don't show up tomorrow, you might as well travel and never return, for you'll be no son of mine!' said Father.

'Well, fine then!' Akufa retorted.

With this, Mother collapsed like a rag doll on the floor, and Akufa rushed out of the house, nearly kicking one of several feeding chickens roaming freely outside. Hand on his stinging cheek, he fought back tears as he made his way towards the noise coming from up ahead. As expected, the square was packed with men, young and old. Some of them still wore their kenga, and they were chanting war songs and breaking into a dance around the large outdoor fire. Three men smoked shisha from a shared hookah pipe in the corner.

Many more sipped buruku, a sweet alcoholic drink made from fermented camel milk, while others showcased their powers. Men flew around, jumped several feet into the air, and raced each other around with incredible speed. As he walked past a gangly old man who was lifting two men twice his size, Akufa asked himself how happy all these men truly could be when their sole purpose was to protect their wives, children, and the village – if it ever called to them. They would never see the world or know the genuine power that came with venturing into the unknown. As he stood near the high burning logs in the centre, he couldn't help but think that tomorrow he would be here wearing his own kenga to mask his unhappiness too, just like all these men.

* * *

At sunset the next day, the entire village trooped towards the square, just as they had done for all young men before. There was no rising dust as they walked the grounds because the rains had come and gone only a few hours earlier. Now, only a dashing rainbow sat comfortably in one corner of the sky while the relaxed golden hue of the sun took the other half.

Mother said this was a good sign. Akufa couldn't be certain since Mother saw good in everything.

Father and Mother led the procession because the day belonged to their son, each of them holding a side of the mask that had been carved especially for Akufa. He was not supposed to see the mask before today. This was the custom. Seeing it meant bad luck would typically follow, and Mother, he suspected, had hidden it well to avoid this. Not that he had even cared enough to look.

Akufa was shirtless, as were all the other men. His attempt at a smile was plastered on his face, and he was wearing a newly made colourful raffia skirt that hung loosely below his waist and softly caressed his shins. Mother had even permitted him to use the scented soap to bathe that morning.

He walked behind his parents, with Talatu behind him and the rest of the village after her. They sang old folk songs as they marched. At the end of their procession, Akufa stood at the centre of the square, tall and very lanky, flanked by his parents. His sister stood at their mother's side, and right beside Father was Akam, the oldest living person in the village. She would act as an intermediary between Akufa and the red gods today because she was next in line to dine with them in the heavens.

No man was allowed to wear his kenga or have it on his person at the masking ceremony of another.

The drumming started, then came the chants from Akam, which were followed by the uniform responses of the villagers. Finally, the fire at the centre was lit. Akufa had been to other masking ceremonies, so none of this was foreign to him. He knew what to expect and what steps came next. Akam handed his parents a small cask filled with a red paste. Mother and Father dabbed their fingers in it before each placing a hand on their son's chest and smearing him with marks while their free hands held on tight to the kenga.

'May this kenga guide your fate and the fate of those around you,' Akam wheezed. 'May its gift be a blessing to you and those around you.'

Akufa's family and the villagers all hummed their response in prayer. Akufa hummed too. Both his parents handed him the kenga as Akam spoke out again.

'This kenga is ultimately the property of the gods, but you must guide it as you will with your life. May the gods bestow their gift upon you.'

His kenga was beautifully carved, truly. It was polished brownish red, the colour of freshly cut redwood and the liquid under the earth. It had frills similar to his father's, except this one was orange with light streaks of green. A fine cowrie sat between the eyes, and around the forehead, carvings in the local tongue were inscribed.

As Akufa held the wooden mask, he thought of how much this meant to everyone here, but he himself was void of any emotion. Nothing sparked inside him. Instead, he envisioned himself riding on camelback, far across the Sahara towards endless sand and further seas.

And just like that, excitement swelled in the pit of his stomach.

There was humming once more in unison as Akufa spat on the mask and threw it into the burning fire. Instantly, the flames sizzled and burned with ferocious intensity – rising higher into the sky with increased brightness. The crackling grew louder as it burned slower until suddenly, a hissing voice could be heard. The embers themselves had come alive, and the flames burst into a familiar song from folklore.

As the fire burned with song, the villagers hummed with it in matching rhythm. And as it reached its final verse, Akufa stood there, unblinking and unsinging – daring the red gods to do their worst now.

'As fast as the lightning that precedes the rain …'

Akufa saw Father's eyes water with pride immediately.

'As invisible as the air you breathe …'

Father, Mother and Talatu exchanged nonplussed looks now. Several of the villagers stopped humming and were whispering to themselves as the fire sang on.

'Please stop,' Akufa whispered under his breath. 'Please.'

He closed his eyes as the fire hissed with finality.

'As strong as a hundred men gearing for battle …'

There was deafening silence as the last flames burned quietly into nothingness, leaving only a small pile of ash and a whisp of white smoke. Akufa's kenga lay there, its carvings glowing bright blue but unburnt from the recent ordeal.

'The protector!' Akam's voice broke the uncomfortable silence.

Cheers erupted from the hundreds of people around. Akufa, dazed, remained on the spot, speechless, with his mouth slightly agape as his parents rushed to him. Father swept him completely off the ground, and Mother planted kisses all over him. Someone ruffled his hair, and he knew it had to be Talatu. When his feet touched the ground again, several men thumped him on the back before hoisting him up in the air once more. They chanted the songs of praises he had only heard in folklore songs as a child. Food and drinks emerged suddenly, almost as if they had been conjured out of thin air.

With immense difficulty, Akufa managed to wriggle his way out of every grip that followed. As he sipped the warm buruku that someone had shoved into his hands, Jola's eldest son was telling him something, but he wasn't paying much attention. His ears picked up the clear words of his parents a few feet away.

'… less than a year for him to get married – we must find him a wife right away.' Father's booming voice was clear as day even in all the noise.

'The most beautiful one,' he heard Mother saying. 'Fit for the protector. Thank the gods, I already spoke to Munife a few days ago.'

'You have good foresight, dear. Her daughter is the pretty one with the blue eyes, right?'

'Yes, yes. Can you picture their children? Oh, gods!'

'She will bear him six, way more than what we could have.'

Mother laughed at this and said something, and Akufa knew whatever it was he didn't want to hear any more. He heard someone yell 'All hail the protector!' at the top of their lungs, and at that moment he truly lost it. He dropped the tin mug that held his drink and hurried towards a pile of large stones before anyone could drag him back. A group of young women giggled as he rushed past them. He rested his head on the rock and tried to catch his breath.

His head was spinning so fast it was a miracle he was still standing and conscious. One gift he might have been able to handle, but three? And as the protector – it was surreal. He wasn't ready to protect anyone, not a family, and definitely not an entire village that would now have to rely upon him. He couldn't.

Without looking back, he started to run, making his way towards the forest. He ran non-stop until a stitch formed, piercing him sharply in the side. He slowed and took gradual steps until he came face to face with a giant redwood tree that had several missing chunks along its great trunk. He sat down and leaned upon it, eventually falling asleep under its protection.

After what seemed like the shortest time, he was awoken by several loud bangs and violent shakes of the very earth he slept on. He jumped with a start and quickly began making his way out of the forest. As the trees thinned, the smoke in the distance became clearer. It appeared to be coming from the square. It was early morning, and although the sky was usually a light shade of blue and orange, it was a frightening shade of red now. There was still dust in the air as he ran towards the centre of the square, faster than his legs could carry him.

There was food and drink spilled everywhere. A sea of bodies littered the square, and the fresh blood from them flowed freely, a noticeable shade that was different from that of the earth.

'No, no, no,' Akufa repeated as he rushed towards the first body.

This can't be happening; it makes no sense. He dropped to his knees beside a dying man. He recognised the face instantly, even with the blood foaming from his mouth and nostrils. It was Bami, the butcher's son. He was struggling to breathe but managed to speak a few words without choking.

'They … came … with big war tanks. You should have … been here,' said Bami amid the gurgling in his mouth. 'We didn't … stand a chance without … without you.'

His eyes rolled to the back of his head with a finality that sent chills down Akufa's spine. No nightmare could have been worse than this very moment. This wouldn't have happened if he had been here. None of the men had their kenga because they had been here, celebrating him. And what did he do? He had run away like a bloody coward.

He wondered if the gods were punishing him for refusing the protector's mantle. But how could they punish him so soon without even giving him a chance to reconsider his selfish act and return to his senses? How could the gods be so callous? The red gods were the cowards here, evil, merciless cowards.

He knelt there ashamed, wishing whatever had taken his people would come back for him too. But wishes weren't horses. Mother had always known this, and now he knew for certain too. His eyes rested on a ghastly scene; bodies of entire families dismembered by explosives, parts of them strewn across the field. Akufa turned his face sharply, away from the horror, but the bloody images of human remains wasted no time in haunting him.

He saw the deep purple of Talatu's fine cloth several metres away. She was still and mostly intact, lying next to two unmoving people he knew he couldn't bear to look at, even in death. Something was overcoming him now. Worse than any physical or mental pain. Worse than death. As he stared fixated on the ground, his eyes met the large symmetrical marks on the earth. He looked wildly around, searching for something.

He walked to the middle of the square slowly, dreading the revelation, for he knew it would now carry new meaning. In the burnt rubble lay his kenga, just as it was before. Ashen, but otherwise completely unscathed. Hands trembling and lips quivering, Akufa lifted the mask and placed it on his face, masking the tears streaming down his face that no one else could witness. The carvings glowed a bright blue as he paced and became one with the wind, gathering the strength of a hundred men and following the visible engine trail that was still fresh on the red earth.

Don't dream, it's over

The boy was dreaming again tonight, just like he'd done every night for the past eighteen years. He was on the streets of the capital and on the lookout for a monster, or monsters, by the looks of today's celebrations.

He walked past a large gang of teenagers dressed in different costumes. Some of them were creative, others were just abominable. One of them, a clown apparently, with his red ball of a nose and matching red wig, raised a toast to the dreamer with the pumpkin lantern he was holding.

The dreamer didn't partake in the costume-wearing of tonight and was instantly recognisable by his face. His reputation preceded him, known for his non-stop efforts to rid the streets of wrongdoers. The youngsters hailed him as they encircled him, but he only gave them his signature salute and hurried off. He couldn't afford any distraction. Evil never stopped, and some people would lurk in the shadows, masking under Samhain to commit heinous crimes tonight.

He heard a woman's scream now, so he bolted through the narrow semi-dark alley with its puddles of urine. A man dressed as a demon with bloody fangs for teeth and large crooked horns poking out from the sides of his head had an angelic-looking woman pinned against the red-brick wall. Her feet dangled uneasily under her flowing white dress as the man held her up by the neck, and the halo attached to her head by a spring was flailing above her.

The dreamer raised his muscular arm and clenched a powerful fist tight, aiming for the visible side of the aggressor's temple ...

Suddenly, the scene spun into darkness, and a loud banging noise came from outside the dream. Something, no, someone, had woken him up.

* * *

It was around the last days of summer in 1996. And even amidst the troubles in the north, Ireland was experiencing a long overdue economic boom dubbed the Celtic Tiger. Immigrants from all over the continent were flocking into the country because wages had seen a drastic increase. Infrastructural developments, too, had been ramped up, and the average life expectancy for residents of the republic had been forecast to reach new heights.

But this prosperity didn't penetrate every corner of the Emerald Isle. Smaller towns and villages around the country weren't basking in this internationally proclaimed transformation.

One such village was Inis Aisling, a gorgeous place by any standard. So breathtaking that legend says it was once the annual playground for fairies when the autumn colours burst. With a population of just under a thousand people, and more than double that number of livestock, most inhabitants of this south-western Irish island depended on the work of their hands. Predominantly farmers, they exported dairy products and various meats. Those who didn't farm worked in the service industry, selling souvenirs to visitors to the island or working in the handful of pubs and traditional fish and chip shops.

But this was volatile employment, since the tourists mostly came in the summer, and summers in Ireland only lasted a week, two if it was an unusually lucky year. So while farming was the more tedious livelihood, the islanders widely regarded it as the more stable option.

It was also the only thing several of the families here knew how to do. Having come from generations of farmers, not passing down the mantle was considered a disgrace and even more shameful if one refused it.

* * *

Tadgh lived in Inis Aisling, and his dad, like all his dads before him, was a farmer. His grandad, like the men before him, had been born in this village. They'd never left the island and had all died on it too. After his grandad passed away, ownership of the land automatically transferred to Tadgh's dad. There was never loss of land, neither had there ever been an expansion. They tended to their sheep and planted potatoes on the farm.

Dad had a very short fuse, complained a lot and found fault in everything. The longest period he went without grumbling was the few minutes every hour he dedicated to rolling his tobacco. Dad was also angry all the time, and that was partially due to him being the object of ridicule for the other farmers. His farm produced the smallest sized potatoes so suppliers purchased his yields last, mostly when they needed the numbers to meet export demand. Half of his sheep had also died over time from poor health.

But what seemed to anger Dad more was the fact that he only had one son, Tadhg. He'd wanted more boys, five or six at least. Big, brawny lads who'd work on the farm to improve the quality of planting and double the current production. Instead, he'd got a son like Tadgh. A small and sickly son with weak bones. 'Some chronic calcium deficiency from birth or just pure doctor's bollocks,' as Dad preferred to describe it. So Dad was furious that after trying for eight years, Mam finally had triplets and they'd all turned out to be girls.

'Girls are a liability,' he'd often say, 'all they do is eat your food, leave strands of hair all over the place and end up in another man's house soon enough.' But he always added that a strong girl was still better than a weak son.

Aoife, Saoirse and Sinead were good girls in every sense, well behaved and always did as they were told. And even though they were quite young, they understood it was crucial they helped Mam with the chores. Tadgh thought it was quite unfortunate that they never had enough time to play with other girls their age. When the triplets turned eight in April, all they'd wanted was a doll to share between themselves. But Dad had rebuked Mam when she'd offered to buy them one. He said that children who played with toys eventually turned out to become lazy blockheads.

'We bought him that stupid LEGO thing when he was a boy, didn't we?' Dad told Mam loud enough for Tadgh and the girls to hear. 'Look what became of that. I refuse to have four muppets running around the village bearing my last name.'

But at least the girls had each other. Tadgh was all alone; he could say Mam had his back, but there was only so much she could do. Dad terrified her just as much. Tadgh always wondered how someone as good-natured as Mam ended up with a man like that. *A real pity.*

Tadgh had applied to three different courses, all in the best university in Ireland. He'd wanted to prove he could do it, and it was also his best chance to leave Inis Aisling, studying through the dead of night and starving himself of sleep and dreams, all because he'd been determined to make it work. He'd come top of his class in the leaving certificate exams in June, and so naturally, he'd got into Trinity College. Tadgh had mentioned it to Dad during lunch last week, a day after the results had been issued, but Dad had pretended not to hear him and instead focused his attention on the meat he'd been gnawing.

After the meal, as Dad headed to the pub and Mam cleared the plates, she'd told Tadgh to be patient, bide his time and try again when Dad was in a better mood. Tadgh sighed in frustration. *That'll be a tough one.*

* * *

Last Sunday, after they'd returned from mass and all six of them sat around the rickety table for breakfast, Tadgh finally renewed the courage to remind Dad about Trinity. He fiddled with the crucifix hanging from the pendant around his bony neck unconsciously. He'd rehearsed and recited his pitch repeatedly in his head, but Dad wanted none of it.

'You're not going to Dublin, boy,' said Dad impatiently. 'I need more hands on the farm, not less. I'll tell you what, put in some more effort here and maybe in a year or two you can go to a college up in Cork.'

When Tadgh asked Dad why he couldn't go to Trinity in October, Dad replied sharply, 'You can barely take care of yourself in Inis Aisling – what would a softie like you do if you find yourself in a thick spot, eh? With all the troubles and the whatnot.'

'The conflict is primarily in the north, Dad. Dublin is safe.'

'I've been listening to the news since long before you were conceived, lad!' Dad barked. 'Dublin is safe, my foot! Not when this government has let all sorts of scum in. That city is now infected with criminals … knackers, atheists and feckin' homosexuals.'

Tadgh knew the only reason Dad needed him here was for the farm so that he could continue working him like a donkey. Dad could neither read nor write, so his only source of news was the radio, and Tadgh was clever enough to know that relying on just one source for information was a perilous business. Dad was living proof.

Dad's faux concern about his well-being if he went to the city was absolutely absurd and downright pretentious. Laughable even, if Tadgh saw the humour in it. And as uncomfortable as this conversation was, Tadhg knew the opportunity might not present itself again, so he decided it was best to carry on.

'But nearly a million people live there, and they're alright. Why can't I go there too?' he asked bitterly.

'Because you're not posh, boy,' Dad reminded him. 'Only posh little pricks live in Dublin, and you don't have half the brains to get through Trinity anyway.'

'But I was smart enough to get in,' said Tadgh quietly.

'For fuck's sake!' Dad pounded the table with both his fists, upsetting all their plates and making Sinead's porridge leave her spoon and splatter across her face and all over the white damask tablecloth.

Dad turned to face Mam. His large face was red with anger. 'You've been filling his head with these stupid ideas. Now the little shit thinks he's so clever.'

He lowered his flat cap onto his head and got up from the table with half his porridge still on the plate in front of him. No one said another word as he grabbed his keys from the old mantelpiece and walked out of the house. Tadgh's jaw tightened as the door banged shut. This was nothing but a perfect excuse for Dad to go to the pub and start early on the pints of Guinness.

Later that afternoon, Mam found Tadgh sitting in the shed. He was leaning against the grimy wall, and his face was buried in between his raised knees. She kissed him on the top of his head and told him she knew how hard he'd worked to get excellent grades, but that Trinity wasn't workable because they simply couldn't afford it.

'Even after the student grant?' he asked, and Mam nodded slowly. 'I'll only need money for room and board, and for that I could get a job. I'll work in a pub or whatever. I heard there're loads of them in Dublin.'

Mam gave him a tired smile. They exchanged a look, and Tadgh knew in that moment that the expenses weren't the problem; it was Dad. Dad would never let him go.

She sang him one of her calming songs, 'Whiskey in a Jar', and at the end, she told him that leaving the village in another year or two to nearby Cork wasn't the worst idea.

'You could go to the Institute of Technology. It's a grand school, and not so far from home,' said Mam softly. 'Your father also needs help on the farm now. There's only so much your sisters and I can help with there.'

Tadgh frowned. 'But I don't want to go to school in Cork. What does he have against me going to Dublin? He's never even been there.'

'Now your father must never know we discussed this,' said Mam in hushed tones, 'but as a young man, your father didn't only venture into Cork on day trips. I met him in Dublin, and the only reason we moved back to Inis Aisling was because your grandad threatened to disown him. We were so happy there, but he was worried about how society would see him as a failure if he didn't return to save his family's farm.' She bowed her head a little now. 'I left my own life behind, and I was pregnant with you. My parents were so ashamed, they vowed to send me to the Sisters of Mercy if I didn't marry your father.'

'You and Dad lived in Dublin?' Tadgh couldn't hide his surprise. He'd always assumed Dad had never lived anywhere else except Inis Aisling.

Mam looked up again at him and nodded. 'We shared an apartment in the heart of the city. Your father was an apprentice, training to become an electrician, and I was a hairdresser.'

'Did you even love him?' Tadgh was starting to feel nauseous now. 'Or did you marry him only because of me?'

'We lived together for three years before we moved here and had you. Of course I loved him. You were born out of pure love, Tadgh.'

Mam used her tender fingers to draw his face near hers, her kind oval face and piercing green eyes, with that wild blood-red hair. Even with her locks dressed to drop past the sides of her head, Tadgh could see fingernail marks and the bluish-purple bruises running from her neck down to her collarbone.

'*Mo laoch cróga*,' said Mam with a tired smile.

'I'm no warrior,' said Tadgh wearily, jerking his head away. He turned to face the field. 'And I'm far from brave. I'm a weakling. Dad says it and all the lads at school said it too. No one ever wanted me on their team during hurling. Not even on the bench as a spare player. They just laughed at me all the time and called me names … terrible names.'

Mam's face contorted into worry. 'I'm sorry you went through all that, and I apologise for all you still have to endure.' Her voice cracked slightly. 'I can't promise to make it all go away, but what I can assure you is that it always ends badly for bullies.'

Tadgh really wanted that to be true because Dad was the biggest bully of all. The bully's face swam in his head now – stone-faced with thick jet-black hair and bulging ice-blue eyes. Tadgh favoured Dad in looks, and this repulsed him immensely. Even those who'd never met him before always recognised him as Diarmuid Murray's boy whenever he was out in the village.

Tadgh would be the first one from his paternal and maternal families to attend university. If he ever made it there, that was. And other than Mam, who'd had to bottle her excitement when she'd learned Tadgh had got into Trinity, no one else thought this was a big deal. Alright, there was the priest too, the one Mam had told, perhaps after a few days of being proud in secret. Father O'Hara had shaken Tadgh's hand after mass, and Mam had grinned from ear to ear, but the triplets were too young to understand.

When they'd returned, Dad had complained as usual. He accused Mam of trying to starve him, to which she'd simply apologised. She didn't mention what had caused them to stay fifteen minutes later than normal. She was used to Dad's temperament and knew what would happen if she ever retorted or challenged him. Tadgh had never ever heard her raise her voice at Dad.

He wished he could fight on Mam's behalf.

Three years ago, he'd tried. It had started on a Sunday morning, after Mam had appealed to Father Moran, the no-nonsense former parish priest, to talk to Dad.

'I know it's hard to believe now, but your father wasn't always this ... cruel,' Mam had told them as she, Tadgh, and the triplets walked home from church. 'Perhaps a man of God can touch his heart and make him see reason.'

It had ended pretty badly. More so than Tadgh could have imagined. Apparently, Father Moran had cornered Dad in the pub a few hours later and harassed him in front of everyone. Dad had cut the drinking with a couple of his mates and arrived home much earlier than was the norm. Tadgh had never seen him so angry. He became an aggressive feral animal, pummelling Mam until Tadgh had stepped in and attempted to hit him.

Dad had lifted him with one arm and slammed him on the hardwood floor. The result had been several broken ribs and a black eye that wrecked his vision for a fortnight. But at least that night he'd still dreamed. Longer even than most other nights.

He'd dreamed that he was back on the streets of Dublin, fighting the unending crime and dealing with scumbags all night. And after he'd put them away, he returned to his fancy house in a good part of the city. There, Mam and the girls were in their bedrooms, sleeping soundly with their bellies full.

Tadgh still dreamed every night, without fail. The dreams always centred around the same theme. Not that he was complaining. In fact, it was the one thing he could say he always looked forward to at the end of each day – lying face up on his fractured wooden bed and staring at the little maps of mould on his ceiling as he escaped into another world. There he was strong and happy and all was well. The dreams provided him with the motivation to work harder on the farm. The more he tired himself out, the faster he would sleep, and the longer he could dream.

* * *

That Sunday morning, Tadgh heard Dad yelling about something shortly after sunrise. He was like a bloody alarm clock, that one, but a severely unpleasant one. He was threatening to flog Saoirse if she didn't stop brushing her hair that instant and get ready for mass.

Dad himself never attended mass, but he insisted everyone else did. He'd instruct them to pray for Ireland and for good harvests, even though he never gave them a punt to offer God on his behalf.

Rather, he spent his own Sundays in the local pub, the Stag's Head. There, he'd waste the entire day moaning to anyone ready to listen about how fast Ireland was going to the dogs or how the current government wasn't doing enough to help local farmers. He'd drink himself to a stupor before returning home after midnight when everyone was fast asleep.

Drinking and driving was illegal all over Ireland, but that had never stopped Dad from driving back and forth in his 1982 Ford Sierra. In between the rattling of the jalopy and the incessant banging on the front door, Dad always interrupted Tadgh's dreams. And if Mam couldn't open the door quick enough, she'd get a slap across the face. She'd learned not to ask questions too, or that warranted another slap.

* * *

The following Sunday, Mam had taken ill and decided she wouldn't make it to mass, but she urged the children to go on. As Tadgh fastened the buttons of his old burgundy waistcoat, he heard Dad smacking Mam and calling her a very dirty word. This happened a lot. They all frequently got smacks at the slightest offence. Sometimes Dad used his belt too. Tadgh was used to it, but he hated it when Dad smacked the girls. And whenever Mam got hit, every cell in his body ignited with rage.

Tadgh heard the kick of Dad's engine driving away as he paced around the living room now with his fists clenched. The news blaring from Dad's radio drowned Mam's soft sobs.

… is facing growing criticism over his sluggish response to the crisis. And in other news regarding the new one-hundred-punt Irish note that was issued last Wednesday, the Central Bank of Ireland announced in a press briefing early Friday that the old note, which has been in circulation

since 1928, will cease to remain legal tender at the end of this year. A spokesperson for the bank confirmed that the fresh note depicting the late politician, Charles Stewart Parnell will be …

Seething at his uselessness and feeling ashamed of himself, Tadgh marched out of the house and went for a walk. He couldn't bear to look Mam in the eye if she came out of her room.

Every day she called him brave, yet every day, he failed her.

It seemed Aoife, Saoirse and Sinead had figured out the coast was clear. Surely, no one would go to mass now. Tadgh saw them file out of the house too. They ran out of the stone-fenced perimeter like prisoners who'd just gained uncertain freedom.

He walked through the empty field, feeling like a character in someone else's story. *I can't keep allowing him to do this*, Tadgh told himself. *I have to do something …*

His eyes were open, but he paid no attention to where he was going. His legs simply carried him as his brain churned out thoughts.

He knew every corner of the island. He'd been born here and had never set foot out of it in eighteen years. Everyone said Inis Aisling was peaceful and beautiful, so how come his own life felt chaotic and ugly?

Newspaper articles and tour guidebooks recommended it as a bucket-list destination. A July issue of *Globetrotters* from the previous year named it as one of Europe's 'top forty places to see before you die'. Ironic, because Tadgh was certain that this place was killing him slowly.

Yes, there were lovely green meadows with their overgrown grasses and wild buttercups that sprouted independently across the wide-open fields. And the waters down at the rocky beach stayed blue even when the days were grey. Everyone doted on the Viking-era castle that still stood in the centre of the village along with some of its ruined fortified walls. Even from where Tadgh stood now, he could make out the fire-truck-red lighthouse that appeared on many of the island's souvenir postcards, and that dramatic cliff edge that doubled as a world heritage site. It was virtually impossible, too, to ignore the eclectic mix of colour from all the ivy-covered houses that sprawled the village's coastline.

Tadgh knew it all. He'd seen it all and nice bright things could eventually become boring, even dull. In that moment, he'd have traded places with anyone outside this island in a heartbeat, for anything that offered him a chance to escape this hell that was his life.

There was a ferry that came and went from the harbour once a week. It was mostly used for importing and exporting goods, but the tourists came on it all the same. The ferry sailed in and docked by the quay on Tuesday mornings and was gone by evening, giving day-trippers enough time to see the entire island. It was the only way the inhabitants of the village could leave the island as well, and a one-way ticket to Cobh cost exactly twenty-four punts. Tadgh knew because he'd checked several times. From there, he could catch the train to any of the big cities.

He would watch from the cliff's edge near their shed as the large boat sailed, imagining the smiling faces of the handful of villagers who boarded it. They were leaving this place, many of them for the first time. Probably on their way to start new lives somewhere in Cork, Dublin or Belfast. Maybe even London or farther away in Antwerp. Once they left, anything was possible.

'One day, I'll be on that ferry,' Tadgh would say to himself out loud. He just couldn't leave Mam and the triplets by themselves. *Not yet ... not all alone with that monster.*

The sound of seagulls and waves would relax him thereafter, and when the ferry blew its horn, Tadgh could almost smell the freedom from afar. His daydream was always short-lived, though, because the sheep would bleat right after, pulling him back to reality.

The eleven sheep he tended to seemed to have it much better than he did. At least Dad spoke to them nicely and was more delicate with them. They also had a marvellous view of the sea anytime they grazed on the lush greens. Sheep didn't have to worry about stupid things either, like passing their leaving cert or the rising cost of living.

Tadgh would watch them, green with envy, as they grazed for hours. Then around midday, and assisted by Patches, their German shepherd, he would guide the sheep back into the shed to be milked. He'd do this until his fingers became sore and almost numb. Then he'd collect all the fresh pints of milk and store them in a dry room. After lunch, he had to join Dad on the farm at the back of the house for more work.

This time they'd till the soil, plant seeds or harvest the potatoes. It all depended on the time of the year. They'd usually work in silence unless Dad was barking at him for messing up a step.

Whenever Tadgh got some free time, he liked to venture near the edge of the cliffs. He'd peek down at the two-hundred-foot drop into the Celtic Sea and laugh excitedly, with his heart pounding, as he watched the angry waves smash into the sharp vertical rocks.

Every year, on the chilly days nearing Christmas, he would stand there tirelessly, protected from the cold by his weathered navy-blue winter jacket as he waited for the low-toned guttural song he knew would always come. Their large dorsal fins were always first to break the surface of the water, and the moment the giants emerged from the water, his eyes would open wide in sheer delight. He'd hungrily follow the group of humpback whales with his eyes as they leapt and slammed their bellies with a tremendous splash before swimming close to the shore in their seasonal hunt for schools of herring.

Seabirds would circle the whales' feeding spot as the leviathans blew fine columns of spray high into the air. Tadgh loved the way their massive flukes and flippers slapped the water as they went along and the confidence they exuded when they danced in and out of the sea, knowing that in that moment they could do as they pleased. There couldn't be anything more liberating. *So satisfying. So dreamy.*

* * *

About seven years ago, when Tadgh had noticed strings of hair under his armpits, Mam had told him that as children grew older, their bodies, minds and dreams changed. Tadgh had welcomed the change with open arms. At least now that he was growing taller, maybe the lads at school would stop picking on him and perhaps welcome him to their group as an equal. That never happened.

From the corner of the field in which he sat today, he could see the island boys play Gaelic football. He sat here on Saturdays after milking the sheep, and the boys met here unfailingly too, every Saturday afternoon.

They were all his former classmates from St Aloysius Catholic boys' school, one of only two secondary schools on the island, the other being Mount Carmel College for girls. The boys were big and strong and had proper sporting gear on. One of them, the fittest of them all, wore a red and white branded jersey and a matching pair of shorts. They ran around the grass pitch, laughing as they dodged and wrestled one another to the ground. Tadgh watched them control and pass the white leather ball tactically to each other with both their hands and feet.

The most popular of them was Padraig Geraghty. Paddy was tall, muscular, and unapologetically good-looking. He drove a shiny green Mini Cooper around the village, and in the summer, he'd cruise the tranquil streets with the roof open, honking for what Tadgh had concluded had to be attention. The trumpeting sound always startled the older women, causing them to drop their shopping bags in terror, but it drove the younger girls into a frenzy, sending them into explosive giggles and flushes of red that continued long after he'd zoomed off.

Paddy was a conceited stud, aware of his capabilities on and off the field. He definitely ate a well-balanced diet, Tadgh thought as Paddy kicked the ball with his thick, sturdy legs. It shot straight towards the posts and under the bar into the goalmouth. A clear product of those healthy meals – quality beef and the freshest milk.

The Geraghtys had the largest farmstead in Inis Aisling. Their farm had a small plant attached to it where they processed and packaged their own milk and meat, and the family lived in an all-white manor on the top of Féar Glas Hill. Word on the street had always been that the Geraghtys struck a shady deal with the Brits four hundred years ago that made them quite rich.

'Feckin' puppets, those Geraghtys,' Dad always said. 'Selling your soul to the oppressors in order to make money off your own countrymen. Disgraceful!' Dad would usually finish by calling them a very dirty word, the same one he called Mam whenever she did something that vexed him. Tadgh hated this word and had never said it.

He remained seated on the grass with Patches scampering around him. As the boys finished their game and left the field, some of them cast him a fleeting look. Conor hinted a nod at Tadgh, but Paddy didn't even acknowledge him.

'You lucky devil,' said Liam, thumping Paddy on the back as they strode off the pitch. 'Think of all the girls you'll score when you start at Trinity in October.'

'Only two more weeks, man, I'm buzzing,' said Paddy. 'All those sexy Dublin birds –I'll be with a different one every single night. Two if I'm feeling up for it.'

Paddy dug his fingers into his blond hair and ruffled the long curls aimlessly, grinning brashly as all the other boys laughed.

'Lads, my folks are away this weekend, so I have a free gaff,' said Colm. Tadgh knew for a fact that Colm had failed maths and English in his leaving cert and was going to have to repeat next year. 'Paddy, Mairead will be there. I asked her to bring her mates too.'

'That's class, man! I'd love to give her a parting gift before I leave for Dublin. She's been dying for it.'

Paddy did something obscene with his tongue and fingers as his friends spurred him on. *Cocky git!* Tadgh couldn't help his jealousy. *Why did Paddy get to go to Trinity?* From the looks of things, he had no intention of going there to study. *Life is so unfair.*

'Tadgh … Tadgh!' It sounded like Aoife.

She was sprinting across the field to meet him. Tadgh sprang to his feet and watched her eagerly as she closed in, her long red hair and tattered yellow dress flowing behind her in the afternoon wind. Patches jumped at her playfully as she stopped beside Tadgh. Aoife was out of breath and her panting exposed her prominent front teeth.

'Come quick!' she said. 'Dad is smacking Mam … boxing her head off and everything.'

'What?'

Aoife looked unsettled now. 'You didn't … show up at the farm after lunch. So Dad came home, angry and yelling and looking for you.'

Tadgh swallowed. *Shit!* He'd only planned to be here for thirty minutes. He must have done well over an hour.

Tadgh ran off as Aoife spoke again. 'Mam tried to defend you. She said, "Cut the boy some slack, Diarmuid!" She called Dad Diarmuid!'

Tadgh was racing to the house, with Aoife running behind him. Patches followed enthusiastically, barking madly at their side.

The door was wide open when he arrived, and Dad had Mam pinned against the wall with his thick hands wrapped tight around her long neck. Her feet barely touched the floor as she struggled to shove him away. Saoirse and Sinead were yelling and crying, begging Dad to stop. Using all the strength he could muster, Tadgh dragged him by the collar away from Mam, who was now sobbing hysterically as all three girls ran to her aid.

Now it was Tadgh who held Dad in a chokehold. 'Let's see how much you love being strangled,' he said through gritted teeth.

Then Tadgh punched him non-stop in the face. The flat cap on Dad's head fell off, but Tadgh didn't stop swinging until he'd hit Dad's right eye and broken his hooked nose. But Dad seemed to regain himself quickly, and soon after, he whacked Tadgh flat on his back and onto the floor.

Mam was screaming now. The girls were still crying, and Patches hadn't stopped barking the entire time. Dad beat Tadgh senseless until he passed out. Mam had to revive him after by massaging his whole body with some hot water and a towel. When Tadgh woke, his head hurt badly and his arms and ribs were sore too. His whole body was literally on fire when he opened his bloodshot eyes.

'*Mo laoch cróga*,' said Mam as she cried and dabbed the old towel on Tadgh's burst lip.

* * *

He was dreaming now, or was he? He appeared to be standing on solid ground but surrounded by pitch darkness. The usual bustling noise, the beeping of cars and the occasional ringing sirens from speeding ambulances were absent. No loud chatter from drunken partygoers staggering across the Ha'penny Bridge either, as they made their way home. There was no crime to fight. There was nothing at all. And just like that, his nights of dreaming were over. He sensed it … felt it … knew it.

Something woke him. No, it was someone. *It has to be Dad.* The person called out Mam's name, Caoimhe, and said a very dirty word after. *It's Dad.*

Furious but wide awake now, and still reeling from the pain of his wounds, Tadgh got up from the bed and walked to the kitchen. He picked up the sharp bread knife from the countertop and made his way towards the doorway.

'You feckin' cunt!' he cursed at Dad the moment the front door swung open.

OLAEDO: WARRIOR QUEEN

The large room was in a massive palace made from sun-dried bricks. Several dresses hung in the open closet racks by the corner, and lots of shoes and beads were on display too. There were ivory figurines on mahogany shelves above the barely used sofa. And its plush, multicoloured cushions complemented the handcrafted brass masks that were pinned to the wall.

Just like many of the other rooms in the palace, this one was quite lavish, and rightly so, for it was 1697 and the height of the Benin kingdom's wealth and prosperity.

Benin was rich with tremendous amounts of brass and vast quantities of iron ore. The land also possessed significant deposits of salt, which meant the kingdom was always open to trade. Benin was arguably the most civilised of all West African kingdoms. Forever battle-ready and defence strong, the empire was so powerful it had caused many others to crumble and long be forgotten.

The door opened, and the veil was pulled to the side. In came a pretty young maiden wearing a bright orange dress. She was holding a fresh bouquet of roses in both hands. Olaedo rose from her four-poster bed and sauntered to the high velvet stool in front of the round mirror.

'Why do you bother? These flowers are better appreciated in the gardens, not wasting away here,' she said as the maid dipped the red and white flowers into the watered clay vase that sat on top of the dresser.

'The Oloi insists, and I do not wish to vex her.'

'Well, you scooping dead flowers from my chambers every week is beginning to vex me.'

'Just let it be, my princess,' came the maiden's soft voice. Desperate to change the subject, she asked, 'How was your hunt yesterday?'

'Terrible, really,' Olaedo said with a sigh. 'I shot an antelope. But it was too big for me to drag back to the kitchens, so I found a guard and told him to take it to the barracks instead. I just hope his unit had quite the feast last night at least … That'll make me feel better about the whole thing.'

The maid frowned. 'I don't understand. Shouldn't you be elated? Last time you only got a small hare, and I remember you were in such good spirits after, you went on about it right until dinner.'

'Exactly! Because I hit two hares last week. Two!' Olaedo shot her maid a frivolous warning look. 'Hares are twice as fast as antelopes, and they have impressive camouflage. A wild hare is the ultimate test for a good marksman.'

'My princess, you've been learning archery since your seventh birthday. The entire kingdom of Benin knows you are great markswoman.'

Olaedo rolled her eyes so high they momentarily disappeared behind her skull. 'Well, I wish the entire kingdom could tell that to my dear mother … Oh, have Forest and Ginger been fed this morning?'

'Ehi is feeding them as we speak.'

'And that dress is lovely by the way,' Olaedo said right after to the maid. 'It would have looked even better had it been red.'

'It's a shame I'm not royalty then, because I actually quite like red, white too.'

'Such a silly rule honestly. One of the first things I'll change if I ever become queen.'

'You will be, but I don't think you should interfere with customs and traditions even then. You could anger the gods.'

'I don't think the gods give a shit about colours of dresses, Suwa.'
Both girls laughed.

'Thank you for the dress, my princess, it's very beautiful. The Oloi saw me in the hall this morning, and she didn't look too pleased.'

'Don't worry about that, I can handle the queen,' Olaedo said flatly, waving her hand through the air.

Adesuwa smiled and said nothing as she delicately fixed threads and adjusted and retouched the tiny pins in Olaedo's hair. As Adesuwa dabbed the final touches of glossy red paste onto Olaedo's lips, the princess stretched her arms out in front of her so that her newly inked tattoos were even more visible.

'What do you think of them?' she asked Adesuwa.

'They're really lovely. I like them.'

'Me too,' Olaedo said. 'Ehi truly did a fantastic job. I look like a warrior about to charge into battle.'

Olaedo twirled her arms in front of the mirror.

'You look like a princess who's about to meet her suitors,' Adesuwa corrected her.

'Osanobua! Must you remind me?' Olaedo said and rolled her eyes. 'I wish I could spend my days on the battlefield, going on conquests with the king's guards. Even the Oba knows I'm an excellent archer, my mother too. But she'd rather die than admit it. Instead, they keep me confined to the palace wearing pretty dresses and getting my hair brushed.'

'I love brushing your hair,' said Adesuwa, stopping her work on the princess's lips to stare at her through the mirror.

'Well, you could always help with polishing my bow – that way we'd still be on the field together.'

'Ah! You mustn't allow the Oba to hear this. He won't be pleased. The Oloi could also have my head. She already believes I'm the one filling your head with wild thoughts.'

'Well, is she wrong?' Olaedo turned to her now, biting her lower lip and batting her long lashes. Adesuwa gave the princess a smile in return and met her gaze, but she turned her eyes away quickly, like a child who had just been caught admiring the sweet treats they'd been instructed never to touch.

The door burst open, and the veil was flung aside. It was the Oloi, dressed in her finest regalia, her long earrings dangling at the sides of her face. 'Why isn't she ready?' the queen asked, looking quite irritated. She looked enraged but was facing the maid only. When no response came from Adesuwa, she turned her heavily made-up face towards her daughter.

'That you're a princess doesn't mean you should keep important chiefs waiting! Don't be rude … and please, for the sake of the gods, put some more powder on your cheeks, dear. You're not a man.'

And with that, she banged the door shut behind her.

'I'm sick of her unrelenting complaints,' Olaedo blurted out to the mirror. 'I'm not interested in any of those men.'

'But you haven't even seen them. I'm sure there are rich and handsome ones out there,' said Adesuwa, sounding as if she was trying to be comforting.

'Suwa, you know I have no use for any of that. To be honest, I'd much rather marry you than end up with a man that'll expect me to stay put like a trophy he won.'

If the princess wasn't so buried in her own thoughts, she'd have seen through the mirror that her maid's fair cheeks glowed a little rosier now.

'Anyway, let's get this done with,' Olaedo said as she took to her feet.

Adesuwa followed her closely behind, the scent of Olaedo's wild hibiscus body oils pleasuring her nostrils.

* * *

The princess entered the hall to quiet overlapping chatter and caught sight of her parents already seated at the end where a great glass mosaic was mounted on the wall. The king was busy mouthing something to the queen, and Olaedo walked steadily until she could hear clearly.

'I've just received word this morning that we are winning the war in Kalabari,' the king said in high spirits. 'The sheer numbers of our troops destabilised theirs and dampened their defences immensely. I told you sending ninety percent of our army wasn't such a bad idea. We will reclaim Kalabari!'

'I was only worried we'd be leaving Benin vulnerable to foreign attack if most of our soldiers were so far away from home,' said the queen.

'Have you seen our great wall?' The king was grinning now. 'Osanobua himself cannot scale it! We have a regiment in the barracks ten thousand strong, and they are led by the most fearsome general. We'll be fine, my love. No human in their right senses will think of attacking Benin.'

'You are very wise, my king, and your word is law,' the queen said, curling her lips.

Olaedo stood a few feet in front of them and cleared her throat to draw their attention to her presence.

'Ah, my Olaedo. Only you could keep the Oba of Benin waiting,' her father said with a hearty laugh. 'If these were the old days, your head would be hanging on a pike, high above the city gates.'

The princess greeted her father with a curtsy and a smile. She met her mother's gaze and bowed, after which the queen rose and strode towards her in all her radiance. Powdered nose high in the air and clutching a handful of her skirt, she approached the still smiling princess.

'Mother, you look like you're here to find yourself a suitor too,' Olaedo whispered when the queen was close enough.

'Darling, I'm already the wife of the most influential man in West Africa,' the queen said in a solid haughty tone, fanning herself with the multicoloured raffia sheet in her hand. 'It's no fault of mine you refuse to put a bit more *effort* towards your looks,' she continued through pursed lips. 'Of course, the blame isn't yours alone. If only you'll let me find you a better handmaiden, I'm sure—'

'Father doesn't look too pleased,' Olaedo said hurriedly. 'I think its best we take our seats now.'

The queen beamed, keeping up her elegant appearance. She even nodded in agreement before leaning to whisper into her daughter's ear. 'I shall not tolerate a repeat of the nonsense you pulled the last time,' she said, waving her fan around in the air. 'If you don't choose a man here today, your father and I will be forced to select one for you. Besides, we'd be doing you a great favour. Your father and I are determined to quell all those nasty rumours.'

The Oloi gave Adesuwa, who was standing faraway in the corner, a dirty look. Then she kissed the princess on the cheek and walked back towards the elevated area that carried the throne. There, she took her rightful place beside her husband – the Oba.

The throne currently consisted of three metal chairs cushioned by embroidered leather. The largest of them in the centre had a golden crown symbol etched to its top while the other two beside it were plain and equal in size. Half a dozen wolves flocked around the foot of the throne the moment the Oloi sat down. Two of those wolves belonged to Olaedo.

The queen stroked the massive head of the wolf that was nearest to her. Sugarloaf, the oldest of the royal pack, sat on its hind legs now, baring his teeth menacingly at the crowd as its owner dug her fingers deeper into his grey fur.

The king sat in silence now, with the expected decorum. He held a bronze spear in one hand and his ceremonial dance sword in the other. All his fingers were ringed in gold. As he began greeting the noblemen that had gathered from all around the kingdom, a teenage courtier rushed to stand directly behind him. The boy was performing his duty, holding up an elaborate bronze crown only a few inches from the Oba's head.

'Thank you all for honouring our invitation and gracing us with your presence,' the Oba said to the now quiet hall. 'On behalf of myself and my beautiful queen, Idia, we present to you, our lovely daughter – Princess Olaedo.'

There were a few more formalities after that, including recounted tales of the great Obas before. And after a ballad that celebrated the current Oba's peaceful and prosperous reign, it was now time for Olaedo to choose a suitor from the twenty-seven men present. She scanned the room slowly. Of course, all of the men here would have already been screened by the royal council, meaning whomever she selected would surely come from nobility. So she would have to settle for looks instead. She could already hear Adesuwa laughing and saying 'I told you so.'

Since she was going to have to do this, she might as well make it worthwhile by choosing a handsome fellow. Her future children might not grow in a loving home, Olaedo thought, but she owed them good looks at the very least. Some of the men here were even older than her father. *The nerve of them*!

Her gaze continued to journey left and right. A few looked alright, but nothing striking. Finally, one man in the third row to the left caught her attention. Olaedo could tell that he was quite tall, even though he was seated. His face was symmetrical with a chiselled, pronounced jaw and a tidy handlebar moustache. He had dashing, sunken eyes and his muscular body filled his clothes so that Olaedo could make out the clear markings of a well-crafted chest. She walked consciously towards him, eyeing him deliberately until she was in front of him. When he smiled, she instantly regretted her decision. The man gave off an aura of hubris. She turned quickly to look at the throne area, but it was too late. The king and queen had risen to their feet, so everyone else stood too. Then the hall erupted in loud, hearty cheers and thunderous applause.

* * *

As she walked down the streets that evening with her new betrothed, Olaedo could indeed see that they were two different people. The only thing they seemed to have easily agreed upon was that the walls of Benin were a humdinger.

'It was Oba Edebiri the Second who ordered it to be built in the year 1457,' Olaedo said proudly. 'He may not have been known for his physical strengths, but he was a master planner and strategist.'

'Wasn't that the same Oba who went insane just before his fortieth birthday?' Osagie asked her.

Olaedo pretended not to hear this; instead, she focused her attention on the wall not too far off.

The fifty-foot-tall structure could be seen even from the lowest point of the city. Now, both of them took pride in the fact that their fortified city could never be attacked. They continued through the narrow streets lit by hanging oil lamps on wooden poles, and Olaedo returned greetings from all the people who waved to her. Several more people came out of their clay houses, roofed with palm fronds, to catch rare glimpses of their princess. Olaedo stuck out her tongue at a little girl who giggled before running back into her house. Osagie, on the contrary, squared his shoulders and kept his eyes straight ahead.

He was the oldest son of the wealthiest iron merchant in Benin. His maternal uncle was also the Olu of Warri, and Olaedo had already been reminded of it twice that evening.

'I, for one, don't think women should be part of the king's guards,' he said to Olaedo after they were greeted by a passing female guard on patrol. 'The military is definitely no place for a woman. The stress of it takes a toll on their bodies and messes with their emotions too.'

Olaedo thought it was best to ignore this, for she didn't want to be seen arguing on one of her only public appearances. So she kept a straight face until she had to smile at a little boy who had been using both his hands to wave at her.

'Golden monsters in the sky, golden monsters from afar – they are coming, coming – coming,' came the drooling voice of a very drunk-looking man as they entered a much quieter street.

He staggered as he approached them. He looked haggard and was clutching a keg tight to his bare, skinny chest.

'They are coming from the sky—'

He tumbled forward in the middle of his song, causing the keg to spill its murky contents onto Osagie's feet.

'You vile piece of shit!' Osagie jumped uselessly now, failing to avoid the strong-smelling liquid. 'These are expensive, new sandals, argh!'

He sent kick after kick at the drunk, who was shrieking at the hits but appeared to be in no state to tender any sort of reasonable apology. Olaedo grabbed Osagie by the elbow.

'Osanobua! Let him be. Can't you see he's too drunk? Let's go.'

He kicked the drunkard one more time after this so that the man rolled into the wide, empty gutter. Osagie sucked his teeth as he wriggled his pedicured toes dry.

'Call me old-school, but I'm a man of tradition, that's all I'm saying. Women should be home, tending to the children and—'

'If you're truly a man of tradition, then you'll know that women have been part of the kingdom's army since the thirteenth century.'

Osagie stopped to look at her, visibly impressed by the knowledge coming out of her mouth.

'In fact, if you're actually as well read as you claim, you'll also know that it was Oba Asoro who decided it was better to have more female guards than males in his army. According to him, women respected the chains of authority and followed instructions better. They were also not nearly as hot-headed or easily distracted as their male counterparts, and thus made better warriors overall.'

'I'm impressed. You certainly know your stuff. And I knew that too, but like I said earlier, that's my opinion and I'm sure it's the more popular opinion too. Look, I admire a strong-willed woman,' he gave her a cheeky smile, 'but be warned, I'm a man who always gets his way.'

'Is that so?'

'With all this fire of yours, I think the gods made you a warrior in your past life.' Osagie laughed. 'Or maybe they're hinting that you'll be one in your next. Fortunately for you, in this one, you were born a princess to the most powerful family in West Africa. And soon, you'll be married into the richest one. You're one lucky woman.'

Olaedo stared at him. He was still quite handsome in all honesty, but Olaedo concluded she would never get used to his accompanying arrogance. It was also obvious that they were both proud, him more egotistical really, so she would have to do her duty to the kingdom and simply tolerate him. She also decided it was best not to push this conversation any further, apart from one last question.

'Why should me being a warrior and a princess be mutually exclusive, though?'

'My dear, you could be a princess or a warrior, but never both.'

* * *

Over the course of the next couple of weeks, town criers rose with the cock's crow, striking their metal gongs and spreading the news of the upcoming royal wedding. All of the kingdom was invited to witness this once-in-a-generation event.

Benin's messengers took the word to other kingdoms, inviting their allies but also informing their enemies.

'It's all just a big fuss really,' Olaedo told Adesuwa as she undressed and got ready for her evening bath. 'If my mother had her way, she'd invite Osanobua and all the other gods.'

'The Oloi only does what every mother would do if their daughter was getting married,' said Adesuwa as she brought forth more hot water in a wooden pail. 'Have you always had that?' She paused to point under Olaedo's neck.

Olaedo told her it was a birthmark and was surprised Adesuwa hadn't noticed it until today. 'After all these years, I'd have sworn you know my body better than even I.'

'Actually, I do,' Adesuwa said as she emptied the water from the pail into the small steaming pool. 'It's my job, after all.'

Olaedo went into the water, dipping her toes first before submerging the rest of her body at once. She rested her back on the smooth edge and lifted her head out.

'Don't be daft – your care for me is more than just a job. I don't know what I'd do without you.'

'I'd do anything for you, my princess. Except follow you into battle,' Adesuwa said with a chortle.

But Olaedo, it seemed, didn't find humour in that, so Adesuwa, concerned, asked, 'Whatever is the matter now? Is it still because you don't wish to marry Osagie?'

'That's not it. He's a cocky, self-absorbed child, but duty forces my hand, so I've swallowed that bitter pill.' Olaedo was stroking her wet hair unconsciously now. 'It's just no matter how hard I try, I can't seem to shake off the weird images in my head. The dreams are becoming more and more frequent these days, and they're never good.'

'And what have you seen this time?'

'I'm standing on a battlefield, kind of. But the battle is on the sea, and the sea itself isn't made of water, per se. It's made of blood and gold.'

'Ah! Blood and gold? How can a sea be made of blood and gold, and how does one even fight on the sea?'

'Don't ask me. I'm sure it's just a stupid dream, but it's frightening all the same.'

'It could be a vision. Remember you foresaw your old horse's death?'

Olaedo scoffed. 'Suwa, that happened one time, and we both agreed it was merely a coincidence. There's no way the gods deemed me worthy to see through their eyes. Being a princess is enough responsibility, I tell you.'

'The length of time doesn't make visions any less potent,' Adesuwa argued. 'And the gods can bless anyone to see through their eyes. Anyone can be worthy of this, royals and commoners alike.'

'Look, I wish I was the seer you're trying to make me out to be, but I'm not. These are just nonsense dreams that are so graphically annoying they wake me up at night.'

'Well, if you ask me, I'd say you should still discuss it with the priestess. She can offer prayers to the gods on your behalf to avert any possible catastrophe. That can't hurt, can it? Or at least, tell the Oloi.'

'No, never!' Olaedo jumped suddenly, sending water splashing around. 'I'll do no such thing, and I forbid you from mentioning anything to her either. I don't need any more of her nagging or unnecessary fussing.'

'You know I would never. She already doesn't like me much. If she had her way, I'd have been replaced a long time ago.'

Adesuwa looked troubled now, so Olaedo reached out and held her hand as tiny soap bubbles passed between their faces.

'I promise you, we'll always be together. Whether I'm in the royal courts or on the battlefield. I promise you, we will.'

This seemed to raise Adesuwa's spirit because Olaedo's words of reassurance made her smile now.

'And I promise that I, too, will follow you.'

* * *

What a waste! Olaedo thought as the rose petals thrown by several unmarried maidens landed on her hair and feet. Today was her wedding day and she had to accept that even though this wasn't what she wanted, the event was quite grand, to say the least. The Oloi had put a lot of time and effort into organising this – Olaedo could see her mother's touch on everything.

Osagie was beaming throughout, like a sportsman on a podium aware of his success and expecting an award to be bestowed upon him any moment now. Olaedo was presented to him, surrounded and escorted by the twelve unmarried maidens chosen by the royal council. She was wearing a flowing white silk dress that revealed her arms and showed off her shiny tattoos. Adesuwa had tied Olaedo's hair into several small knots using colourful threads, and now a fine bronze tiara sat comfortably on the princess's head, twinkling here and there under the sun. And as was customary with all royals, multiple red beads covered her wrists and ankles while longer versions of the same beads were wrapped around her neck and dropped past her breasts.

Tradition insisted that all weddings, even royal ones, take place out in the open, under the sky and the watchful eyes of Osanobua. This was the only way a marriage could be blessed. And now a spectacular parade began. It started with the heavily armoured royal cavalry galloping synchronously. They were followed closely by the foot guards all dressed in war attire and carrying their weapons as usual.

Next was the procession consisting of the kingdom's chiefs, at the front, the proud father of the groom. Lastly came the slowly dancing matriarchs of Benin singing old marriage songs in the Bini language. Lines and lines of tables held all sorts of food and drink, and everyone was welcome to indulge, except the Oba, who, according to the Benin people, in all his divinity never ate, slept or washed.

Throngs of well-wishers from across the kingdom were gathered outside the palace. Some of them climbed trees, hoping to catch a glimpse of the rarely seen mighty Oba, his noble queen and their gorgeous princess. Dignitaries, too, from far and wide were arriving, and the Benin chiefs came bearing gifts, pouring them at Olaedo and Osagie's feet in hopes that the powerful new couple may remember to grant them personal favours in the future.

The Olu of Warri and his Olori arrived in person in a large carriage drawn by four healthy palomino horses. Servants and guards escorted then, around thirty strong, and they brought more gifts than Olaedo thought was necessary, including a few ounces of gold, a full cart of yams and a herd of goats.

Several other kingdoms from across the continent sent forth their own regards by means of representatives. The Alaafin of Oyo's delegates had travelled the road for six days to deliver two white horses, sixteen bags of freshly harvested wheat and a pregnant Nile crocodile.

When it was time for the chief priestess to perform the joining ritual, a hollow sound like a loud gong ripped through the surrounding area. At the same time, a thick blue beam shot out from the sky, all the way to the ground in the centre of the courtyard. Descending from the beam came a massive metal and glass vessel in the shape of a gigantic pyramid that threatened to block out the sun completely. The royal courtyard was enormous in its own right, but this strange vessel easily filled a third of it. Its sides were rimmed in thin flickering golden lights. And now it hovered only a few feet from the ground. From its protruding chunky base emerged a smooth metal staircase that lowered firmly to the ground.

The doors slid open and the atmosphere felt immediately hostile. Dozens of incredibly tall, dark, uniformed people trooped out in clean formation. But as they marched closer, it was clear that they weren't people at all – they weren't, in fact, human. Their suits were made from an unknown fabric, and their metal boots pounded the earth with every organised step.

They could have passed for humans if not for the cubes they had in place of human heads. They appeared to lack necks too. The cubes, made of a glass-like material, sat flat on their square shoulders. There were tiny openings on the top of their heads that allowed the aliens to emit eerie, electronic sounds. Inside the cube, a bright gold, almost yellow substance that looked like a gel moved around slowly in the centre. The matter swirled faster around the cube as the aliens began to communicate.

An exceptionally loud echoing voice sounded. 'Surrender and this will be easy.' It came from the cube of the alien in front. 'Where is your leader?'

The alien was pointing a strange weapon. The Oba came forward after his behest for Benin's guards to stand down.

'I am Oba Eghosa the Third, king of Benin, grand commander of the guards and sovereign of the Edo empire. You have trespassed into our land. Make yourselves known at once or risk—'

A streak of blue light flashed from the weapon, and a loud bang followed. The Oba fell flat on the ground, and a shapeless patch of red spread quickly, soiling most of his white dress.

'You are in no position to threaten or negotiate,' the alien said. 'You can either surrender or die. We are here for brass. Anything that stands in our way shall be eliminated instantly.'

The alien lowered its weapon, which was mostly glass with hints of metal, as it marched forwards with scores more following behind.

Olaedo was the first to run to the Oba's side and, when he gazed at her, the divine king was no more. She only saw her father, vulnerable and obviously panicking. 'Do not … abandon … the kingdom,' he stuttered to her. 'Your people … need you.'

The Oba coughed and more blood spilled onto his front. The wailing queen had reached him too, falling to her knees as she planted kisses and tears on her husband's face. But he only coughed out more blood and doused the Oloi's face in it. A dozen guards arrived, two of them swooping their king up while the others shielded him. They whisked the king out of sight and towards the palace, with the queen running behind them.

Chaos ensued.

People ran helter-skelter, and the rest of the king's guards gathered, forming a tight formation of their own, cavalry and foot soldiers alike, one thousand strong and led by General Isibor, who rode out in front of them and unsheathed a sword from his waist. To Olaedo's horror, she saw the laser beams from the alien guns piercing through the strong metal armour of several Benin guards.

The Olu of Warri and his queen had already been shielded under the safety of their carriage and were making their way towards the palace gates. They were about to go through when one of the aliens shot at them. The gun used this time was even larger than the one used on the Oba. The beam hit its target, blowing the Olu's carriage to smithereens and sending blood and flesh from humans and horses flying into the air.

The chief priestess ran around in complete panic, beads flapping and slapping against her bare torso. 'The gods are punishing us. We must pray for forgiveness. Osanobua has shown his wrath!'

A stray beam of light from the enemy hit the priestess directly on the shin, severing her leg completely in two. Amid the ongoing pandemonium, Olaedo rushed towards the palace and into the royal quarters. She needed her bow and arrows. Forest and Ginger must have smelt her because they ran to meet her just as she was entering her chambers. She swapped her tiara and beads for weapons; the recurve bow that was made from polished Tunisian yew and layered with buffalo horn. She strapped her quiver to her back and rushed out through the halls once more. A firm hand grabbed her. It was Osagie, and he looked angry.

'Where the hell do you think you're going, are you crazy?' he asked her quickly. .

'Are you blind?' Olaedo eyed him in complete disbelief as Forest growled and Ginger howled. 'Can't you see what's happening out there?' she continued. 'You expect me to cower under the bed in my chambers while my kingdom is under attack?'

'Olaedo, get back into the palace this instant!' Osagie said, turning his head around wildly. 'Guards! Where are all the damn guards!'

Olaedo slapped his hand away. 'They're out fighting, and it's still *princess* to you, by the way. We're not married yet!'

'But we will be.' Osagie looked stunned, and his voice became gentler. 'What sort of husband will I be if I allow my wife go out to fight those ... those things!'

'I'm a princess of Benin first and a warrior for my people. Anything else is secondary.' And with that, Olaedo took off again.

The scene outside had escalated. Several people lay dead already, many civilians and a good number of the guards too. In comparison, only a handful of the aliens' corpses sprinkled the battlefield. At Olaedo's command, her wolves went forth, attacking anything that looked inhuman.

She caught sight of Adesuwa, who was striking one of the fallen aliens repeatedly with an axe until it lay motionless. Thick golden liquid oozed out of its shattered cube. Adesuwa stood upright again, meeting Olaedo's eyes and managing a small smile. But her back was turned and so she didn't see the enemy coming for her.

'Suwa, behind you!' Olaedo yelled and Adesuwa ducked.

The princess fired a bow straight at the attacker's head, breaking its cube and causing it to fall where it stood.

Someone behind her pushed her with great force, making her plunge headfirst and hard onto the ground.

'What are you doing?'

She looked up to see Osagie charging towards one alien and slicing it neatly across the torso with a machete.

He dropped his weapon and picked up the fallen alien's gun, admiring it hungrily as he spoke out. 'While you're protecting the backs of others, someone has to protect yours.'

He smiled at her as he offered his free hand. Olaedo took it, rising to her feet and nodding curtly at him. 'Thanks.'

'There'll be many ways to thank me later,' Osagie said with a wink. 'Osanobua! This is one hell of a sophisticated weapon.'

He fiddled around with the buttons on the side and nearly took out his own foot when a beam accidentally shot out of it and cracked the ground open. Osagie threw the gun away quickly and rushed to pick up his machete again before returning to stand beside Olaedo. Adesuwa, too, had joined them now; she was still holding her gold-stained axe. They flanked their princess as she ran forwards, drawing arrows and firing shot after shot as she swept through the field. Not once did she miss.

But it wouldn't be enough, Olaedo thought. These things – whatever they were – had more advanced weapons and a bloody strong defence. She looked at the alien ship in the centre of the courtyard, and her heart sank to rock bottom as she saw several smaller battleships fly out of it. Alien soldiers rode inside the flying ships, and their shots were more deadly than anything before. Olaedo gasped as three shots from one of them brought down a huge chunk of the Benin wall. She heard a scream near her, and when she turned around, she saw that one of the aliens had just shot a little girl. Olaedo rushed towards the girl, but she was already dead. Feeling more rage than ever before, she chased after the culprit, pinning the alien to the ground and pummelling its cube until it shattered. Her hands were bleeding, but she kept going until she heard Adesuwa call to her.

'My princess. It's done, it's alright.'

Not too far away, Olaedo saw a firebomb being hurled at a pack of aliens, who thankfully didn't seem to be immune to the flames. She cast a nod towards the courtier that had been responsible for this, and a hand tapped her shoulder from behind.

'Princess Olaedo, you're wanted back in the palace.'

It was General Isibor. He stood tight-lipped but eyed Olaedo's bloody fists out of the corner of his eye. His face, too, was a bloody mess, and his long sword was still dripping with gold. It was obvious his horse had fallen in battle because he was standing on his feet now.

'What?' Olaedo asked, unsure if her ears had just failed her.

'Order from the Oloi.' General Isibor didn't meet her eye as he spoke. 'She wants you safe within the palace walls and beside the Oba.'

'Why, so we can both cry uselessly as we watch my father bleed to death?'

Olaedo stared at the general's lined face; she studied the way his lips tightened and saw a muscle at his temple twitch. When he met her gaze, the light greys of his eyes betrayed him by darkening, and she knew his next sentence would be grave.

'It's not looking good for the king … the Oba won't see another hour. I'm under strict instructions to return you to the queen's side. I understand you may—'

'No, I don't think you understand, General. Was it not under your watchful eyes that I learned archery?'

'And you are an excellent archer, my princess, but—'

'Now our kingdom is under attack and we're quite possibly outnumbered – only Osanobua knows how many thousands of them are inside that thing. And you want this war to be short one less fighter? No! As long as I breathe, this is where I shall remain. Whatever happens.'

Olaedo loved her father, dearly, but this was no time to grieve. *Grieving would do no one any good now*, she thought. The cold voice inside her head sickened her, but she knew ultimately that it was right.

Adesuwa, meanwhile, looked tense as her eyes silently darted from the confused general to the furious princess.

Osagie spoke now. 'Well, General, you heard the princess.'

'The Oloi will be—'

'The queen will be fine,' said Osagie with a sigh.

He held out his machete, cracking a confident smile and jerking his head at Olaedo. All four of them charged as one, taking down as many of their enemies as they could. Two scores of guards followed behind them, flinging several more firebombs far towards the front so that the aliens screeched in a high-pitched electronic sound as the explosive fire met them. Their skins and cubes melted as they fell to the ground in a heap. In retaliation, the aliens on the other side of the field attacked, sending double the number of Benin guards to their deaths.

Near the base of the ship now, Olaedo observed an orb under the belly of the vessel. It had the familiar golden mass swirling inside it and appeared to be protected by some sort of glass shield. A part of it had to be inside the ship, Olaedo concluded. She had to go in and investigate herself. The sooner she stopped these aliens from coming out, the better, or the entire kingdom could be slaughtered within the next few hours.

'I still can't wrap my head around this,' Osagie told them as he dodged a beam from one alien and ripped through another. 'Where did these things come from? All my years of reading the texts and I've never heard of such atrocious creatures.'

'And what could they possibly want with our brass?' Adesuwa spoke now. 'They're clearly not of this world, so it makes no sense why they need it.'

'That's it!' Olaedo whispered to herself as she narrowly escaped being hit. 'They require it because it's not on their world,' she blurted out. 'But they clearly need it to survive.'

She looked at the orb under the ship once more. *The answers must lie inside.* This was going to be a near impossible feat, a foolish attempt too, quite possibly, but she had to try.

'Princess! What are you doing?'

'Olaedo, have you gone nuts?'

'My princess, please!'

But their screams fell on deaf ears because Olaedo had already climbed the stairs and made her way into the ship. It was an impressive barracks with a series of hallways and stairs. She hid for cover as she made her way deeper in. More alien soldiers were coming down elevators from the top of the ship, and several more were shouting commands in a language that made no sense. She saw another battalion of aliens enter the smaller ships and disembark, ready to go out and wreak more havoc. She had to shoot her way through many until she reached a large room with a golden glow. The metal walls in here gave off some sort of pulse. Almost as if it were alive or breathing. Olaedo struggled to explain the feeling to herself at first. *Sentient.* She shrugged the eerie feeling. The room was empty of aliens but filled to the brim with dials, buttons and flat screens displaying indecipherable alien text.

Whatever they were, their technology was several light years too far for Olaedo's brain to even comprehend, so she turned her attention from this and focused, instead, on the golden light.

The glow was coming from the orb, which was actually a gigantic glass bowl. The top half of it was indeed here and, even more shocking, wasn't protected by any shield. Instead, it lay open with the golden liquid inside it. At the bottom of the half orb, she could see the tiniest fraction of a thicker, faster-moving gold-coloured lump. Something jolted inside Olaedo's brain and it all made sense. This was brass – melted brass.

This was what powered their ship. This was what was inside all the aliens' cubes, sustaining their lives. It was what they needed to survive. The sound of boots hitting the metal floor approached. Without thinking, Olaedo aimed and shot arrow after arrow, chasing the speeding brass in the alien bowl with her slender wooden missiles. But it was as if the thing knew it was being attacked because it spun around even faster. So far, it had all been futile, so when she withdrew the last arrow, she took a deep breath.

'You need to get this,' she told the arrow quietly. 'There'll be no Benin kingdom if you don't.'

She fired and the sharp head of the arrow met the brass clean, ripping it open like a wound and sending a wave so strong the ship rocked and Olaedo lost her footing. The door slid open and a horde of aliens fell; the bright gold in their cubes grew duller and fainter until they lay unmoving. The once pulsing walls became still. Ordinary.

She emerged from the ship to see that the other aliens were falling now, the ones closer to their source being the first to go. The ground was covered in blood and endless trickles of brass as cubes shattered. A sea of blood and gold, she thought.

This was what the gods had been trying to show her all along.

Stepping over the charred and broken remains of aliens, Olaedo found Forest whimpering beside Ginger. She picked up the dead wolf in her arms. Once upon a time, her fine golden coat had been the envy of the pack; now it was soaked in its own blood and barely recognisable. She walked sombrely to the rest of the crew as more aliens fell around her. She looked up and saw an alien whose golden light was also fading. It clicked the button of its gun and Olaedo's life flashed before her eyes because it was all over, but someone pushed her out of harm's way. It was Osagie, for the second time that afternoon.

He was on the ground now, struggling to breathe as blood poured from his mouth and nostrils. The alien who fired the shot had long fallen, but Osagie had taken the final beam it had sent to finish Olaedo.

Olaedo pressed the gaping wound with her already bloody hand, but her efforts were useless. The blast had hit Osagie in the chest and ruptured his heart.

'My warrior-princess,' he said as he gave Olaedo one last blood-filled toothy grin.

* * *

The kingdom buried all its dead and gave Oba Eghosa a befitting royal funeral. It took nearly two years for Benin to rebuild its city walls, but they did because they had a strong sovereign. The people used their bare hands to ensure that the new wall was higher and tougher. They used Benin clay but included the remains of the fallen alien ship – metal and glass.

They also invested time and resources to learn about technology. The university of Benin was founded, with the first department of extra-terrestrial studies in Africa. This way, they could never be attacked by land or sky, and if that ever happened, they would be ready.

Many of their strongest soldiers had fallen, and most of their valuable figurines had been destroyed, but Benin kingdom remained, along with all its brass and its new warrior queen.

A Tale of Two Cities

Ruga had been an immensely wealthy city three hundred years ago. Its streets were paved with the finest cobblestones and lined with grand, majestic buildings with pointed arches. Great spires of stone shot out into the cityscape alongside mighty rounded halls with shiny brass cupolas crowning them. Their interiors, finished in exquisite Ruga signature style, had superb chandeliers and high vaulted ceilings that were meticulously crafted to perfection.

Even the lamp posts of Ruga were interesting works of art and marvels to behold.

Elaborate open gardens with an array of well-tended flowers were scattered around the city, and Ruga's wide boulevards were lined with kissing canopies of healthy oak trees that stretched on for miles. The shiny floors of the open plazas gleamed under the sun, and beautiful handcrafted statues stood on bubbling fountains in their centres.

The air was clean, crisp, and smelled richly of expensive fragrances, authentic chocolate, and freshly baked bread. It was a magnificent city by day, just as it was regal at night. The exact age of the city was unknown, but in its prime, scholars had found records – rune paintings on rocks that dated back to the era of the first men. Ten thousand years old, at the very least.

A majority of the people in Ruga had magic and thus were known as magicians. They lived and breathed magic, and their city and lives thrived as a result. There was an institute of magic that catered to children, teaching them all sorts of magical arts until they reached adulthood. Every aspect of magic imaginable could be learned there, from alchemy to spell casting to sorcery and runes. Students also mastered necromancy, divine arts, meditation and the skills of illusion as they went along. By the time they had completed their education, every magician was as skilled as their ancestors that had come before them.

Magic was also safely guarded and preserved. To ensure its survival, large public libraries could be found in every nook and cranny of the city. Each library held several hundred books, scrolls and scripts from the beginning of time. Bells tolled upon every birth and with each death. This was how the city had functioned, without change, for thousands of years.

In Ruga, you were either born with magic or without. There were no two ways about it. It could not be acquired, neither could it be bought. And in fairness, most of the population possessed magic from the moment they came out of the womb, but life is anything but fair.

Certain bloodlines seemed to possess no magic for unknown reasons, meaning magic was hereditary. If one's parents had no magic, their offspring, too, carried that emptiness. And because people with magic never intermarried with people without, the product of such breeding remained unknown.

For those unlucky enough to be born without magic, their lives were, quite simply put, hell. These people were known as the *faceless* and struggled in all aspects of life. Their magical brothers and sisters, whom they called mages, never even looked at their faces. The faceless were ignored, spat on and kicked to the other side of the river by the edge of the city where they lived in indescribable conditions. They could never find jobs, and putting even one meal a day on the table was considered a luxury. Still, a few lucky faceless men and women made their way into Ruga.

Initially, they came as farmers to help cultivate the lands and pluck the harvests, but soon they climbed the ranks, to an extent. The faceless men now drove chariots, conveying mages from one place to another in grand style, while the faceless women worked as personal maids and cooks. This meant that, in time, the faceless could be found in the homes and offices of every mage family. And while the conditions were still terrible, those who managed to attain this life considered themselves somewhat better off than the rest, who were still scrambling to get in. To keep more of the faceless out, and the stench they brought in with them, the magicians built a wall across the river so high that it surpassed the mountains.

The numbers of illegal immigrants were controlled, but over the years, many more risked ingenious ways of sneaking in, even if it led to their painful deaths during the treacherous river crossing and wall climbing. As the years went by, the number of faceless inside Ruga continued to grow. The hours they were expected to work even doubled, but their wages became significantly reduced. The magicians cited fair competition. It was also word on the streets that the mages didn't entirely need domestic staff but offered the faceless jobs simply out of the goodness of their hearts.

This system continued for the next two hundred years before the faceless formed a united front, a union of sorts. And then they planned their rebellion. The leaders of these groups were comprised mostly of descendants of the first immigrants. It pained them that after all this time, nothing had changed. Many of them now owned small businesses and had a life their ancestors could only have dreamed of, yet they were treated as nothing more than vermin by the ruling mages.

Decades of meetings in secret locations along with the passage of both oral and written knowledge forced the faceless to create a new power of their own. At first, they called it *New Magic*, but as their formulas advanced and solidified, it came to be known as technology. The faceless continued to meet whenever they got the chance, testing prototypes of their machines and mixing refined chemicals until they achieved more stable versions. They did all this work in a laboratory located behind a building that doubled as a cobbler's workshop. This shop belonged to a faceless man, and the mages never patronised such low-life businesses.

The magicians in all their splendour had become complacent. They thought nothing of the other people they shared their city with, and so faceless technology continued to gain ground, brewing right beneath their raised noses.

The new technologists created explosive chemicals so potent that a few litres of it could reduce several streets to rubble with just one hit. They built handheld machines that shot bullets faster than the mages could write runes in the air in order to cast counter spells. This marked a declaration of war from the technologists. Bitter and proud, the mages proclaimed there would be no forgiveness for their former slaves. Men, women or children. Such disobedience and treachery could only be met with triple the labour and, in fact, no pay at all. The new technologists, however, were confident in their own new magic, so they stood their ground.

It was either that or death.

And thus, the three-year war began.

* * *

The magicians were caught completely off guard by the magnitude of the premeditated attacks. They also grossly underestimated the power of this new magic, and they suffered several deadly blows. With their population now drastically reduced and their properties tragically destroyed, it was a catastrophe too great to recover from. In the end, more than half of Ruga was blown to smithereens. The techies, as they were later referred to by their former overlords, specifically targeted the magicians' libraries and archives first, a deliberate act that would eventually cripple the future of magic and wreck Ruga's economy for generations to come.

The magicians, who once greatly outnumbered the faceless in terms of population, were now nearly on par with the technologists. And as the mages laid their dead to rest on a large scale, the techies returned to the far end of the city, over the wall where their ancestors had dwelled many years before.

It was general knowledge that the techies had plundered what was left of the devastated city, carting away heaps of gold as well as the twelve books of magic, the very ones that all branches of magic had stemmed from. Legend said they survived because they were the only texts that couldn't be destroyed by either magic or technology.

And so it happened; the technologists had taken the very source of all magic, stashing it away in their new home – their old land. And in this new city, their technology advanced, allowing them to thrive beyond measure.

The vestiges of the great wall still remained, and through it, it was easy for the mages in Ruga to see the tall glass and steel buildings that nearly brushed the skies of New Port. The shiny spires glimmered both day and night, piercing the clouds like desperate colourful needles.

Meanwhile, in Ruga, things had changed. In the many years of scholarly barrenness, magic had suffered and dwindled, losing most of its value and potency. The only magic that remained was meagre, the crumbs of what had been passed down orally and haphazardly over the years.

Many mages secretly yearned for the glory days, but they knew better than to dwell on these dreams. Old things had passed away, and it would be easier to accept this and move on, and most of them did just that. But some couldn't let go. They met in secret, changing locations every time so as not to risk any exposure. They mostly met in covered rooms under ruined buildings. There was no shortage of those here so that was easy enough. The difficult part was retaining their numbers and morale. Every meeting meant one less mage, either lost to dwindling faith in the cause or emigration to New Port.

A lot of mages now trooped there in numbers to seek employment. They worked in factories mostly. Apparently, jobs were aplenty in New Port. It was hard work, but there was no hope for a decent life in Ruga, so this was fine for many. The lucky ones worked in the homes and offices of techies as domestic staff.

Some of those who stayed behind formed a small group to burn the flame of hope. They met once a month at full moon, the day magic was supposed to be at its most potent, to practise their craft and retell stories of the old days. They called themselves the New Magical Order or NMO for short.

One such mage was Bise. She always led these meetings and she seemed to have a constant look of frustration on her face, an expression that was clear when she spoke too.

'Twenty-two ... twenty-three.' Bise's shoulders slumped immediately as she finished the count with her finger. 'We're down two people from the month past.'

She handed a stack of new pamphlets to the young man in front, who in turn passed them around.

'Tamara thinks this is all a waste of time,' a girl called Ibinabo said from the back of the room. 'She said there was no progress.'

Bise sighed.

'And my brother just got a job offer in New Port. He left two days ago. He's a barman there now, good money and lots of tips too,' said another young man closer to the front of the seated group.

Bise couldn't recall his name; he was one of the two who joined two months past. To Bise's irritation, his announcement was met with smiles and congratulatory cheers.

Bise shook her head several times, waiting for the chatter to drop so she could continue her address. 'It's a pity,' she said, 'powerful magicians being reduced to nothing but servers and cleaners. We used to be at the top, ruling with magic and might.'

Someone at the side sniggered. It was Hasani. '*We used to*, in case you've forgotten. We're powerless now,' he said, looking around the room. 'Look at us, meeting in the leftovers of our once splendid halls. Practising simple runes to illuminate rooms and shield ourselves from the rain. All this talk of past power is why more and more people are losing faith in the cause.'

'What about pride?' Bise asked him. 'As magicians, we must carry ourselves with grace and hold our heads high. Magic will always be superior to any stupid technology.'

Hasani laughed and Bise swallowed in annoyance because she knew the laugh was born out of sarcasm.

'Tell that to our ancestors who lost the war to the techies.'

Hasani stood up and walked to the front so that he stood beside Bise. He was much shorter than her, but his voice carried undeniable charisma. 'Their stupid technology is putting food on a lot of our tables since we flock there for a better life. I say we think of how to find employment there rather than wallow here licking old wounds. Magic is gone.'

Several people nodded their agreement, and Bise felt herself fuming with rage.

'We will get our magic back and you all shall eat your words,' she said, trying to ignore Hasani altogether.

'Three years I've been coming here,' Hasani continued. 'Every month, without fail. Yet all I hear is the same tired dance with no concrete plan. You tell us if we fail in our uprising, there'll be no magic left by the time our children are born, but I say if we continue in this futile journey to reclaim magic, we'll all starve and our children will come into Ruga to meet even worse hunger.'

There were a few murmurs of agreement within the group, and Bise caught some of them nodding their heads.

'Not to mention, we are playing a rather dangerous game here—'

It was Tinah, a sharp-tongued girl, who took a turn to speak now. Her burgundy beret made her stick out like a sore thumb. She had got on Bise's nerves at every single meeting since she joined over a year ago. Bise didn't like her at all. She never trusted people who wore bright colours, but she also knew the NMO desperately needed the numbers.

Tinah pressed on to more nods of agreement. 'If the techies discover our plan, they'll ban the lot of us from ever entering New Port, and they could strip away our rights to work there forever. That will shatter many livelihoods.'

'Pray tell, Tinah, how will the techies find out our plans if someone in this room doesn't go ratting us out?'

Bise eyed her warily, but Tinah just shrugged before adding, 'I'm just saying. What shall we do if that happens?' Tinah shifted in her seat, and Bise noticed she was wearing a lemon green skirt. Her dislike for the girl now multiplied tenfold.

Tinah turned her head slowly from side to side, looking at the other members of the NMO. 'I mean, even in the days of the great magic, under the brightest of moons, our spells were unable to bring forth food. I'm just saying,' Tinah finished with a pout to her lips before throwing both her arms up in the air with dramatic flair.

'Please, guys, let's not forget the purpose of this group,' said Bise. Her voice was breaking as she addressed them all again. She was getting so angry that her head was trembling with every word she uttered. She bit her upper lip when she saw Hasani had opened his mouth to speak again.

'Bise, everyone here can cast an illumination enchantment!' he said, reigniting the argument. 'Actually, everyone in Ruga can do the same tired, boring magic that doesn't put bread or stew in our bellies, so please, *grand mage*, tell us what else is new and why we should be here instead of drinking root beers under the full moon.'

There were several chuckles after Hasani finished.

At this point, Bise had had enough. She was sick of their incessant complaining and constant childish behaviour. Month after month, she had been here for the last five years. And at every meeting, she had reassured them of future success, but some of them seemed hell-bent on planting discord. It was her duty, after all, as founder of the group, to separate the wheat from the chaff.

And so she spoke out in a steady voice. 'Anyone who has lost faith can leave now.'

Hasani was the first to rise to his feet, alongside Tinah and the man whose name Bise would never care to remember. *Good riddance!* Bise thought as they left. A few more got up, including one or two Bise could have sworn were forever loyal to the cause.

As Bise watched half the class empty, she hurled every curse word she knew behind them. 'Enjoy slavery, useless bunch of idiots!'

To those that remained, she read a story from her ragged notes. It was the one about how it had taken eleven mages only six days to build a grand new hall. Then they took turns drawing runes in the air in an attempt to see who could illuminate the room the brightest.

Later, as Bise walked home with the loyal members of the NMO, she couldn't help but notice the fascination in the eyes of her cohorts when jets of fireworks shot into the night, splattering the sky above New Port with poster colours. There was clearly some sort of celebration going on there. This wasn't special, Bise thought as she turned her attention to look at the moon instead.

The techies, it seemed, always had a silly reason to celebrate something.

'It's Founders' Day!' she heard one member of the NMO say cheerily to the group as a multitude of drones took to the skies to form the words neatly with their lights.

There was no mistaking the longing in his voice. That he could even register any sort of positive acknowledgement for the day that signified the loss of magic for his own people made Bise sick to her stomach.

The admiration on the other mages' faces was even more painful to watch. *I just might be alone in this fight*, she told herself, and it was a daunting revelation, one she had always carried at the back of her mind. But even if it was the last thing she'd do, she was going to do everything possible to bring magic back to Ruga.

* * *

As the weeks passed, the numbers in the NMO continued to drop. A lot of the members had relocated to New Port, especially the youth, who seemed to be leaving in droves. It was like an unstoppable pandemic sweeping across their city, sucking away the only magicians who might have considered joining in the fight for their birthright.

Older magicians weren't spared the bug either; they, too, were running to New Port in search of menial jobs.

The process of moving to New Port wasn't as easy as it appeared. The documentation was particularly tedious and even more bureaucratic. It also cost a lot of money to apply for work permits, money most of the people in Ruga didn't have. Worse still, the government in New Port issued a quota every month, and New Port's embassy here in Ruga adhered to it to the letter, making the permits even more coveted.

Mages who wished to obtain work permits had to book an appointment several months in advance with the embassy, a small modern office on the first floor of a renovated building down in central Ruga.

After which, it took an average of three calendar months, and approvals could never be guaranteed. Word on the street was that the techies didn't need Rugan workers since they already had technology for that. They only did it out of the goodness of their hearts.

* * *

On one bleak and cold day, the type where the birds of Ruga forgot to sing at sunrise and the sun did nothing but shy away all day, Bise walked to the market to get cans of vegetables. Most of the food consumed here came frozen and packaged from New Port, the prices nearly doubling the moment they reached the ruined city. The land here produced bad crops almost unfit for consumption all year round. Magicians said it was the after-effect of the radiation from all the bombs that had contaminated Ruga's soil.

An old man walking a donkey greeted her. The animal was dragging a wheeled cart. Its contents sent a wave of shock through Bise. Damaged potatoes and cocoyams still covered in sand lay scantily around, and flies followed and feasted on the few decent patches that remained on these so-called fresh harvests.

As Bise entered the noisy plaza, she scanned the stalls with her basket in hand. Everything so far looked unappealing, but she made her way towards her usual stall. Madam Bianca's prices were the same as the others, but at least here, Bise wouldn't need to go through rounds of useless haggling.

There was a man before her, so she waited patiently for her turn. She stared from her basket to her nails, pretending not to pay any attention to their interesting conversation.

'I say it all the time,' said Madam Bianca as she automatically selected some carrots from the mix for her customer. 'If only the best of us could storm New Port and take back our books, it's all we need.'

'Ah, Madam Bianca,' the slouched man who was nearly as old as the shopkeeper said. 'We'll be dead before we finish crossing the October bridge. And what makes you think the books are even there? All these years, someone ought to have seen them. It's a tale we all grew up with, but that doesn't make it true.'

Madam Bianca gave him a snarky laugh, not one stemming from the desire to gossip, but that of a wise woman who'd rather not say too much in a bid to prove herself. 'I'll tell you this,' she said. Her voice dropped several notches, and Bise tilted her head carefully, desperate to catch every last word. 'My sister's son saw one of the books himself, nearly lost his job for it.'

The man let out a small gasp. 'You don't say.'

'Oh, yes.' Madam Bianca clarified. 'He happened to be cleaning an old cabinet that was unlocked in the mayor's home office when he discovered it. I'm telling you, the mayor nearly took his eye for it. He was transferred to another building the very next day.'

'So, if he saw one of the books, it would mean that, quite possibly, the others were there?'

'All twelve of them, if you ask me. The twelve can't be destroyed, after all – that's no myth but a fact.' She threw some onions into the same basket after fiddling with the small pile on her table.

'I always thought that part of the story was nothing but an old wives' tale.'

'I may be old, but alas! I was never married,' said Madam Bianca scornfully as she handed the man back his basket. 'And I tell no tales.'

The old man, who looked quite abashed now, bid Madam Bianca farewell and nodded politely at her before taking his leave, allowing Bise to make her way to the front of the table.

'Hello, my dear,' said Madam Bianca, barely throwing her a second glance.

And even though Bise's answer never changed, Madam Bianca asked her all the same. 'Local or foreign?' she asked, first pointing left then right.

Bise jerked her head towards the woman's right-hand side. Madam Bianca gathered cans of different vegetables from the cart that extended out of her stall as Bise complained about the recently increased prices of them. Madam Bianca told her that things were better now than they were two decades ago. Apparently, the hyperinflation then coincided with an embargo placed on Ruga by the government in New Port. The results of this meant a famine that lasted nearly two years, forcing several mages to sell some of their children to childless techie couples. Apparently, it was a painful scandal everyone old enough had chosen to forget.

'Parents needed money to feed their other children, you see,' Madam Bianca said darkly. 'Be grateful for today, my dear girl, things are much better now.'

In the end, Bise collected her basket from the trader, frozen-faced. She combed through the insides of her pocket, withdrew seven nickels and handed them to Madam Bianca, who counted them professionally with a quick rattle.

'Happy summer solstice!' Madam Bianca said in subtle dismissal.

Summer solstice, Bise thought. *Gone were the days when that actually meant something to us.* In the old days of magic, the streets of Ruga would have shut down from the loud songs, colourful parades and vibrant display of magic. These days, people drank palm wine quietly in their homes, if they even remembered to mark the day that is.

She walked in silence until she reached the end of the plaza. For the second time that afternoon, she remained as inconspicuous as she could in order to gather information. This time around though, she was eavesdropping on a group of friends. One of the boys among the group of three was boasting about his time in New Port, where he had been working, cleaning and changing sheets in a hospital for the past seven months.

Bise trailed them at a reasonable distance as they walked through the streets. Sometimes, she followed closely behind because the noise on the streets threatened to muffle their voices. The girl among them had finally got her own work permit after waiting for a decision for nearly five months.

'I'm just glad it's here now,' she told her friends, who appeared happy for her. 'I'll be working in the newly elected mayor's house.'

'Ah, that's why your application took even longer,' the boy who worked in the hospital said to them. 'The mayor's house requires additional background checks. You're lucky, the wage there is fantastic too – you'll receive nearly twice what I earn at the hospital.'

The girl squealed, and Bise rolled her eyes.

'I don't even care about the wage just yet,' the girl said again. 'I heard the mayor's house comes with the highest level of exposure, like steady promotions and other transfers within the city council offices.'

'Yes, yes, that's all true,' the boy from earlier said.

'Fair play to you,' said the second boy.

At that moment, Bise had the brightest idea. She walked faster, pushing hard through people in order to keep up with the friends.

The group reached the ruins of an abandoned opera house and stopped in front of the wide steps. Bise ensured she was still within earshot. They continued their discussion carelessly, unaware of Bise, who was leaning like a fly on the wall by the corner of the dried-up fountains. The hospital boy, whose name she had come to learn, was talking about Nuclear Servicing Day in New Port.

'It's the one day in the month we don't work yet get paid in full,' Ovie told his friends, who were now listening keenly.

He was telling them about all the money he'd saved in the past months and how he'd been this close to buying a rechargeable scooter of his very own.

'Unfortunately, mages are forbidden from purchasing any form of technology,' he added, looking rather downcast. 'Everything is registered, so there's no tricking the system. Some jobs allow you to handle tech though, like cleaning jobs, but that's about as far you could get away with.'

He went on to explain all he knew about how technology worked in New Port. The huge nuclear plant in the centre of the city was responsible for powering the city's infrastructure. Every piece of technology in New Port was infused with something called a power chip. And since everything from transport to weapons and electricity needed these power chips to function, the service would force a shutdown from dusk until midnight on the last day of each month.

'Argh! I can't wait to start making money. Come on! I'll show you the permit.'

The excited girl beckoned her friends to follow her into the empty building so she could show them her prized possession. Bise rushed in after them, throwing her hands in the air the moment they were all out of public view. The three friends looked at Bise, petrified as they watched her hands quickly sift through the air with a skill they assumed had been lost to the ages. One after the other, they dropped to the floor as Bise mumbled under her breath and cast large golden runes in front of her.

Three of them now lay motionless in different positions as they would have typically gone to sleep in their own beds. Bise walked towards them, casting an additional memory spell upon them all, before retrieving the yellow document from the girl's bag. There was no photograph on it other than a few lines of the girl's personal information and an inked signature. Bise peered at the scribbled sign again as if verifying its authenticity. She folded the paper in half before tucking it neatly into her basket, leaving the three young mages on the marble floor that had long been overtaken by stubborn weeds.

* * *

Halfway home, Bise detoured into the garden of remembrance, passing the towering marble mausoleum for Sekyen – Ruga's most celebrated grand mage – and setting down her shopping basket on the brown grass next to a baobab tree. She retrieved the yellow paper from it and moved it to the safety of her inner jacket pocket. She felt something else as she did. She pulled it out to see that it was even more old and wrinkled now. She stared at the very parchment that had inspired her to start the NMO. Bise carried this on her person at all times – a gentle reminder of what drove her and what she was fighting for.

The parchment contained the texts from one of the lost scrolls of chaos magic. It was the only full scroll that had ever been found. Over the years, several other pages and scrolls had been pulled out from the rubble, but they were always either half torn or severely burnt in parts. Except this one.

It used to be displayed in one of the rooms in the only museum in central Ruga before Bise stole it six years ago. She was certain no one would miss it; besides, she was putting it to much better use than any of the scanty visitors to the museum ever would.

It was this page from which the contents for the first pamphlet she distributed to the NMO was culled.

The page spoke of the spell of doom, one Bise preferred to call the spell of annihilation. It described the effects of the spell in graphic detail, but unfortunately, omitted the runes and incantations required to cast it.

'The spell of doom can only be cast by one magician at a time. The magician must be of sound body, mind and spirit during the ritual in order to bring forth the runes of destruction.

A doom spell is useless if the magician who casts it has a blood relative anywhere within a three-mile radius.'

Her eyes shifted to the bottom half of the parchment; this part, she had intentionally refused to add to the first pamphlet.

'Classified under chaos magic, the spell of doom is highly corruptible and is capable of tainting the minds and darkening the spirits of even the most powerful of magicians.'

Bise slipped the parchment into the other side of her jacket as she stared at the large empty fountain in front of her, completely lost in her own thoughts.

No one else in Ruga was strong enough, only she.

She had a plan. She had a purpose, one she felt with renewed certainty every morning when she heard the curious magpies tapping away at the glass of her bedroom window with their black beaks. She had never shared her deepest desires with anyone, not even with her father. He wouldn't have understood anyway; he was too ... simple-minded.

She had once contemplated telling the members of the NMO but look how that turned out. They were all weak and didn't have the willpower. She wanted Ruga to be filled with magic once again, truly.

Bise had always known she was special, different from the other mages.

She wanted nothing more than to be grand mage. In the centuries past, there were a good number of them in Ruga, one for every major field of magic, but if magic returned, when it returned, only she would be deserving of that title. After what she was about to do, that would only be right. Fitting too.

Yes, the books were gone, but that was only a convenient excuse for lazy magicians.

How come she could read and write runes better than anyone else?

How come she could mix potions and herbs without any help?
How come she could tie her incantations tightly together?
Because she was better than the rest of them.
Bise, the grand mage.

* * *

The flat Bise shared with her father was on the fourth floor of a dilapidated twelve-storey tower block. It was one of many tucked away beside the Hill of Five Sisters. A good distance from the city centre, it was among the few residential neighbourhoods that survived unscathed during the war.

It only had three rooms – a bedroom for each of them where they slept and kept whatever belongings they possessed and a living room they both shared. In Bise's opinion, the only good thing they had going for them was the beautiful furniture in their living room. Bise's father was a famous carpenter this side of the city.

The bathrooms, which were shared by all the inhabitants of the fourth floor, were in the middle of the common hall that was seldom used. Occasionally, the children of the fourth floor gathered there, inventing games to pass the time.

The kitchenette was against the wall at the end of the living area. The room was a fairly decent size. It had an old armchair with intricate carvings around its wooden edges and was covered in a heavily stained green fabric that had become more worn and stained over the years. Bise hated it so much that she never sat on it. She made use of the nicer, newer ones. She knew her father would be seated on it, however. He was a creature of habit, after all ... extremely predictable.

Bise opened the front door and was accosted by the familiar acrid smell of tobacco mixed with cheap air fresheners that permanently lingered in the room. All her clothes held this stench, and she despised this too. Her father's voice greeted her as she entered, but he might as well have just spoken to the walls because she ignored him. His smoking pipe was resting on the flat arm of the chair as he read a copy of *New Port Today*.

'Happy summer solstice!' He coughed a few times before continuing quietly. 'Strangely enough, today was the slowest it has been at the workshop all week.' When Bise said nothing, he spoke again. His voice was dry and serious. 'I locked up early. Not a single customer all day, not even to mend a footstool ... this economy won't be the death of me.'

It won't, Bise thought. *It's all this smoking that'll kill you.*

'You're still unhappy with me?' he asked her.

Bise said nothing, dropping the basket on the cooking table with an unnecessarily loud thud and walking past him to push open the window. Her father flipped a page of his newspaper.

'The living room needs ventilation, and I've told you to stop reading that shit,' she said through gritted teeth.

She didn't turn to look at him as she walked back towards the kitchenette, but she was certain he was staring at her. He hated when she cursed and, frankly, it was all she seemed to do these days.

'You know I like to stay informed,' was all he gently said.

'Why are you spending money we don't have buying newspapers from New Port?' Bise's voice was rising now. Her father hated this as well.

'There's never anything helpful in them anyway,' Bise said as she took some cans out of the basket and stacked them on the overhead shelf. She kept two, one tomato soup and one can of mushrooms in brine, which she would use to make their dinner.

Her father stood up now, all pale and gaunt, with his bald head attempting to scrape the ceiling. There was a haunted look on his face.

'My child, you must let go of this anger before it consumes you from the inside out.'

When he spoke like this, it only fuelled her anger even more.

'Baba, aren't you tired of living like this?' Bise asked him. 'Because I am!'

'If you mean without magic, we've lived like this now for over a century,' her father said calmly. 'Even my own grandparents weren't born during the period of the great magic, so how can you be so bitter about a life we never experienced?'

'Because I have magic flowing through my veins.' Bise flashed her fingers in her father's face. 'I've been practising my runes and spell casting, and you've even said my knowledge of the arts is impressive. It was the potions I brewed that nursed you back to health a fortnight ago when you were burning with fever! If only the rest of you would take this as seriously, we'd reign supreme once more! Magicians were born to rule, not cower in ruins and beg the techies for scraps!'

Her father was eyeing her closely, a cautious look in his eyes. 'We're all out there trying to earn a decent living,' he continued in his reasonable tone. 'Many of us are simply facing reality.'

'I'm sorry, but I refuse to accept this reality. Tell me, Baba, don't you ever long for the old days? When even the water in the pipes of our homes was rich with magic.'

Her father shook his head slowly. 'Bise, my dear, those days are gone now. And I share your plight, I really do. I, too, wish things could be easier, but all this … anger. Your anger is misplaced.'

He told her that he understood, and that many years ago, he, too, was on a similar path.

'So, what changed?' Bise asked him.

'I grew up,' he replied simply. 'I learned to accept the hard facts. This path of vengeance, nothing good can come of it.'

Bise switched to a matching low tone in a bid to coax him into siding with her ideology. 'The techies took everything from us, and it's high time we took it back.'

'But we stripped them of their dignity first,' her father said.

'No!' Bise insisted, her volume increasing again.

She felt her temper rising as she turned her back to her father and fiddled with the stove. 'All we did was open our homes to them and offered them jobs, but they got greedy and destroyed everything we'd built over the years.'

Bise turned back to look at him, and his face was full of concern. 'Bise, every dog has its day. Moreover, if they knew about your planned uprisings, they would argue the same thing.'

Her mouth opened slightly as she looked at him. 'You know about that? How?'

'My dear child, I'm old … not blind.'

Her hand automatically pressed her jacket, brushing it slightly until she felt the paper behind it. 'I swear to you, I will bring magic back to Ruga. I'll return us to glory and make all magicians proud.'

The look of concern on her father's face quickly changed to one of disbelief. 'I'm sorry I failed you as a father,' he said quietly. 'You must forgive me.'

Bise's face immediately softened upon the words. She shook her head vigorously. 'Baba, none of this is your fault. You're the most perfect person I know.'

It was his turn to shake his head. He didn't even look at her when he spoke. 'Oh, don't say that. You have no idea the things I've done. It was very difficult for me after your mother passed away twenty years ago … I had to do everything so we wouldn't starve.'

He was fighting his tears back, and in that moment, Bise could see beyond the wrinkles lining his face; here was a man who had been forced to carry a burden for so long. It looked like guilt. It almost even resembled shame. The tears were trickling down his face when he finally spoke again. 'I am proud of you. I always have been …'

He sniffled. This was the first time Bise had seen her father cry. Her acts of rebellion couldn't possibly be hurting him so, could they?

She stood there, lost in thought and pondering so deeply that she didn't notice when his hand reached out and gently caressed her cheek.

'… and no amount of magic is required to prove that.'

Bise clasped her hand on his. The calluses on his palm tickled her smooth skin. 'It'll be alright,' she assured him. 'I'm certain I can do more magic now than all the mages in Ruga combined.'

Her father swallowed and then frowned.

She pressed on. 'I've been practising, Baba, day and night, I've been practising magic. I have the potential to become a grand mage, I know it. Wouldn't you want that for me? You always speak of how much you believe in my potential and that I can achieve great things. This is it, Baba!'

He bent his head. 'You misunderstood me. And perhaps I misled you,' he said slowly. He told her he had seen her notes and pamphlets, and that the magic in them was neither a mystery nor a discovery.

'No one bothers because it's useless magic,' he said. 'Even the techies don't consider it a threat, they describe it as parlour tricks.' Her father pointed at the newspaper resting on his chair.

Bise pushed his hand away from her face. Her brows were furrowed, and she looked like an angry animal ready to pounce at any moment. She walked to the stove and turned it off, leaving the pot of boiling water still bubbling. He would be making his own dinner tonight. She had zoned out, but she still caught snippets of her father's words as she walked away. His voice was still gentle and pleading, as always. As she shut her bedroom door aggressively behind her, the banging sound brought her to yet another stark realisation.

Her father too, it seemed, was definitely a lost cause. She obviously was alone in this. And even with all her zeal, this truly frightened her.

* * *

The heavy chimes of bells rang in the distance the following morning as Bise hurried down the cracked stone path of the desolated edges of Ruga. A new mage had just been born. Although the bells of death rang in a similar way, there was a subtle difference in their notes still, and mages like Bise who had heard the sounds thousands of times could always tell.

She had rushed out of the house early that morning, packing as quickly as she could. She had been unable to do so the night before because she had gone to sleep pretty early. She had intentionally forgotten to mention to her father the previous day that she would be leaving, partly because of their argument but mostly because she knew he would try to make her see reason. So she had avoided him for the most part, only seeing him for the dinner she eventually still had to cook but saying nothing more than a few words.

There was no time for distractions.

The sun hadn't even risen as she rummaged through her wardrobe less than an hour ago. She had stuffed only a handful of clothes and important items into a duffle bag she never used. She wouldn't be needing many items anyway; she wasn't planning on staying too long in New Port.

She left no explanatory notes behind for her father. It was better this way.

There was a spring in her step as she neared the sparsely populated end of Ruga. Dressed from head to toe in black, the bottom of her skirt swept the dusty road. She had a good feeling about it all. Robins and skylarks sang their sweet song and even the sky seemed to agree with her because it was lighting up nicely now, with beautiful warm morning colours.

She passed a ruined library, noticing the crevices in its walls. Beside it were large open spaces surrounded by partially standing blocks. Small heaps of stones lay scattered around, like skeletons of the grand structures that once stood in their place. Down the same street was a manor nearly in its original form, except for the missing roof that was never replaced. It used to be the residence of a grand mage renowned in alchemy. These days, the bottom floor served as a children's hospital with the arch in the front entrance now a haven for termites who had built spiralling hills around it. On the other side of the road was a cemetery, its shabby tombstones stretching as far as the eye could see. There was a cenotaph in the centre. It had been erected after the war, in honour of the one million magicians who fell to technology.

A bit further down, on both sides of the road, men and women toiled away on their farms. Their children were pushing barrows of dying crops and racing back towards the market square now. The one who arrived there the fastest may fetch a small profit; the rest of them would have to try again tomorrow.

Bise smiled at them as they ran past her. *Soon, things will be better,* she comforted herself. Finally, she reached the October bridge that marked the boundary between the two cities. She looked back at Ruga one last time. Up close, the vestiges of the old city walls were still quite intimidating, although severe cracks ran across it and several puncture marks lined it from top to bottom.

This was the first time she had ventured towards the border in all of her twenty-two years. As she crossed the bridge, she took some time to admire the alabaster statues of the famous grand mages on either side of the stone railings. The mages held lamps with both hands, and their heads were stained with dried droppings from all the birds that used them as resting points.

When she reached the end of the bridge and the beginning of New Port, she saw that the techies had a wall of their own – a much shorter fence with neatly stacked metal poles linked together by razor-sharp barbed wire.

Hypocrites, she thought. She approached the narrow gates, and her attention shifted to the digital screen screwed to the top with fast-scrolling text. 'Welcome to New Port … please have your documents at the ready.'

She was officially in technological territory, and here her name would be Veshima Dikachi. There were six counters in the middle of the gate with equal spaces between them and long queues before them. She joined the line for the fourth counter, and it was past noon when it reached her turn.

The sharply dressed uniformed guard seated behind the glass gestured her forward with his forefinger. He looked extremely bored and sounded it too. 'Purpose of visit?' he asked drily in a thick accent.

'I'm here to work,' Bise replied instinctively. She could see the half-eaten sandwich that was wrapped in an aluminium foil and tucked behind a small stack of blue papers.

Bise assumed he was used to hearing that sentence because he didn't even look up at her when he spoke again. 'Course you are.'

He was looking at a screen Bise couldn't see, but she presented her document to him. She wanted this over as soon as possible. The sleeping spell she had cast on the real Veshima would be wearing off in a matter of hours. Bise also couldn't say for sure how potent the memory charm she'd placed on the lot of them would be.

'Mayor's office, eh, Veshima?' he asked her with a raised brow.

'Yes,' answered Bise.

She forced a smile that failed to reach her eyes. The officer typed away on his long keyboard as short pinging sounds came from both sides.

Panic instantly overtook Bise as she looked and noticed other Rugans placing their fingers on small machines that beeped once. Of course, there was a verification process before entry. She had been foolish to think this would be a smooth sail.

'Right fingers here,' the officer said to her, yawning and pointing towards the small machine on his desk.

Bise did as she was told, albeit slowly. The flat panel on top of the device beeped twice after its glass blinked red. The officer looked at her and sucked his teeth; he was frowning too. At that moment, Bise considered making a run back to Ruga. In the split second that followed, she factored in how high her chances of survival would be if she tried to run through New Port's gates instead. After all, the entrance was right there, open and waiting for her.

Surely she wouldn't get very far, she told herself. The techies with all their sophisticated gadgets were prepared for people like her. She knew, though, that the only way she would go back to Ruga today was if she was dragged back there, kicking and screaming.

'The other fingers, please.'

Hands visibly trembling now, Bise placed her left fingers flat on the same board. It flashed red again before making the same beeps. The officer let out a groan like a wounded animal. 'This bloody thing is broken again!'

He had turned to face his colleague on his left.

'Mine did the same thing this morning,' the female officer called back to him from inside her glass. Her voice was slightly muffled. 'It's hit or miss nowadays, really. I've been saying we need new readers for some time now, but no one listens to me.'

She shrugged and turned her attention to the mage boy in front of her.

'Here you go,' the officer said as he handed Bise back the yellow paper. 'Make sure you report to the nearest immigration office as soon as possible, preferably within twenty-four hours but no more than forty-eight. They'll stamp this for you in there. Failure to do so will result in the cancellation of your work permit which, in turn, could affect your temporary residency and can end in deportation.'

Bise couldn't believe her luck. She even thanked the officer as she hurried through the gates with a sigh of relief. The plan was back in motion once again. She saw the other arrivals hop on the threaded staircase that climbed upwards through the terminal, so she got on and allowed it to take her up towards the exit at the top.

She stepped through the wide opening and onto the streets of New Port. It was unlike anything she could have imagined. Here she was, standing under a dense forest of skyscrapers, each building competing in height with the one next to it. Vertical screens ran the length of their sides, flashing colourful videos, images, and massive dancing texts. There were nearly as many cranes in the sky as there were buildings.

The streets were wide, allowing for the free passage of quiet electric vehicles, and the pavements were covered in clean-cut interlocking granite tiles. There were several small fully automated machines hovering inches above the ground. Their speakers issued gentle warnings when they got too close to people as they went around, sweeping and sucking the dirt off the roads. Bise stood on the spot watching them go, so frozen and struck by it all that she didn't even notice when she was nearly run over by a group of teenagers hurtling past on hoverboards. They only drew her attention when other pedestrians on the path showered curses after the unruly rascals.

It was easy to tell the mages apart from the techies. Her lot were dressed like her in mostly plain, loose clothes. Mages only knew three colours – white, black and grey, nothing flamboyant like the citizens of New Port, with their very colourful clothing. Their clothes were way too form fitting too, Bise thought, casting some of them disapproving looks as she walked on. Everyone here appeared to be rushing off somewhere. A train stopped at one of the sheltered, numbered stops. Commuters hurried in and out before the metal doors slid close with a ding and the train picked up pace again, towards the elevated monorail.

A middle-aged couple wearing matching cyan jumpers in front of her stopped in the middle of the pavement where they'd been walking their keen dachshund and locked lips without a care. Bise rolled her eyes as she circled around them and continued along her way.

She looked to her right; a big glass building, perhaps six stories high, had several colourful stickers that formed the words: New Port Technological University (NPTU) – City campus library. Through the clear windows, several young students around her own age were shuffling around with folders, and others had their faces buried in the flat screens stuck onto the polished wooden desks in front of them.

The very thing they took away from us, Bise thought. The techies had denied generations of mages the chance to learn magic, yet here they were, enlightening the minds of their own youth with technology. Her blood boiled near the tipping point. There was a stinging pain in her palm, and she looked down to find she had been clenching her right fist so tight that her nails had dug into them and marked the skin there.

She turned her focus inside the library once more. One girl threw her head back in a fit of laughter after a male counterpart standing next to her said something.

Enjoy it while it lasts, Bise thought with a smirk as she continued down the pavement. *You won't be laughing for much longer, stupid techie girl.*

A group of young women chattered loudly among themselves as they danced lightly in front of Bise and towards their destination – a large white dome-shaped building by the harbour front. Their bizarre-looking dresses were almost as shocking as the loud music that blared out of the poled speakers around the dome.

From the promenade, Bise could see mega vessels sailing at sea, probably carrying goods and passengers between the seven islands of New Port. She followed the signboards and met a roundabout. There was a tall statue on top of a fountain that shot jets of dancing water from its many nozzles. Curious, she crossed over until she was completely dwarfed by the structure. It had daisies surrounding its base that spelt the words *Idan Hyrhel*.

Idan was a heavily bearded man standing on a large flat wheel holding a conical flask. He was stroking his moustache and staring at the flask with a pensive look. Bise read the words that were engraved onto the front slab of the basin.

'Necessity, the mother of all invention'

Her nose crinkled in disgust.

Of course the techies would celebrate all of this. They probably taught their children that they were the victims in this story. The anger inside her only heightened when she heard pockets of laughter not too far ahead. Groups of aged techies were soaking themselves in some of the several open thermal baths stacked in tiers across the gigantic canyon. She turned to the opposite side, towards where the signs guided her to the city council district. This street comprised of buildings all constructed in a similar grand style, with wide front steps, bronze domes and symmetrical arches.

'Pfft!'

There was zero inspiration here, Bise thought as she eyed the buildings in disapproval. These were nothing but blatant rip-offs from Rugan architecture. She would especially enjoy watching them crumble into heaps of ash.

She turned into a cul-de-sac. There were no other buildings here, only street lights lining the long, well-manicured lawns in the middle of the straight driveway. Attached to their edges were hard, green plastic banners displaying the symbols of New Port, which made Bise instantly sick to her stomach – a white bubbling conical flask in the centre of a gear icon.

Finally, she reached the mayor's residence, another replica of the other buildings a short distance away. A section of the exterior was covered in scaffold, and about half a dozen men were screwing, screeding and repainting parts of it. She climbed the front steps and came face to face with a stern-looking man with beady eyes. He was dressed in a navy-blue uniform that had two metal strips running across both shoulders. Bise handed him her work permit before he could ask. The man's eyes travelled from the paper in his hands to Bise's face.

'It's not stamped,' he finally stated the obvious in a drawling uninterested voice.

'Bad reader at port of entry,' Bise said to him without breaking eye contact. 'But I'll be doing that first thing in the morning.'

He scanned her thoroughly with his eyes, but Bise remained unflinching.

'First thing,' said the guard.

He stepped aside to let her pass, and the high front doors slid open to reveal a large room, where a smiling older woman was already waiting for her. The woman's greying hair was rolled into an elegant bun behind her head, giving her the look of an experienced, responsible secretary. Her plain clothes had some colour to them, but Bise could tell instantly she was a mage. There were dark circles under her eyes that must have come from many years of tears, and when she shook Bise's hand to introduce herself, it was obvious she had once ploughed some of Ruga's toughest fields. There was barely any time to soak in the ambience before Veliane led her to the mayor's office. Bise didn't mind this one bit. Time was of the essence, after all. When the woman spoke again, Bise heard the distinct New Portian accent.

'As you can imagine, the mayor is a very busy man, but he insists on meeting every new member of staff personally.'

'Naturally,' said Bise.

Veliane turned to Bise and cocked her head. 'That jewellery won't fly here, dear,' she said pointedly, now eyeing the sides of Bise's face as if checking for more piercings.

Bise removed the silver bull nose ring and stowed it in her pocket.

'And you will only address the mayor as his lordship,' Veliane added before knocking twice on the door.

The first thing to catch Bise's eye was the armchair in the far-left corner of the room. It looked exactly like the one back in her father's flat, and it even had the same carved designs on its polished wooden edges. Parts of it were covered in the same green fabric too, but this one was tidier and clearly better taken care of. It was so alike, Bise nearly swore it had to have been made by her father, except he wasn't the only carpenter in Ruga, and certainly New Port had to have its own fair share of skilled artisans, she reminded herself before withdrawing her attention from the furniture.

As expected, the office was well decorated with pictures, award plaques and contemporary art. A carbon fibre telescope attached to a steel tripod sat in the corner with its lens facing the large window that allowed for an uninterrupted view of the cityscape. There were shelves of books too, lots and lots of them. The mayor, however, was much younger-looking than Bise had pictured him. *Definitely in his early fifties.* He was surprisingly shorter too. He had been pacing around when they came in and had a glass of brandy in one hand; the bottle, half full, was on the table.

He was bespectacled and spoke with a permanent brooding expression on his strong face. Bise could tell she was one of many staff who came just as fast as they went. She looked around the room, collecting as much visual detail as her brain would allow. Everything had a digital lock in here; her plan was looking unpromising.

At first, the mayor gave her a sweeping look that Bise believed had to be curiosity, but when he didn't break off, she thought it plain rude. His gaze lingered upon her face until Veliane broke the silent tension and introduced Bise as the new cleaner. The mayor, still eyeing Bise tenaciously, asked her name again.

'Veshima Dikachi,' Bise repeated carefully.

This seemed to put him at ease for whatever reason because, after that, he had very few words for her.

There were strict protocols to adhere to, even for cleaning a stupid office. She was only to clean the office floor and surfaces of cabinets and safes. She was to touch nothing else and wasn't allowed to move anything around.

'Service day is two days away,' the mayor, now seated behind his desk, told her. 'Veliane will bring you up to speed anyway, but you are not to clean on that day. There will be no need to even enter the office. You'll be paid a full day's wage, of course.'

He turned his attention back to the tablet on his table and poked lazily at the screen. When Bise just stood there, the mayor looked up at her and then spoke to Veliane directly. 'That will be all,' he said casually, dismissing them both with a lazy wave of his hand.

That night, as Bise lay on her single bed down in the staff quarters, she could barely sleep, torn between the excitement of her accomplishments thus far and the worry of not finding the twelve books of magic in time. Still, if she ever needed a sign that she was on the right track, this was it. She truly believed that her ancestors, who had set her on this path, were laying the groundwork for her.

How else could it be explained that this month's service day coincided with a supermoon? And it was only that evening that Veliane had told her the mayor's office had opened the sought-after position because she, Veliane, was retiring in one month. She had served the mayor's residence and office faithfully for the last twenty-seven years.

Having worked with five mayors past, it was time for her to return to Ruga and spend time with her grandchildren.

Bise smiled now as she punched her flat pillow into shape. Veliane didn't know, but she had proven herself more useful than all the other NMO members put together, and for that, Bise swore to ring the bells of her death personally whenever Veliane decided to go and join the fore-mages.

* * *

The following morning, Veliane woke Bise up and showed her around the building. It comprised of both private and official spaces and had a whopping thirty-six rooms spread across its four floors. Bise was assigned the mayor's residence itself on the fourth floor because she was taking over for Veliane soon. The residence held the mayor's private quarters, a personal office and enough rooms for his family whenever they visited from Gombe, a smaller island nearby where the mayor's family primarily resided.

'Have you met his lordship's family yet?' Bise asked as they exited one room and prepared to enter another.

'I've met her ladyship,' Veliane said, eyes twinkling with pride. Bise could hear the excitement in her voice as she rambled on. 'The current mayor used to be New Port's ambassador to Ruga, and coincidentally, I used to clean their apartment back in central Ruga. One morning I arrived for work and her ladyship was gone. Months later, I heard she had delivered a baby girl. The ambassador was posted back to New Port after that. He only took up office three weeks ago, and, like many busy mayors before him, he'll want less of his family here, I assume. I'm looking forward to meeting her ladyship again after over twenty years, and their daughter too, of course, who shouldn't be too far from your age, actually. I've been informed they'll be visiting sometime tonight. With the power out and the city at a standstill tomorrow, I can only assume they'll be much safer here.'

— 233 —

She filled Bise's head with more information, some of it insightful, but most of the rest Bise thought was quite useless. Veliane showed her how everything was done the rest of that day, and Bise focused hard, determined to learn as quickly as she could so they could keep the tour moving.

'Wow! You're a fast learner,' Veliane praised Bise as she recounted the steps to be taken for each different security protocol. Bise smiled and nodded back at her.

After a quick lunch in the basement, they spent the rest of the afternoon going over the buttons of the three cleaning machines Bise would mostly need for her daily tasks. The session ended with a presentation from Bise, demonstrating the multiple buttons and toggles on the whirring machines to Veliane, who was very proud.

In the evening, after the mayor had retired for the day, Veliane took her to the same office as yesterday. Bise watched gingerly as Veliane swiped her access card on the door reader. The mayor didn't receive official guests here, apparently; that room was down on the second floor.

'That's his favourite chair,' said Veliane, pointing and causing Bise's eye to find the familiar-looking armchair in the corner. 'You must polish the wood once every month. I'd suggest the day after service day so you have a nice routine. He likes to sit there and think, so dust daily and polish monthly. I've polished the handles of that very chair myself, more times than I can count. His lordship has had that chair since his days in Ruga.'

Veliane eyed the chair with a doting expression across her face. A small smile formed between her thin lips. 'I mean, I don't know the story behind it, but it is quite a lovely chair, isn't it?'

Bise nodded but said nothing as her heart began racing. She was too disoriented to speak.

Alright, so the former ambassador bought a piece of furniture from her father during his time in Ruga. *So freaking what?* Bise thought. After all, her father was the best carpenter in all of Ruga. That should come as no surprise. This was sheer coincidence, it meant absolutely nothing!

Veliane ventured deeper into the room and Bise inched behind. To Bise's annoyance, she kept running her fingers over surfaces and raising them to her face as she walked, as if checking for dust.

'We never enter here in the evenings,' Veliane started again. 'Today is the exception because I need to show you some things, but we only clean early in the mornings before the mayor starts work. He is an early riser, you see,' Veliane mentioned to her. 'He starts his day here shortly after sunrise, and around noon, he goes down for meetings in the bigger office. After tomorrow, one of the in-house technicians will give you a special access card for the doors. Other than our quarters and the kitchens, you'll be given another card that only grants access to the elevator and onto this floor, nothing else. Stairs are for emergencies only.'

Veliane walked ahead again, so Bise followed her diligently. She stopped abruptly and turned to face Bise. 'Oh, don't forget to get your permit stamped and make a copy too, you'll need that for subsequent entry and exits. The immigration office is closed tomorrow but get the original copy to me the day after that. I'll need to submit it to admin as soon as possible.'

Bise nodded her understanding. She wouldn't even be here after tomorrow, but sure.

She scanned the room as she had done yesterday, but today she had more time to look around. She asked Veliane several more questions pertaining to the cleaning of the room as an excuse to scout it for longer.

In the end, she knew the position of things. She counted four small safes and two large ones, eleven shelves, two mid-size cabinets and a fine mahogany table with two drawers underneath. With all the added security in the room, she knew that if the books were locked anywhere in this building, they would be in this very room.

'How far is Ruga from here?' Bise asked.

She had already done her rough calculations, but she needed to hear it from someone else, especially someone who had made the trip several times back and forth. Bise needed to be certain her plan would work.

'It's at least five miles to the bridge of enlightenment.'

So Bise's calculations had indeed been accurate.

'Why?' Veliane asked her. 'You're not homesick already, are you?'

Bise pretended to be embarrassed at this by refusing to meet Veliane's eyes as she smiled nervously.

'Ah, sweet girl, remember you're here to work and make money so you can have a decent life whenever you decide to return to Ruga. So, eyes on the prize.'

'I know why I'm here, don't worry.'

'Good! It's decent work here and much better than working in the warehouses or factories.'

'Oh, I am a lucky girl,' said Bise, grinning rather broadly.

* * *

On the night of service day, Bise gobbled down her food so she could leave the staff dining table early. The mages usually stayed behind an extra hour after food for some small talk. A complete waste of time if you asked Bise. Because the lights weren't working today, they all ate their dinner under the white light from the battery-powered lanterns scattered around the room.

Including Bise, there were thirteen domestic staff, all of them mages. Veliane was the oldest among them, and Bise could see that the others looked to her as a mother figure of sorts. Veliane was looking pleased with herself this evening as she sat at the head of the table. There were a bunch of keys hanging low on a chain around her neck.

Keys to the rooms upstairs, Bise thought. Thank the ancestors, she had a well-mapped-out Plan B.

As they all ate, Veliane checked with them, ensuring everyone could see their plates clearly and asking if the mashed potatoes were creamy enough.

'I still don't understand why we can't just use an illumination charm,' Bise had said through mouthfuls of food. 'It's much nicer. I mean, we're alone here and it's harmless.'

The mages at the table all fell silent as they exchanged frightened, knowing looks.

'It's forbidden!' Veliane hissed, looking around pointlessly. 'Even the mention of magic in New Port could have you deported and banned from future entry.'

'Oh, I'm sorry,' said Bise, even though she wasn't. 'I didn't know.'

'Fair enough. I mean, how could you?' Veliane smiled at her. 'You've only just arrived, but now you do.'

As usual, Bise simply nodded her understanding.

'Well, it's going to be an early night for me,' she announced to the other twelve mages shortly after before rising to her feet.

'No … stay a little while with us,' said a young man with a pointed chin at the foot of the table, who clearly fancied Bise. 'You couldn't possibly be tired, today of all days.'

'I don't know, I find that I always tire faster on days where I do nothing.'

The mages all laughed, and Bise knew this was her cue. She waved them goodnight and hurried to the staff quarters. In the privacy of her room, she went through her belongings and retrieved the small drawstring bag from it. Inside were all the ingredients she required. Smooth powder that was once an adult buffalo tooth, a shrivelled liver of a female chimpanzee and a vial holding three drops of tears from an alpha wolf.

The exact measurement to hold my body weight …

She set her mini basalt mortar and pestle in front of her and pulled a strand of hair from her head, then she knelt to pound the liver, crushing it into grains. She transferred this into a glass hip flask and added the other components, including two ounces of water. Then she heated the small flask under a lighter and cooked for six minutes until its contents bubbled and became an odourless indigo syrup. She gulped the potion down with a slurp.

I have exactly half an hour!

Bise dashed through the corridors and up the stairs, past the neon lit emergency signs, and to the mayor's private quarters. The security cameras at the top corners of the halls were missing their tiny power lights. *Perfect.* When she reached the door leading to the hall for the private offices, she tried her luck by turning the handle, but just as she'd expected; someone had locked it manually with a key tonight.

So she said the incantation under her breath and walked confidently into the wall. It felt like going through a silky sheet of ice. Her body crossed the bricks easily, like air itself.

The main door for the office was unlocked now, with its dead pin pad. All she'd had to do was simply turn the handle and let herself in.

She cast an illumination spell once inside the office and went to work immediately. The warm golden light followed her, bobbing up and down near her head.

The dead pin pads also meant she had unrestricted access too. So cabinet after cabinet, she opened. Safe after safe. But none of them had contained anything of interest until the last. It was the small safe closest to the lonely green armchair. Once open, she knew, even before she saw the book, she knew. Something surged in her, like a tiny jolt of electricity coursing through her veins.

Her breath slowed, but her heart raced faster as she retrieved the heavy book from the depths of the safe. There was only one book here, but it was enough because right there, embroidered on the thick leather cover, were the golden rune symbols.

ΔΔΦ⊇ξυℵΘ

Bise never cried, but she wept now as she hugged the book tightly to her bosom. She was gazing at the very foundation of magic. *The original before all others.* The first, even before the legendary eleven. The book that was protected by a magic so ancient and powerful nothing could destroy it. She flipped through the heavy pages, basking in the comfort and security they provided her. Her eyes searched hungrily; she knew exactly what she was looking for.

The supermoon was visible from here and the large windows of the office provided her with uninterrupted views of its brilliance.

She found the page she required for the spell and, knowing what needed to be done now, she faced the moon and laid the book wide open on the table.

Bise wrote the runes confidently in the air, muttering rapidly under her breath so that complex golden symbols formed in front of her. She moved her fingers so adeptly that it was unreasonable at this moment to say magic was not alive. Only glancing occasionally at the open book now, she pushed the runes aside as she cast them, piling them around until she was surrounded by golden lights of her own making and rendering her illumination charm from earlier completely superfluous.

The runes swayed gently as Bise finished the incantations.

This was going to obliterate the city of New Port along with everyone in it, except for the single square foot on which she stood.

The mages here would end up in the wreckage too. Painful, but necessary for the greater good. The mages in Ruga would start anew with her as their grand mage. They'd be thankful to her for liberating them, for putting them at the top once more. For bringing magic back. All would be well, just as it was three hundred years ago.

As she prepared to release doom past the four walls, she heard heavy footsteps approaching. In all her excitement, she'd left the door ajar. She wasn't scared though; she was the one holding all the power here. In fact, she wanted the last thing the mayor saw before he became a pile of dust to be a mage girl – the same one he had dismissed with a wave of his hand because she was just another hungry working-class girl from Ruga. A wicked smile formed across her lips as the door opened. She was going to show him her cheap parlour tricks.

'Father?' said a female voice. 'Is everything alright? I was passing by when I saw the reflection of a strange light and wanted—'

Bise smelled hints of strong lavender perfume before the silhouette came into focus. The girl was holding a battery lantern that projected a bright white light before her. She lowered her lantern, and her face contorted in horror upon meeting the golden runes dancing between her and the mage girl.

With a desperate flick of her finger, Bise tried to send the spell out through the walls so it could cause the annihilation it had been created for, but to her frustration, the runes didn't budge. Instead, they gradually fell to the carpet where they faded into nothingness.

Bise stood there dumbstruck, her mouth drying up as she stared at the floor in front of her in disbelief before slowly raising her head to face the techie girl. Her sister.

DEMONS AND AN ANGEL

I will never forget that day. The afternoon was unusually dark, and thick clouds gathered in their fullest, deepest grey. I remember the heavy whooshing of rustling trees and the strong smell of petrichor. When the heavens finally opened, the rain was unlike anything I had ever seen. It was as if the creator himself was trying to tell us that he had reached his limit. He'd had enough, or she – only a female creator could have been so patient with us, so merciful to us for this long.

The heavy rains seemed like punishment, only it was not severe enough for the crimes in this city. Not even close.

Under the heavy downpour, I made my way to the secret meeting point. There, my brethren awaited me. They never began without me, especially on such an important day as today.

Today was crucial; today would change everything.

I apologised to my brothers and sisters for my tardiness; it was very unlike me, but my reasons were valid. When I was certain I had been forgiven, I took my seat in a prominent position.

My role was key.

We all placed crowns of thorns on our heads. Blood flowed freely down our faces. The pain reminded us of the importance of our purpose.

The conclave began. Few spoke but many agreed. There could be no disunity now, not today. We had all worked hard, through countless debates and many a disagreement, to reach this consensus.

In our meeting place, we also wore white Venetian masks coinciding with our black clothing. I had no knowledge of the face of the person next to me and they did not know mine. No birth names were used either. We trusted only our familiar voices to convey the message. We trusted the process. We trusted each other.

Our city had been riddled with sin for far too long. Dirty, unspeakable sins. Fathers lay with their daughters, and brothers with their own brothers. People slew one another for the slightest transgressions, and there was stealing, drugs, gambling and prostitution. It was all so brazen, so shameless.

There was no law and order, only chaos and evil. We had all lost our way, even us, the righteous twelve.

I knew this because I, too, had sinned; for this, we all had to be reborn. All of us. The city had to die first so that it may live. The creator willed this.

No one was without sin in this city, not one soul.

In the last sixteen years, there had not been a single new birth. Not for lack of trying, but because the creator had made it so. It had been the first of many plagues to come, a sign that the creator had forsaken us. We should have taken heed and done this much sooner.

Now the city was tainted. Everyone, young and old, was stained – completely drenched in unforgivable sin.

As we concluded our talks, I picked up the black case I had come along with, the very one that held the dangerous contents of my own design. This case was going to be our road to redemption. And after today, every single one of us in this room would be a martyr.

I stretched out my hand towards my brothers and sisters and, one after the other, we shook hands. We exchanged the same words around the dimly lit room.

'Until we meet again in the great beyond.'

I walked out of the room first, removing my mask to breathe in the rotten air one last time. The rain had stopped, but the smog had taken its place. I ignored people on the streets, and they did not engage me either. My eyes caught the distressing, vulgar graffiti freshly drawn on the side walls of the decaying low-rise buildings, but my brain ignored it. It was going to be of little importance after today.

When I reached the docklands, I made my way down the deserted staircase that led deep into the narrow underbellies of the city.

By detonating the bomb here, I would be ensuring that the very foundations of the city were shaken so that it would fall. No person or thing was to be saved when the bomb's timer ticked to its end.

In the darkness, I heard the cries of a woman, so I followed the sounds to investigate. When I reached the source of the noise, I retrieved a small light from within my clothing and flicked it on. There, on the grimy stone floor, was a young woman with her legs apart. The bottom of her dress was a mangled mess of water and blood.

'Impossible!' I exclaimed instantly; I was unsure if it was my own eyes that deceived me. The woman was heavily pregnant and appeared to be in labour.

'What is this?' I asked.

Even I was taken aback by the stupidity of my own question, but it was one that needed to be asked. The woman saw me, and her face became full of fright. I suspected that if not for her condition, she would have fled immediately. I drew closer to her, and she trembled the more. Her violent quakes seemed to have nothing to do with the child's imminent arrival. She was scared of me.

'Please, I beg of you, not again,' she said through gritted teeth before closing her eyes tight shut to push.

'How are you with child?' I asked her, still utterly perplexed.

There were burning questions in my mind, and I demanded answers. She was pregnant, not deaf and dumb.

'How?' I asked again, and my voice echoed through the man-made cave.

'This is my third child in four years,' she said amid fast-paced breaths. 'I'm begging you, don't take this one from me.'

She pressed her chin down to her chest to push some more. 'Help me, please!'

Although I was still reeling in confusion, I let go of the case and dropped to my knees instinctively. The burning questions were still there in my head, but I tried to calm her as she continued to push. There was more fluid now, and I reckoned I was about to pass out at any moment. However, it was not too long after that when a hale and hearty babe came forth.

As the baby girl cried, her mother laughed – a laugh that did not last long because the woman seemed to remember my presence. In her tired eyes, I saw the fear from earlier return.

I threw both my hands in the air and said nothing for a while. I must have looked quite out of place because my mask was hanging down my neck and the crown was still upon my head. By now, my whole face was covered in blood.

I allowed her to swaddle her babe in peace before I resumed my questioning.

'Tell me how this is possible.'

I hoped the babe would stay quiet because I was keen to hear the woman's every word. She told me again about her several births over the years. I would not have believed her were the proof not before my very eyes.

'I'm not alone.' She sounded convincing when she spoke. 'There's been lots of other women too, some of whom I know personally.'

I barely had the chance to put forth the obvious next question before she told me.

'It's why the maternity wards are empty, because people like you come to take the babies. I don't know how they do it, I don't know how they know, but they always find us no matter where we hide. At least two of your kind always show up to take our babies at birth. They've taken all my babies!'

I shook my head vigorously, but in her eyes, distrust lurked.

'People like – me?'

'Exactly like you.' She pointed towards my chest. 'Dressed in black, wearing those masks and talking all righteous.'

I felt a chill that swept my mouth dry.

'I don't know what they do with our babies. Tell me what you've done to my babies!'

I was standing on my feet now, glancing down at her. My light in the corner illuminated a bright patch on the brick wall, and it allowed me to see the woman's eyes flashing. She was no longer afraid or distrustful, only disgusted.

I felt the same way.

'What will you do to my baby now?'

'Nothing,' I told her. 'Your baby will live.'

The look of surprise on her face was a clear indicator to me of how badly our society had fallen. I expected her to be relieved, but instead, she looked incredibly distressed, and when she spoke, her voice was dark, shaky and foreboding. 'But the others, they won't let us be. They'll find us, they'll come for her.'

The woman was panicking, and the baby, who was still attached by the cord, was crying now, as if she, too, was sharing in her mother's plight.

'No, they won't.'

I carried the case and made my way back out to the city. I did not even bother lifting my mask to cover my face this time. I needed them to see my face.

SPACE RACE

Most days, you're up all night because sleep eludes you. A lot of thoughts are swarming inside your head, and the weight of them won't allow you to close your eyes in peace.

Some days, it's because you worry about your mother, and on other days, it's that unpredictable future of yours. Today, however, it's your father. You miss him so much, but you dare not bring this up with your mother. You know she understands, but it's been five years now, and she needs you to move on. She has told you oftentimes in the past that such is life. Bad things can happen at any time, and it's usually out of our control.

You suspect that is her own way of coping. Her way of toughening you up, in preparation for when she finally leaves you too.

Panic is filling you as you imagine your life without her. The weight in your head is slowly making its way down to your chest until it reaches the pit of your stomach. That's it; you won't be getting any sleep tonight, that's for sure.

You stand up and walk around the pod, glimpsing yourself in the vertical mirror. People swear you are pretty, but this pretty face has never put food on your table. The dark circles under your eyes are even heavier than the week before. Your hair is still wild and frizzy but even bushier than ever, and you've lost a significant amount of weight. Age, too, is no longer your friend. You chuckle nervously because you know you're still quite young, but it's the air here. It does this to everyone.

Your name is Aurora. Growing up, your father reminded you every so often that it meant beautiful lights. You believed him because he never lied to you. You'd seen pictures of the vivid green lights dancing in the black sky in one of the many books he gave you. There had been mountains, plains, rivers, and mighty oceans. Forests too. But your favourite picture was the one where a herd of cows with bells tied to their necks grazed on a lush open field near a high waterfall. The tiny text underneath had read 'Cows grazing in Swizz Alps, Lauterbrunnen, Switzerland'. It's hard to imagine that something so beautiful once existed, water flowing freely until it dropped several feet through the hills and rocks. That must have been amazing.

But your forefathers destroyed it all, so now, all those natural things are gone, along with the Earth itself – the home of your forefathers.

It started with the pandemics, and then came the flash floods. The wildfires became rampant too, until all the forests were wiped out. Not long after this, war broke out between countries and territories, each of them trying to fight for whatever few resources were left. But it was too late at that point; the earth was already dying. It was not until the ground began melting off the very surface of the earth that the people realised they had broken the Earth beyond habitation. The damage was irreversible.

Now, nearly a hundred years later, you and forty thousand others live on the strip, a piece of land floating in space that had been built by humans a decade or so before Earth's final days. The survivors, people who had made it onto the thirty-three shuttles before Earth's destruction, escaped and landed here.

The strip is somewhere between Mars and Jupiter. It is just over four miles long from the north to its narrowest point down south and around two miles wide. The structure itself is stable except for occasional slight tremors caused by passing meteoroids. The air here is still unforgiving to humans, even after all these years, and the slightest exposure to it could be lethal. If you're lucky, you may get a nasty bout of Pluto's flu, which is treatable but a bloody costly expense.

Indoor spaces are climate controlled, but outside that, thin pressurised bodysuits have to be worn under clothes, alongside special gloves, made of the same elastomeric fibre material because the human skin still hasn't adjusted to this brutal atmosphere.

As expected, suits vary in quality, so you get what you pay for. Coats and jackets are a norm here too, but that one is mostly a fashion statement.

There are no resources on the strip; it's only man-made, after all. And even if there were, you are certain humans would mess everything up again, just like they did on Earth. People here mostly learned about the old world through the small museum in the central atrium. There are videos and pictures on the large screens there. There are books too and glossy magazines with select pages only accessible through the thick secured glass. You, on the other hand, learned much more from the books your father left behind for you. He had inherited them from his own father, whose father's father had brought them with him from Earth.

You know the famous fairy tales of the old world and have read all of Shakespeare's works. Some lines you even know by heart because you'd spent most of your childhood poring over the pages. Most of those books are gone now. Over the years, you've had to sell them, one by one, in order to survive with your mother. Only one of them remains, a severely worn-out copy of *Our Planet in Pictures*.

Everyone says you should be more thankful to be here, but you see no particular reason to, because life here is tough. The days are repetitive, and there is neither day nor night, but people use the old system of Earth – it was arranged that way as a coping mechanism by the first settlers, you like to think. A day is split into twenty-four hours, with mornings, afternoons and evenings. Monday to Sunday exist here too, along with the twelve months of the year.

The price of oxygen is sky high, and the food tastes like crap, because like everything here, it is manufactured in a lab. And only rich people can afford nice cuisine like steak. The cows are needed for dairy, so slaughtering them can only be done for big, big bucks. You'd love to try steak one day; it's one of your many heart's desires. You work in The White Rabbit, a posh restaurant down-strip where you often get a whiff of it in the kitchen. It smells heavenly. The last manager was a nice man and used to hand you some of the leftover tripe on Sundays after the fancy women from Nathgar, who were always dressed in their heavy jewellery that twinkled under the golden lights, finished their lunch. Their husbands were some of the most senior members of the establishment. Judges, ministers and directors.

'The rich housewives of Nathgar' you and the others in the kitchen called them. The housewives came along with their pets and occasionally ordered more food than they could eat combined. You always had to clean up animal hair afterwards, and you were particularly thankful for the sensible woman among them who had an iguana.

Sulman had been kind to you, and he'd never asked for the things most men ask for in return. On the occasional excessive days, you even got some extra food with tripe to take home to your mother. All your privileges stopped with the new manager though. He was a dickhead, and that was you putting it lightly.

You work Tuesdays through Sundays from noon until evening, and from evening till midnight, you work your second job at the concert hall on the fourteenth floor of the ultra-pod. This is the only way you can afford to survive on this damn strip.

Your hours there are spent in the cloakroom; it's easier than the restaurant but the pay is much less, and the people there never tip. *Selfish pricks*, you think. You take the fine coats of laughing men and women who are always excited to pay an outrageous number of units to watch people sing and play instruments. And when you hand them back their expensive fur, leather and silk items at the end of the night, they never look at you or even say thanks.

Rice flakes and wheat biscuits are the staple foods here. Sometimes you throw in some fruit and vegetables, especially on paydays. Those are still quite pricey but cost less than beef, since they multiply much faster than cows.

Water is a scarce, precious commodity and thus heavily rationed. Everyone has to pay for it, but in your district, the pipes only run once a week in the mornings. So, every Tuesday, you wake up even earlier than you ought to so you can store the running water in every container and jar you're able to lay your hands on. This is the only day you can shower, just before you rush out to your shift.

In the nicer parts of the strip, you've heard water flows through the pipes up to four or five times a week. You could never confirm this since you know no one from any of those districts, but you believe it because some of those posh fuckers actually keep potted plants.

One time at work, you overheard the chef and his assistant in the kitchen bragging to each other about the rich people they'd provided home service to. You don't get on with either of them, but the one you dislike the most claims he'd once cooked for a man who had an eight-hundred-litre fish tank full of exotic fishes inside his mega-home pod.

The other chef had laughed hysterically. 'Dude, that's just insane. No way that's true.' The assistant doesn't believe him, so they argue some more.

You know it's true though, because you know the exact mega-pod the head chef is referring to. When you were a bit younger, you read in one of your books that water fell from the sky back on Earth in the form of something called rain. Sometimes it was so heavy it even flooded the streets. It's absolutely mental to imagine this now. Your ancestors must have had it so good.

Medicine is a different story altogether. It's near impossible to get some even when you have the units to pay for it. It seems so many people suffer the same ailments in silence. There is a widespread theory here that members of the establishment – the powerful men and women at the helm of affairs, keep things this way in order to decongest the overpopulated strip. *That's cruel if it's true*, you always think.

You know that the strip was originally intended to house ten thousand of Earth's richest, but plans changed at the last minute. The rich needed people to serve them in their new home, after all, just as it had been on Earth. So most of them came along with their nannies, butlers and chefs.

These workers in turn negotiated a pathway for their families, and on voyage day, several more people showed up at the launch site. They pleaded desperately to be allowed onboard, and many of them tried forcing their way in. In the end, only a few succeeded. Upon arrival, nothing changed. The poor remained poor, serving the rich and building the residences with their hands while the wealthy stayed on top, passing down their units and valuables to ensure aristocratic continuity.

You have a degree in mathematics and astrophysics from the University of Applied Sciences, but it is useless for work since every second person has the same qualification. *You're nothing special*, you remind yourself.

The Milky Way is always on display above, and truthfully, it is quite beautiful and never gets old. But even that is never enough to lift your spirits from the reality that is here.

As you make your way to the restaurant with your small tank strapped to your back, and your backpack fastened over it, filled with a change of clothes for your other job later, you pass by a large poster. It has been pasted to cover the entire side of a kiosk pod, but you pay it no mind; you've seen the likes of it splattered across the streets every year now. Nothing new here, just another competition for men willing to risk their lives in a dangerous race.

Your day is like every other before it. You do your shift and endure the endless screaming from the short-tempered manager and irritated chefs. Every day, they find ingenious new names to call you. It's derogatory, but you take it all in stride; you don't have any other choice. You need this job.

When you reach your other job, you breathe a sigh of relief. At least you have the chance to sit down here. You take their coats and thank them mechanically as you do, because as your manager never fails to remind you, you only have this job because the guests are kind enough to come along with their coats.

'Adigo, can I take off an hour earlier today? I think I'm coming down with the flu,' you say to your manager halfway through your shift.

She eyes you with her usual incertitude as the high-pitched voice of a soprano comes through from the hall.

'You can do whatever you want,' Adigo tells you begrudgingly. 'But just so you know, I won't be approving any sudden time off like this in the future.'

She is also quick to remind you as you leave that you will not be paid for the missing hour. 'Your contract doesn't include any sick leave,' she says to you point-blank.

You rush as fast as your legs and the busy streets permit you. The pharmacy closes on the dot at midnight, and you need to make one stop before that.

You arrive at an old mega-pod that once functioned as a private warehouse – a place you've frequented more times than you would have liked over the years. These days, it is used as a flea market during the day but serves another purpose at nighttime.

It is full of shifty-looking men and women ready to prey on desperate people. Officially known as the night market, it is also infamously referred to as *the underground*. The place is notorious for its dodgy transactions, and everyone on the strip knows the inhabitants pay a *fee* to the establishment so that the enforcers can turn a blind eye to its illegal operations.

You ignore the annoying catcalls that come as you walk into the underground, but a tall woman jumps in front of you, blocking your path. She is trying to sell you something dodgy.

'This is cloud-nine material, baby,' she says croakily and smiles at you with blackened teeth. 'It's fresh off the block. Trust me, you can't get better anywhere else on the strip. But you're a lovely-looking girl, so I can give you three for the price of two.'

She opens her greasy palm to reveal the handful of drugs in her possession. *Definitely opioids.* You shake your head quickly at the sight of the round white tablets and continue your walk down the large pod.

'How much will you give me for this?' you ask the first person that approaches you.

The unkempt man is watching you hungrily as you pull out something from your bag. Instead of showing him the book you've just retrieved, you grip it to your chest.

'Well?' he asks you impatiently. 'Ya ganna show me or nah?'

You stretch the heavy book outwards, allowing the man to flip through some of the pages. His eyes grow wide with excitement, but he seems to catch himself quickly before he speaks.

'Two units!' he announces.

'What?' Your voice is louder than his. You feel instant anger. You suspected this could happen, but not to this extent.

'Mister man, this is worth twelve units,' you say to him, frowning. 'Ten at the very least. Look at the patterns on the cover.'

'Ha! Maybe you haven't been here in a lang, lang time. Collectors don't pay good units for 'em no more. The market fa books ain't as profitable as 'fore, 'tis quite slow now.'

'What's your best offer, please? I'm in a hurry.' You regret this immediately as you say it, but you are indeed in a hurry; you have less than thirty minutes before midnight.

'I'll give ya three,' he says to you as he tries to snatch the book from your hand.

'Hey! Not good enough,' you yell louder than you planned to.

Several people look in your direction now, and the man seems to have become annoyed. 'Okay. Try someone else then. Let's see if they'll give ya more than me offering.'

'Alright,' you hiss. 'But give me eight. I'm sure you know this is a very valuable book. Look at it.'

You flip several pages open for him to see, hoping to attract him with the clear, full-page image of a bullet train speeding past a snowy Mount Fuji.

He glances at it and shrugs. 'Last offer is four units, only 'cos ya a very fine girl.'

He is licking his lips now. Four units is just barely enough to buy two months' supply of the medicine you require, but you have about twenty minutes now, so you nod slowly, painfully. Your throat is sore as you watch him count the units before handing them to you. When his fingers touch yours, he strokes them with a sly smile that immediately makes you feel like you need to take a shower.

'Come again next time,' he yells at you from behind as you sprint out without a backward glance.

You make it just in time, and as you walk home with your lighter bag, you're so downcast you aren't paying attention to your surroundings. A man riding in a cruiser throws a very dirty look at you because you had not looked when you crossed the street. The woman seated behind him in the cruiser is saying something to him and they laugh as they zoom off.

Your heart is broken, and there is no other way of putting it. This was the last book in your possession, one of the last fragments you used to hold on to your father. He would be rolling in his grave now, and all his fathers before him.

A few people call you as you near your district. You're well liked enough mostly because your mother has been popular here for years and the people respect her. A woman smiles at you, but you don't smile back, mostly because you barely see it, but even if you did, manners would change nothing; you'd still be poor and your mother is still dying.

You try not to cry as you think about it. Living here with no friends is lonely as it is. You can't imagine your mother out of the picture.

You're well into your district now, and the best way to describe it is deprived. Lomzar is the least desirable place to live and, ironically, it is right beside the more upscale Nathgar. To utilise the limited space on the strip, districts were built in clusters of piles, and each pile had several pods stacked on top of it. Some piles exceeded three hundred metres in height, and the only way to build new piles now is by knocking existing ones down.

Older districts with more affordable residences were always the first to have their piles demolished to make way for shinier new pods that most people would never be able to afford.

You continue down the road that separates the districts, and you can't help but stare into one of the brightly lit, spacious mega-pods on your right. It is easy to estimate the wealth of the owner quite often by what they have occupying their space.

You see several arowanas and angelfish swimming in a large tank in one of them, while Vincent van Gogh's *The Starry Night* is hanging boldly on the wall of another. The number of units that could fetch makes your head spin. In another, you count orchids in three porcelain vases sitting on the window ledge. Those things probably got more water than you and your mother combined. Small fury starts to build in you.

You step on a piece of paper. It's just a smaller copy of the one you saw earlier, but your eyes automatically read the bold letters on the top and you do a double-take. Impossible! You stop dead in your tracks to look again. You even pick it up and hold it closer to your face so there's no confusion.

'One Thousand Units for the Fastest Person!'

Your eyes weren't deceiving you. The prize units have doubled this year. You're not sure why, but you suspect it has something to do with the centenary celebrations. You decide on the spot that you'd like to enter.

The space race, as it's called by everyone here, is a highly competitive tournament hosted every year on Landing Day, the anniversary of human settlement on the strip. It is also dangerous, so dangerous that although women aren't forbidden from registering, no women have ever competed since its founding sixty-two years ago. The participants are always daredevils, speed-loving men in the fastest cruisers. The race consists of one lap only, from the far north of the strip right to the southern tip. But this takes nearly an hour because racers have to go past several obstacles and roadblocks as they try to reach the finish line without being knocked off the course, or worse, the very strip itself.

There is a bitter taste in your mouth as you think about it. There are several reasons your mother will forbid this, but you can only think of one major one. Your eyes drift to the smaller print at the bottom. *'All participants must be over eighteen to enter and are liable for their own protection. There is no insurance provided in the event of any crashes, accidents or a fatality. The organisers are not liable for injuries sustained to racers or any damages to their cruisers.'* Your gaze shifts back upwards on the paper – the entry fee is three units. You don't have it, but you'll have to find it. If you win this race, it'll change your life and that of your mother too. But the knowledge of it could also kill her, so for that reason you'll be keeping your mouth shut, at least for now.

When you enter the micro-home pod, your mother is there, lying quietly on her bed. You remove your worn-out gloves, tossing them aside without caring where they'd land. You've worn the likes of them every day for most of your life, but something about covering your hands feel most unnatural. Next, you unfasten your oxygen mask and drop your tank on the floor with a thud as you always do to announce your presence.

'Aurora,' she croaks.

She looks even older than ever. The average life expectancy on the strip is sixty. Fifty-one for the residents of Lomzar. Your mother is about to turn fifty, and you are only twenty-three, but it feels like you've been alive for twice as long. You remember when her illness started. It had begun just like any other case of Pluto's flu, and you thought it would fade as quickly as it came, but weeks passed and she only deteriorated. Medicine after medicine, nothing worked. By the time you could afford to take her to the hospital, her condition had become terminal. It was a rare thing. The doctors didn't even have a name for it yet. The air was to blame, they told you, people reacted to it differently even under the safety net of oxygen.

'It's one of those things we still don't fully understand,' the doctor had said to you after the last of six different test results.

'We could still monitor her and conduct further tests, but I don't think her situation will improve, I'm sorry.'

And that was it. She was dying; they didn't know how long she had either, only that the very expensive medicine they prescribed could help keep her stable, on some days.

'You're an hour late today,' she tells you with a faint smile.

'I had to restock your pills.'

You drop the bottle beside her. She is blind. The wicked ailment robbed her of her sight too. She breaks into a slightly bigger smile.

'But how can you afford this now? Your wages are barely enough for rent and food. Did you sell off something again?'

You say nothing as your eyes fill. And in this moment, you're glad she doesn't have the eyes to see your tears. 'Nothing I'd miss.'

Your brittle voice gives you away, and she's on to you now. When she speaks, your heart shatters to pieces.

'You shouldn't have sold it,' she says to you quietly. 'That was all you had left of your father.'

You want to yell at the top of your lungs and tell her that you are well aware, but instead, you reassure her that it meant nothing.

'It's just a book, Mom.'

'I don't know why you bother with me.'

As she turns her face away from you, the callousness of her words hits you so hard you jump from the bed and stare at her in silence. She is trying to hide her tears, but she is doing a terrible job at it. Several emotions are piercing you at once, and it's hard to decide which of them to attend to first. So you sit down beside her again and take her hands as you promise her that everything will be alright. She forces one more smile and tells you that she believes you, even though her empty eyes tell a different story. The one where a tired woman is losing faith.

You can't blame her; you are losing all faith too. It's the strip, it does that to everyone. You wait by her side until she falls asleep, and then you make your way to the basement. The garage for your pod is here, and it has a sliding door that leads directly towards the streets. You pull back the tarpaulin to reveal a very dusty cruiser. Your mother doesn't know this is still here. You were supposed to have sold it three years ago along with the cruising simulator.

You stare at the large dent on its side and run your fingers slowly over the paintwork. The front plug will need replacing, and the glass is cracked in various places too, but you think you can fix it. Your father had been a fixer, and your mind darts back to all the time you shared with him here. He spent most of his time working on cruisers. The man could resurrect dead racing machines with his skill. And because you spent several hours at a time here with him, you learned most of it too.

For your eleventh birthday, he built you a cruising simulator. He told you there was nothing like it on the entire strip, and you believed him because he never lied to you. You had sat in it right here in this basement, racing through the streets of the strip, reaching the topmost speed and laughing to your father's delight. It was the first thing your mother made you sell after your father died; you were so angry at her for making you sell a part of your father and you resented her for years, but you grew to understand.

It was also why you swore to yourself never to sell this.

You push the small window open completely, and the smell of peppermint escapes into the air, filling you with instant nostalgia. This cruiser belonged to your father. He was carefree and smart and knew a lot about everything. His laughter was loud and contagious; you remember that more than what he looked like.

You touch the dials and buttons, careful not to push them too hard. If you sold the cruiser for scraps, it would be enough to get you by with medicine, rent and groceries for five, six months maybe, but after that, it'll be back to square one. You needed a better plan, so you make your decision there as you stand. It's risky, yes, but still the better plan.

* * *

You are paid every fortnight Saturday. So, on the next Sunday after payday, you head to the registration centre before noon. You're already dressed for work just in case you run late. You meet several men there in the short line when you arrive, and a lot of eyes are fixed on you. Someone asks you if you're lost, and another asks you to bring them coffee. One particularly huge man with bleached hair and bold tattoos on his face, near the front of the queue, keeps casting you dirty looks. He turns back to look at you again, and you see his muscles threatening to rip his shirt. He smacks his lips and rubs his palms together just in time for the men around him to start making lewd remarks directed your way.

You maintain a poker face the entire time. After you pay the fees and put down your details, you try to hurry off, but one man grabs you by the wrist and pulls you aside. 'Aurora?' comes his gruff voice.

You study him. From his oversized denim jacket to the stingray boots of his feet. Despite the trendy dressing, his salt-and-pepper beard betray his age. His nose is broken, and his right eye is swollen and shut; the left one is bloodshot red, and there is a fresh small stitch above the corner of his lip. You suspect he is one of the fighters that frequent the infamous Saturday night underground wrestling club.

'Sorry, who are you?'

'I was right, then,' he says, looking rather pleased with himself. Rough voice notwithstanding, his tone is kind. 'I thought it was you. I wasn't sure, of course, since I haven't seen you since you were about six or seven.' He smiles now. 'I used to call you beautiful Aurora. I see not much has changed.'

Your look of impatience should be visible to him as you stand there quietly, waiting for him to make his point. You don't have the mental capacity to get yelled at by your manager today.

'My name is Abas. I was a friend of your father's, but I'm sure you don't remember me.' He eyes you with his good eye, and when you don't respond, he asks you why you're choosing to participate in such a dangerous race.

You speak, reminding him that you owe him no explanation, since your reasons are yours alone.

'It's not a safe tournament for people like you,' he goes on to say, but you cut him short before he can say more.

'Because I'm a woman?'

'Aurora, I mean no disrespect, truly, but you're … just a girl. You're young with no driving experience …' He is gushing out his words with a hysterical look on his face. 'This race is no joke – drivers die, and no one will even bother to stop. There aren't any rules out there on the track, and those competitors are wild, desperate beasts!'

'Mister Abas,' you say as respectfully as your patience will allow. 'Women aren't prohibited from entering the race, are they?'

'No, but—'

'Then I'll be entering, but thank you for your concern, although misplaced.'

You start walking, but then he grabs your wrist again before you can make any progress. 'I heard your mother is sick. Do you need some money? I can help—'

'Thanks a lot for your generosity, but we don't need your charity. I'll still be entering the race.'

You make to leave, but he pulls you back once more. You're feeling the tightness of his grip, so you grit your teeth as you turn back to face him. You are frowning, and he is frowning too, his tone becoming more serious.

'Your father won't want this!' he spits.

'You don't know what my father wants. He's dead!'

You pull your arm away and walk off sharply; this time you know he won't try to stop you, but you know he is watching you as you fume along the way.

* * *

In the days that follow, you buy the bits and pieces you need and begin working on the cruiser in the basement. You do it as discreetly as possible. Your rent is past due because you used the units meant for it to pay for the registration fees. You've staked everything on this, so there is definitely no turning back now.

You're getting even less sleep than you usually get as a result of the anxiety that is crippling you and the repairs consuming your free time.

Yesterday, you considered quitting everything altogether. It's better to cut your losses and pretend this never crossed your mind, but you remember Abas and that big oaf of a man that probably had more muscles than he had brains. You'd go ahead with the race just to wipe the smirk off his face and prove to Abas you could.

Now that you dwell on it, you remember vaguely the man who used to visit this basement and stay for hours with your father when you were a child. It might have been Abas, but what did it matter now? He hadn't visited in the immediate years before or after your father's death. He had no right to show up now and offer you his words of wisdom. He seemed to need it more himself, considering the state of him.

But then, you go on thinking, who would take care of your mother if you died in the race? Perhaps you hadn't thought this all the way through and you're just being selfish. You're doing this for her is what you tell yourself.

You step back to look at the cruiser. It's fixed now. You hop into the cabin and start the engine; you don't even realise it but you're beaming with pride.

* * *

There's one more day before the big race, and unfortunately, the event doesn't fall on a Monday. So on Tuesday, right after your weekly shower, you head to work as usual. Only this time you ask your boss at the restaurant for the day off.

'I'm sorry it's short notice, but it's an emergency,' you say to him as you follow him from the kitchen to his office. 'I've asked Agnes, and she's happy to cover for me.'

But your manager wants none of it, and he yells at you. It seems this is his favourite pastime. As he continues to scream at the top of his lungs, you realise this is all unwarranted. The man has had a problem with you from day one, and so you quit, right there where you stand. The mild horror on his face is a win for you, though. It's also the last thing you see before you return to the changing room to clear out your things.

You know even as you walk out that it'll be impossible to make ends meet with only one job. This is also quite the worst possible time to find new employment on the strip, but the deed has been done. Also, nothing will be stopping you from competing in that race tomorrow, not even the fear of being jobless afterwards. You reach the concert hall three hours earlier than the start of your shift here, which is good because you'll need the time to go put some finishing touches to the cruiser anyway. You've already braced yourself for another round of resignation because Adigo is just as big an asshole too. But to your greatest surprise, her response to your request is the opposite of what you had expected.

'You can take the rest of today off too.'

Her tone isn't joking, and her face isn't devil-like either. You can't believe your ears. She comes close to you, and her voice sounds supportive. 'I understand a *crazy girl* from Lomzar is competing in the race this year,' she says to you now.

You open your mouth to speak but quickly decide against it. There is nothing to say. But she wishes you luck as you leave the hall to several arriving, coat-wielding guests.

* * *

Your mother is still half asleep as you prepare to leave the house on race day. You put on your green second-hand fleece jacket. It's the only one you own. Then you kiss her tenderly on the cheek before dashing out. Several stunned eyes are on you as you cruise down your district and towards the centre. You're certain your mother will hear about it before the race proper begins. All racers must gather in the centre first to check in before making their way to the starting point far north of the strip. If you're being honest with yourself, you're a smoking ball of nerves.

When you reach the racetrack, the big man is glowering at you from his shiny red cruiser. He smiles right after but it's a cocky one, and you can see a full set of finely cut silver teeth. Apparently, he has won the last two years in a row. Abas, too, is eyeing you and your cruiser from inside his. A lot of people are coming around to your cruiser, and many of them stare at you as if you've gone completely bonkers, especially the women. Others smile as they wave at you, and a few even take your hand and shake it. You somehow manage to garner some cheers from the crowd when your name is called. It feels nice, however lacklustre it is.

You can see your name on the list of racers up on the massive screen overhead. The ages of the racers are there too. You're the youngest of the lot and the youngest to ever compete, apparently. You almost forget now that you're also a woman. The significance of the other facts seemed to have drowned this.

Husky's name is right at the top. He is thirty-seven and the projected winner for this year. He also seems to be a fan favourite judging by the sizeable round of applause he receives. Your name, Aurora, is right there at the bottom of the list of twenty-four. You take slow, deep breaths as the announcement begins outside, and it's not long after that you see the flashing numbers counting down.

Your father tweaked the engine before his final race. He competed five times and never got very far because he refused to modify his engine, even though everyone else did. And when he finally did tweak it, he overdid it. The speed he'd rightfully feared was what eventually killed him. Now you sit behind the same engine, aware of the power it has. The numbers flash to zero, and all caution is thrown to the wind as the loud roaring of cruisers fills the north strip.

All twenty-four mini spaceships hurtle down the road, hovering only a few inches from the ground and blasting out red, blue and orange flames from their exhausts. The cruiser is even faster than you previously thought but you're in control, mostly. You look around; you have to be in around tenth place, maybe. With each cruiser you pass, you notice a look of either disdain or embarrassment smeared across the face of the man driving it. You don't smile or gloat, though; you remain focused.

Massive cones pop out suddenly in all directions as you continue down the winding course. You miss one of them by a whisker and nearly crash headfirst into the bottom floor of a pile of office pods. You must slow down, even just for a bit, or you'll be out of the race before you reach the top five.

Immediately the road straightens again, you step on the pedal, slapping it until your feet feel the bottom of the cruiser. There is another bend ahead, even sharper than the last, and if your calculations are right, you're definitely in fourth now. The cruiser in front of you is so fast it's a green blur as it paces from side to side. The road curves. This is your chance. Your feet and hands are busy, your brain, too, lights up. Your whole body is working overtime.

Your mind goes to Newton's laws of motion, and you remember weight distribution. You sink yourself as low as possible in your chair with your upper body straight. You and your cruiser are one. You must remain balanced as you try to gain the desired mass. You jerk the transmission lever just as you turn right, but you tilt your body to the left with your foot still jammed to the pedal. *Fucking risky, Aurora.* The engine rattles dangerously and the severity of the turn unnerves you momentarily, but it worked. *Of course it worked!* You've propelled past the green cruiser. A fine boost, but there's still work to be done.

There's just one cruiser between you and Husky now, but the driver isn't going to let you pass him that easily; he's pretty fast too. The roads begin to twist again, and it becomes even narrower as the three of you cross into the southern point.

There are no piles here, just a slender road with light poles and cameras on the top. The road continues to thin even more as you go neck and neck with number two. He nudges you with his cruiser, and you drift off the course. The impact forces your head forward and back so fast, a sharp pain follows instantly. If anything shifts you off the road, the lack of gravity will send you plummeting into space where your tank and glass will shatter, leaving you to choke on the nothingness until you're dead within seconds.

A painful way to go and not how you plan to. You're too close to fail.

So you press on, and now you only have Husky to contend with. There, not too far off, is the finish line. You can make out the last two poles casting their warm golden lights upon the black-and-white line. Husky is well aware and fully prepared because two sharp piercers extend from the bottom of his cruiser. He is moving from side to side too, and if you get too close, he'll ensure your cruiser is wrecked to the teeth.

The winding roads have come to an end – only a straight, smooth pathway remains. The people watching from the tall stands on either side are cheering. Your cruiser can go a tad faster, but it's too risky; you need an opening. You speed to the left when Husky moves to block your right, and now you are side by side.

It is obvious that you're not the only one with the accelerator pressed down to the extreme. The look on his face is aggressive. You're panicking because this is a make-or-break moment. There will be no prize units for second place, and next year will be a little too late to try again.

Husky desperately nudges your cruiser. There is no fair play here; you understand this more than ever now, so you hit him back with the side of your own cruiser. The equal force from you and him is the only thing holding the both of you from falling off the sides. The finish line is a mere eighty metres away, give or take, and you're getting ahead now; it's slight and gradual, but it finally happens. You're in front of Husky, but only by inches.

You don't need to glance back to tell he is boiling with rage inside his cabin because you feel the firm bump from behind as his cruiser rams unapologetically into yours. He knows he can't win, so he is determined to knock you past the finish line and off the course, off the strip.

Your heart is pounding in real time because your life is about to end just as you are due to make history. With each hit from Husky, you're nearing the finish line, but also heading uncontrollably towards your death.

You close your eyes and see your father; he is laughing that loud laugh you remember well, and your mother, too, is on her feet. She is smiling and looking much better than you've ever seen her. You take your foot off the pedal, and your father's laughter becomes louder, surpassing even your engine. You jerk the lever to its rear, the same lever he designed, and it brings you to the side of the track with a jolt, past the finish line. But it provides Husky with an unstoppable path so that he jets into the abyss. You see his face briefly as his cruiser whirls past you, aware of what he has just done to himself. You don't smile or gloat though; you're too focused on being the winner.

And as the other cruisers come to a halt behind you, you see people rushing out from the stands and cruisers alike, each of them attempting to greet you first. You cover your nose with the oxygen mask before opening your cabin. You know its inside your head, but still, you embrace the small gust of peppermint as you breathe in. Your teary eyes are clouding your vision, but you look up just in time to catch the text flashing boldly on the large screen above: 'AURORA', and it is surrounded by vivid, dancing green lights.

Acknowledgements

I'd like to say a big thank you to my earliest beta readers – my sisters, Sam and Thia.

Your unwavering support pushed this book right through to the very end.

Also, to Stephanie, who gave me the inspiration for one of my favourite characters.

Many thanks to my later beta readers too; a dozen close friends and family. Your feedback was thorough, yet kind.

And lastly, I'd like to say cheers to the shy Irish sun. Your elusive nature inspired the first of these stories and gave me this book's main title.

ABOUT THE AUTHOR

Born and raised in Nigeria, Dexter had always loved writing. As a young boy, he would travel to faraway planets and distant lands of his own creation.

These days, however, he keeps his travels mostly on Earth, because being an adult is expensive enough. Except for the odd times when his mind still wanders.

Dexter is, till this day, quite fascinated by clouds and lives somewhere on the east coast of Ireland.

Dearest Reader,

Thank you for purchasing a copy of THE DAY THE SUN VANISHED. I had so much fun writing this book, so I can only hope that you had even more fun reading the stories. I considered naming this book Dream Collection, and even after deciding against it, the manuscript itself carried that name for the longest time. I eventually named it THE DAY THE SUN VANISHED because that was the very first story I wrote in the collection and it was Kofi's journey that set my pen to hundreds of pages worth of paper.

Most of the stories started as scattered day and night dreams. I would then flesh them out during my waking hours — filling the character gaps with people I know or have known, things I'd heard or imagined hearing, and places I'd visited or at least thought I had. I scribbled down on paper napkins in the middle of dinner at restaurants, typed into my old computer on airplanes, dictated to my phone while sandwiched in packed underground trains and even took mental notes when an interesting enough idea came to me while I was in the shower.

Now a lot of my dreams didn't make it into the pages of this book. But I don't believe I'll ever stop dreaming, and since I have no shortage of people and events to draw inspiration from, I have no doubt that there'll be many more stories to come. So, see you soon!

With gratitude and love,

Dexter.

Printed in Great Britain
by Amazon

31349469-f26b-450e-a949-ca7ceaa79593R01